A THOUSAND PERFECT ~~LIVES~~ LIES

A THOUSAND PERFECT ~~LIVES~~ LIES

NEW YORK TIMES BESTSELLING AUTHOR
MONICA MURPHY

PENGUIN MICHAEL JOSEPH

UK | USA | Canada | Ireland | Australia
India | New Zealand | South Africa

Penguin Michael Joseph is part of the Penguin Random House group of companies whose addresses can be found at global.penguinrandomhouse.com

Penguin Random House UK,
One Embassy Gardens, 8 Viaduct Gardens, London SW11 7BW

penguin.co.uk

Published by Penguin Michael Joseph, part of the Penguin Random House group of companies, in association with Mayhem Books, part of Entangled Publishing LLC 2026
001

Copyright © Monica Murphy, 2026

The moral right of the author has been asserted

The Mayhem Books name and logo are trademarks of Entangled Publishing LLC and are used here under licence

Penguin Random House values and supports copyright. Copyright fuels creativity, encourages diverse voices, promotes freedom of expression and supports a vibrant culture. Thank you for purchasing an authorized edition of this book and for respecting intellectual property laws by not reproducing, scanning or distributing any part of it by any means without permission. You are supporting authors and enabling Penguin Random House to continue to publish books for everyone. No part of this book may be used or reproduced in any manner for the purpose of training artificial intelligence technologies or systems. In accordance with Article 4(3) of the DSM Directive 2019/790, Penguin Random House expressly reserves this work from the text and data mining exception

Edited by Rebecca Heyman
Interior design by Britt Marczak
Printed and bound in Great Britain by Clays Ltd, Elcograf S.p.A.

The authorized representative in the EEA is Penguin Random House Ireland, Morrison Chambers, 32 Nassau Street, Dublin D02 YH68

A CIP catalogue record for this book is available from the British Library

HARDBACK ISBN: 978–1–911–75328–5
TRADE PAPERBACK ISBN: 978–1–911–75329–2

Penguin Random House is committed to a sustainable future for our business, our readers and our planet. This book is made from Forest Stewardship Council® certified paper.

ALSO BY MONICA MURPHY

The Players

Playing Hard to Get
Playing By The Rules
Playing to Win

Lancaster Prep

Things I Wanted To Say
A Million Kisses in Your Lifetime
Promises We Meant to Keep
I'll Always Be With You
You Said I was Your Favorite

Lancaster Prep Next Generation

All My Kisses For You
Keep Me in Your Heart
You Were Never Not Mine

Single Titles

Pretty Dead Girls
Daring the Bad Boy
Saving It

This book is for the self-protective, independent ones who learned to trust themselves first before they could rely on someone else.

A Thousand Perfect Lies is a twisty murder mystery with lots of family drama and romance. However, the story includes elements that might not be suitable for all readers, including parental alcoholism and abandonment, underage drinking, recreational drug use, consensual physical intimacy, bullying, and murder. Readers who may be sensitive to these elements, please take note before confirming your enrollment at Wickham Academy.

CHAPTER ONE

"Hey, babe. Gimme another beer."

One of the cheesy tourists from Tennessee has a leer on his somewhat handsome face that makes me want to roll my eyes, but I contain myself. He came into the bar with his friends to watch college football on a Saturday afternoon, and they're loud. Obnoxious. They can't stop checking me out, either. Why are they all like this—flirtatious to the point of unbearable?

I need every dollar I can get, so I flash him a smile. "Coming right up."

I head toward the bar, where Doug, the owner of this fine establishment, has already placed a fresh bottle for my customer on the counter. I offer him a grateful smile, and he lifts a whiskered brown chin in acknowledgment.

I set the bottle on my tray before I head over to the table where the three pretty-faced college boys sit. Their focus is stuck on the big-screen TV playing the game, one of them shouting a string of curse words when the ball gets intercepted.

"Got a lot of money riding on this," the one who ordered the beer mutters as he checks his phone. I can tell he's on one of those online betting sites.

I deliver the beer in front of him, making sure I bend over the table as I do, flashing them a boob shot thanks to the deep V of my T-shirt. Anything to get tips.

Two out of the three notice, their gazes now glued to my chest. So typical.

"Thanks," the other guy mumbles, finally giving me his attention.

"Need anything else?" I glance toward the TV and see the game is almost over. Meaning these customers are going to leave soon, and I hope they give me a decent tip. But they're young and probably not big spenders, despite what their popped collars and chunky silver watches would have me believe.

"No thanks," one of them tells me, his tone dismissive. I guess tits are less fun to ogle once the mouth above them starts talking.

I leave their table and head back to the bar, setting my tray on the counter with a too-loud clang. Doug joins me, sucking his teeth like he always does when he's about to complain. "It's slow today."

Nodding, I glance about the space, noting the empty tables. A couple of regulars sit at the other end of the bar, continuously sipping from their drinks while also watching the game. Not that they care what's on the TV. They're here every single day, rain or shine, game or no game. I can't imagine this sort of life. Shuffling into the same dingy bar day in and day out. Talk about depressing.

Despite the lackluster crowd, I'm still a bundle of nerves, trying to build up the courage to tell Doug this is my last shift. Most of the time, I feel like it's a pity position anyway, but I don't like the thought of leaving him high and dry. I'm a lot of not-nice things, but unreliable isn't one of them. I've never had the luxury.

"How's your mom?" The sympathy in Doug's voice is obvious. Long ago, when I was a little kid, they used to date. Back then, she was a mostly functioning adult and not a complete mess like she is now. Doug came into our lives and paid attention to me, unlike Mom's other boyfriends. Treated me like I was his own kid. Showered me with attention and gifts, but never in a creepy way. No, more like he actually cared.

Until Mom ruined everything and accused him of cheating on her. Doug's not a cheater. His mistress is this bar. He has to work constantly to keep up with his bills and doesn't employ much of a staff. When I came to him a year ago desperate for a job, he reluctantly gave me one, even though at seventeen, I'm not technically old enough to work in a bar.

He pays me under the table in cash, which I really appreciate as well.

"She's doing okay," I lie.

It's easier than telling him the truth and admitting she's in bad shape. That an opportunity arose for her to go back to rehab, and I don't have the strength to turn it down, even if it means I have to drop everything and fly halfway around the world. Hard as I've tried, I can't crush the hope that maybe this time it'll stick. Maybe this time she'll want to get better. Do better.

Doug's gaze is assessing, never straying from mine. He sees too much—always has. It makes me want to squirm, but I keep still. "You sure about that?"

"Yeah, I'm sure." My voice is firm, but he looks like he wants to argue. When the door slams, the tension breaks and we both glance toward the entrance. The college guys are gone, their table a mess, a couple of soggy dollars left behind.

I fight the disappointment that threatens to swallow me whole and turn back to Doug. But I guess if there's enough disappointment to go around, I might as well share it. I paste on a bright smile and dive in. "Look, I don't know how to tell you this, but…I'm leaving town for a few months. You'll have to find someone to cover my shifts."

He gives me a look, one that says he hopes I've finally decided to leave. He hates my life almost as much as I do. His voice rises with interest. "A few months? Where you going?"

If he was anyone else, I'd tell him it's none of his damn business. "Um, I'm going to go see Peter."

Doug's eyebrows shoot up his forehead. "Really?"

I nod, knowing how absurd it sounds. Why would I suddenly cross an ocean to spend time with the sperm donor who abandoned me and Mom? Frankly, Doug's been more of a father figure to me than Peter ever was. "He says he wants us to have a relationship."

Lies. All lies.

The truth? Peter Vale has a problem, and he thinks I'm the only person who can solve it. In exchange for my help, I demanded he put Mom in rehab. It's the one way I can justify giving *anything* to a man who has not only given me nothing—he's actively stolen from me. Because if it weren't for him,

Mom would never have lost herself at the bottom of a bottle.

He owes her this.

He owes *me* this.

And he agreed, but with demands of his own. We traded terms back and forth like lawyers, not like blood relatives trying to mend fences. In the end, he agreed to my two non-negotiables: Mom in rehab and our rent paid for the next three months. He made all the arrangements. Now I have to leave. Tonight.

Glancing around the room, Doug pulls his not-so-secret pack of cigarettes from beneath the counter and lights up, taking a deep drag before blowing out the smoke. "You sure you're not getting scammed?"

"By who? Peter?" Probably, but I'm scamming him, too. "Nah, he needs me this time."

"Well, just take care of yourself. You came in last in the parent lottery." Doug's opinion of my parents isn't the best, and I get why. "I always wanted something better for you, Billie. Leaving is probably best, you know? As long as you don't end up somewhere worse than here."

"Don't worry about me." My smile is weak. "I've got this. I'll be fine."

"Uh-huh." He pulls out his ashtray and taps the cigarette against the edge, sullying the chipped white dish with a streak of ash. "Just—be careful, Billie. Feels like no one is watching out for you."

No one is, I want to tell him, but instead I offer a shallow nod and reach around to untie the black apron I wear when I'm working. "I have to go."

"You give me notice and then leave immediately?" The

hurt in his voice almost undoes me. Doug doesn't do feelings—he does sarcasm and bar tabs. He looks like he wants to say more but can't figure out how.

I reach up, twist the thin silver hoop in my nose, and pretend not to notice. Pretending helps us both. "Not like you're swamped." I wave a hand at the near-empty bar, then head for the back and grab my bag, tossing my apron in the laundry bin for the last time. I nearly miss, and it hangs over the edge like I feel—half in, half out, not sure where I belong.

A minute later, Doug pushes his way through the swinging door.

"I need to pay you," he says, voice gruff. He heads over to the small safe he keeps next to the rickety old desk and taps at the keypad, opening it with a *click*. Within seconds he's standing in front of me, a fistful of cash clutched between his fingers.

"That looks like too much," I start, but he shoves it in front of my face, cutting me off.

"Take it, Billie. Not like I've got anywhere to spend it."

"Maybe on rent?" The temptation to grab the cash and run out of the building is strong. It's definitely more than I've earned in the last week.

"I've got that covered. Just take the damn money. You're the closest thing I've got to a kid, and—" There's an odd shine in Doug's eyes. "I just want you to be okay." Before things get too deep, which will make both of us want to crawl out of our skin, I grab the money and stuff the wad in my backpack.

"Thank you." I check my phone, and my chest tightens. I need to leave. "I gotta go. See ya around, Doug."

For a second, we just stand there—both of us knowing this

goodbye is more than it seems. I half-lift my hand, not sure if I should hug him or wave. He just nods, a quiet agreement that it's better to keep it simple, and turns back to the safe.

I take the out, push through the swinging door, and don't look back.

I make my way between the tables and chairs, pausing just long enough to scoop up the soggy dollars those jerks left as my tip. Only when I'm outside do I feel like I can breathe again, and I release a shuddery exhale, hating the dread settling over my skin like a heavy coat.

Then I remember I'm getting out of here, and the tiniest flicker of hope sparks to life in my chest. This is my chance to get away. To change my life for the better. That's what I have to hold on to. A fresh start. Sounds like a cliché, but my life has been one long sequence of bad clichés: Child of a single mom too busy drinking her sorrows away to do much parenting. Absentee dad thriving with his new family an ocean away. Smart enough to go places, according to all my teachers, but too broke to travel. I've survived through all of this mess so far, because that's what I do. That's what I am.

A survivor.

I'll probably never see Doug again, I think as I make my way down the sidewalk, headed toward my apartment building. There's an uncomfortable pressure behind my eyes at the thought, and I decide to send him a text when I'm settled again. Just to let him know I'm okay. Nothing too mushy.

I sidestep a broken-open Styrofoam container spilling greasy noodles over the street as I take a left off Seventh Avenue. Wrinkling my nose at the scent of rancid garbage and piss, I wonder if other cities smell like wilted hot trash and bodily functions, or if it's unique to this part of New York. It's disgusting, but I know we're lucky to have this apartment at all. We're close to Penn Station, which on the plus side means I can sometimes hear strains of music from concerts at Madison Square Garden. On the minus side? Pretty much everything else.

It's not glamorous, and it's not fun, and it's not even especially tolerable most days, but this *is* my life.

Or it was.

Until a certain someone came crashing back into my world and demanded I come see him. Help him. He must've been downright desperate to ask for *my* help. I wish I could take some pleasure in his pain, but even I'm not jaded enough for that. Not when his reason for reaching out ripped both our hearts in two.

I'm halfway down the block when one of my neighbors on the front stoop across the street shouts at me. "Hey yo, Billie! How much will it cost me for a smile today?"

"Oh I don't know, Sammy," I yell back, pretending to root around in my front pocket. "Can you make change for this?" I hold up my middle finger like it's a five-dollar bill I just found. I'm barely able to contain the smile that wants to stretch across my lips. This is our love language, slinging insults at each other.

He just laughs, calling, "Aw, next time, Billie, next time! Get home safe, girl."

I keep walking, spotting Mrs. Espinosa up ahead, struggling with two heavy bags of groceries she's practically dragging along the sidewalk. I jog to catch up with her, take one of the bags and heft it in my arms, then run up the stairs to our building door and tap the code to unlock it before holding it open for her.

"Thank you, Billie *dearest*." She lays the sarcasm on thick. She hates feeling like she can't run her normal errands, and I know she never wants help, but I always worry she's going to bust open one of those bags and spill her stuff everywhere. "You know I can handle it."

"Oh I know, Mrs. Espinosa. I only wanted to see if you had any Cracker Jack in here." I peek inside the bag and spot the familiar box. No one else I know eats it, and I'd never even heard of Cracker Jack until I found a box in another one of her bags a couple of years ago.

"Don't you dare steal my only treat." She slaps at my hand as I dig into the bag with what she calls my dirty little laugh.

"I would never." Once I walk her to her door on the first floor, I offer her a quick wave and head up the stairs to the third floor, not bothering with the elevator. It's old and rickety and hot as balls.

When I enter my apartment, I pause for a moment, taking it in. There's Mom sprawled out on the couch, dead to the world. Either asleep or passed out drunk, I'm not sure. She better be easy to wake up, though, because we need to leave soon.

Walking over to the couch, I tighten my jaw. I shake her shoulder, and her hazel eyes flutter open on a soft groan.

"It's time," I tell her, my voice firm.

She lurches upward, running her fingers through her snarled hair as she watches me move about the room. I pick up the garbage littering the coffee table and shake my head. I won't miss living in this chaos. I head to the kitchen and toss out the leftover fast-food wrappers and empty paper cups, then check the fridge, relieved to see it's mostly empty. Nothing will spoil in there while we're gone.

Mom yawns and stretches as I shuffle around, straightening shit and tossing out empty bottles before I stand back to take in the room again. This place is as clean as it's going to get. Besides, we've only got about half an hour before we need to leave.

At my urging, Mom takes a quick shower while I grab a duffel bag and start packing for her, shoving stuff inside that she'll probably need. She's barely able to think straight and depends on me for way too much, and I know she's not going to protest what happens next. Not really.

Hopefully.

Once I'm done with her bag, I go to my room and finish packing my own stuff, though I'm not taking much. Just enough to fill my black backpack. A few changes of clothes, a toiletry bag, and all the freaking money I've saved up over the years. I open my door, stopping short when I find my mom standing directly in front of me.

"Don't forget this," Mom says, her familiar British accent thick with emotion. Her mousy brown hair is dripping wet from the shower, and her skin is waxy and sallow, but at least she's already got some clothes on. She's holding that stupid photo of the four of us on a cliff, standing under a giant tree with smiles on our faces. It's a moment in time I can't recall, but that's never stopped Mom from acting like this photo represents my most precious memory.

Her voice still sounds like London—smooth, proper, with a careful lilt I used to try and copy when I was a kid. I'd trail after her around the apartment, practicing my *what-evers* and *bloody hells* until she laughed and called me her little parrot. I wanted to be just like her. But then her world cracked apart, and I forced myself to be nothing like her—flattened my vowels, sharpened my rs, built myself an American accent thick enough to drown her out.

I even slashed the dull brown hair we share with thick blue streaks, as if color could erase the parts of her still hiding in me.

"You want to take it with you?" I reach for the chipped gold frame, to pack it with her things, but she shrinks back. She stares at the photo with that lost look in her eyes that she always has when she glimpses into the past, at a family that doesn't exist anymore.

"No." She firmly shakes her head. "You should take it with you."

"I don't want—"

Mom cuts me off by shoving the frame in my hands, and I have no choice but to take it. I stash the photo in my backpack. I'll throw it away later—I don't need the reminder. I don't live in the past like my mother does. Besides, where I'm going, being her daughter is even more of a liability than usual.

"Ninety days," I remind Mom. She makes a face but doesn't say anything. "It's only ninety days, and then everything will go back to normal."

The lie falls easily from my lips. Not the ninety days part—that's true, only because it's all I could get Peter to agree to. No, it's the "back to normal" line that I know is a lie. Nothing is going to be normal ever again.

Not if I can help it.

Taking one last, long glimpse at the too-small, too-dark apartment that we've lived in for years, I kick the door shut, thankful I had the foresight to demand Peter prepay the rent for the next three months. I might have agreed to let him blow up my life for the foreseeable future, but eventually, I'll need somewhere to come home to.

Even if that means returning to this shithole.

But first, I gotta take my mom to rehab.

...

The woman sitting behind the check-in desk at Merciful Mary Rehabilitation Center taps away at her keyboard, her brows drawing together as she studies the computer screen. Nerves eat at my insides, making it hard to stay still. I want to run. Flee this sterile lobby and take my mom with me.

My father better not have backed out of our agreement. I don't trust him, and why should I? He's not a good man. If he was, he would've taken care of me. Would've tried to establish a relationship with me for my entire life, not just now, when he needs my help.

"It looks like your mom's stay is prepaid in full," the woman finally says, her gaze lifting to mine. The flood of relief turns my knees liquid. "We have a room reserved for her. Is she ready?"

"Let me go talk to her." I push away from the counter and approach Mom with tentative steps, not wanting her to freak out. I settle onto the couch beside her, grab hold of her hands, and clutch them tight.

Mom frowns, and I offer her a reassuring smile. "I've got to go, and you're staying here. They're going to help you, Mom. Clean you up."

A trembling sigh passes her lips, and she hangs her head, her fingers tightening around mine. "It won't work, Billie. It never does."

Her voice is small—the kind she used when I'd cry over a scraped knee. I can almost hear the old softness underneath the damage.

"It might," I say, trying to sound steadier than I feel. "You just have to want it this time."

Mom shakes her head, a wet laugh catching in her throat. "You don't understand. The memories will come back."

Her eyes search mine, pleading, but I don't know what she means. "You mean Dad?" I ask, then pause before adding, "Or Isla?"

She flinches, like I've brushed against an open wound. We both rarely mention my sister's name. At fifteen, she's only fourteen months younger than me. Irish twins, Mom used to say. But Mom just shakes her head. "You don't understand what happened," she whispers. "What we did. If I could undo it all—"

"Mom." I squeeze her hands, cutting her off before she can spiral. She's never actually said what happened back in England, but honestly, who gives a fuck at this point. We've been in the States since I was six. Unless her and my dad killed somebody, I'd like to think I'd be able to get over anything if it meant being there for my own kid. That thought has my next words coming out a little harsher than I intend. "We all have shit we'd undo if we could. But you can't keep drinking away the past. You have to deal."

Tears spill over, quick and hot, and she turns her face away from me. "Just go then. Not like you care anyway."

My throat burns, but I force my voice to stay calm. "That's not true."

My stomach cramps into angry knots. My mom loves to twist every word until you don't know what's real anymore. I know it's not on purpose—it's just how she survives. She clings to pain the way I cling to control. Maybe that's our family inheritance—holding tight to the things that feel like help but only hurt us in the end.

I stand and let her fingers slip from mine. "I love you, Mom," I say, meaning every word, even when it hurts to say it. To feel it. She doesn't look at me. "Bye."

After sending the woman behind the counter a meaningful look, I exit the building. I lean against the brick facade, heave a sigh, and close my eyes for a moment. The rush of city traffic goes whipping by, making the air stir, and I open my eyes, surprised my mom isn't standing in front of me, begging me to take her back home.

I push away from the building and flag down a cab. Normally I'd take the subway, but I don't have it in me to be underground right now—not when this might be the last time I see New York for who knows how long. When I'm settled into the back and the driver has the address of the private airfield entered into his GPS, I open the Notes app in my phone and start a new note titled PETER PAYBACK. If that asshole thinks I'm going to spend a single dime of my own hard-earned money pulling his ass out of the fire, he's got another think coming. The way I see it, he could compensate me for every dollar I've ever spent and that wouldn't even begin to cover the compensation I'm owed. After all, he's responsible for Mom's demise.

She's never been able to get over him.

So I guess it's true what they say—there's no accounting for taste.

Me? I hate Peter Vale. It's a burning fire that lives in my gut, always there, flickering to life whenever I think about him.

Like now.

I lean back against the cracked seat and put my earbuds in, a sign to my driver that I don't want to engage in conversation. I open my phone and check my texts, but I don't have any. Then check social media. I haven't posted in months. I'm more of a lurker—a spy who checks out other people's lives but never posts about her own. Not that anyone cares. I've been doing online school since I was a freshman and already got my high school degree an entire year early. It was easy. School is a joke. A racket.

One I'm going back to like an idiot, but sometimes we have to do things we hate to help the people we love. The people we let down.

Not Peter. That guy can go fuck himself.

But Isla? Isla I let down, and now my sister desperately needs my help. And by God, I'm going to help her, no matter what it takes.

When we finally arrive at the private airfield, I pay the driver in cash and record the amount on Peter's tab. I climb out of the car, sling my backpack over my shoulder, and head into the small building, my voice monotone when I tell the woman sitting behind the desk my name.

"The plane has been waiting for you." Her nose wrinkles like I stink as she studies me over her glasses. I'm wearing my typical uniform: black-and-burgundy-striped tank top and black jeans with knockoff Doc Martens, layers of silver necklaces I love to pile on, and bracelets in every material from leather to metal to string on both wrists. I flick my dark hair away from my eyes, frowning at her. Her disapproval is a sharp top note to her floral, overly sweet perfume.

Well fuck her.

I offer the woman a curt nod and stride outside like I own the place, running on pure instinct. The plane is waiting for me, just like she said it would be. The aircraft's stairs are down, and a man stands by the base. His gaze narrows on mine as I draw closer, a fake smile slowly turning up the corners of his mouth.

"Miss Winters?" I stop short, the name catching me off guard.

For a heartbeat, I almost correct him—then I remember the deal I made with my dad. And just like that, Billie Vale no longer exists.

I'm Belinda Winters now.

The name feels awkward in my mouth, like I've just taken a too-big bite of ice cream and I have to wait for it to melt a little before I can chew or swallow or even breathe. I remind myself that Belinda *is* my legal name, though hardly anyone's used it in my living memory. My grandmother's maiden name on my mother's side was Winters—a factoid Peter shared like he has any right to mine and Mom's family history.

"Yup. That's me." I nod once, gripping the backpack strap extra tight, trying to hold steady against a sudden wave of nerves. I can do this. I haven't let myself feel afraid for years, but that bravery only works in the face of all the old familiar terrors. Mom not waking up from a blackout. Getting evicted. Never finding a way out of the shitty circumstances that have defined my life so far.

This is new. Different. Foreign.

I'm going to need a new kind of bravery. And I'm going to have to fake it until I figure it out.

Starting right now.

"We're ready for you to board." He makes a sweeping gesture up to the open plane door. I practically run up the stairs, pausing as I enter to take in the luxurious interior of the private jet my estranged father arranged for me.

It reeks of wealth and power, and as much as I hate to admit it, wealth and power smell good. Expensive. The cream-colored leather interior and sleek lights are a far cry from the industrial-looking sardine can–sized planes I've seen on TV. Plush carpet squishes under my boots, and I have the unhinged urge to take them off and sink my toes in. I throw myself into a seat and drop my bag into the empty chair next to me. I strap in, politely refusing the offer of food and drink from the smiley flight attendant.

My chest tightens painfully, and I absently rub at the space above my heart. Peter Vale owns this plane. A plane that has its own private flight attendant and staff. A plane that's at his disposal at any time, day or night. Meaning he could've come to see me any time he wanted to, but did he?

No. Never. Not once.

I only know what he looks like because of photos on the internet. His voice was totally unfamiliar to me until a couple of days ago, when I picked up a call from an unknown number. *I need you*, he said. I laughed when I heard those words.

Please. He doesn't need me. He doesn't even *know* me. He's just using me, which is fine.

I'm using him, too.

The moment the pilot announces we're preparing for takeoff, I tense up. I don't remember the only other time in my life when I flew—back when I was six years old, and Mom couldn't stop crying, and we were leaving England behind for our new life in America. Our new life...alone together. Without Peter. Without Isla. Clenching the armrests, I take a deep breath, telling myself I'm fine. The plane won't crash. Thousands of planes are in the air right now. This is nothing.

But it feels like everything.

I'm a knot of nerves through takeoff, but when the flight attendant finally says it's safe to move around the cabin, my grip loosens and my shoulders drop away from my ears. Maybe I'm still shaking inside, but I'm doing it—I'm moving forward. I'm committed now. And if there's one thing I've learned from years of taking care of someone who only ever breaks promises, it's how to keep mine.

I unbuckle, grab my backpack, and make for the bathroom at the back of the cabin.

I yank open the door and close it behind me with a metallic *click*.

Staring at my reflection in the mirror, I take a long last look at the old me. Billie Vale may have boarded this plane, but Belinda Winters is stepping off it. I can't be me anymore if I'm going to have any hope of pulling this off. Might as well lean into being *her*.

I take out and unzip a tiny, satin-lined bag before I start removing my jewelry. The nose ring comes out first, then my rows of three tiny silver hoop earrings in each ear. Next, I peel off the necklaces, not bothering to untangle the chains before dumping them in. I shake off the bangles, then undo the tiny clasps of the smaller bracelets, dropping them in the bag with the necklaces. I straighten and stare at my reflection, taking in the heavy black eyeliner, thick mascara, and pale foundation I wear. I use the last of my makeup wipes to smear it off before I wash my face, scrubbing until my skin hurts and my cheeks glow pink.

There's one more piece to this puzzle, and it might be the most important. I pull out the box of hair dye I bought at the Duane Reade closest to Doug's bar, and follow the instructions, praying I don't damage my hair so badly it all falls out. As I add the color, I stare in the mirror, repeating the same words over and over.

"Belinda Winters, Manhattan socialite." I make a face. Like I'd ever say that to someone. "Yes, hello. I'm Belinda Winters. Belinda. Yes, from Manhattan."

I keep repeating nonsense phrases until I find Belinda's voice. "And then I said *you have to stop, that's not our yacht!*" Higher, I think, and a little brighter. "I mean seriously, Malta is so 2022." A touch more nasal. "Where'd I get this bag? I mean, it's vintage Givenchy, so like…heaven, I guess?" Annnd there she is. Belinda's laugh tinkles like a bell made of sunshine and generational wealth.

While waiting for the color to set, I pick up my phone and archive all my social media, wiping myself from existence with a few taps on a screen. I suppose Peter has a team of people who could vanish my online footprint, replacing it with the newly formed New York socialite I'm now supposed to be.

God, this all sounds like a nightmare, but one I'm determined to conquer.

Once the timer is up, I wash my hair by leaning into the tiny shower and using the handheld nozzle. The water pressure is shit, and it takes forever to rinse the color out. The water swirling down the drain runs dark and strange—like I'm watching the last version of me disappear. When it finally runs clear, I grab a towel and dry my hair as best I can. Then I turn toward the mirror, and my mouth drops open, my fair skin turning even paler when I see my new color.

Oh no. It looks freaking *terrible*.

Dear old Dad is going to kill me.

CHAPTER TWO

I jolt awake when the plane touches down, glancing around the interior in confusion. It takes me a minute to remember where I am and where I'm about to go, and my nerves flare up, my stomach churning. I can't tell if it's from hunger or nausea.

"The plane just landed," the flight attendant says, appearing in front of me looking fresh and beautiful. Her simple charcoal gray uniform doesn't have a wrinkle in sight, while I'm a rumpled mess, with the badly dyed hair. And I'm pretty sure I left a drool stain on the plain black T-shirt I changed into after my hair color fiasco. "We should be disembarking shortly."

"Thank you," I mumble, afraid to speak too loudly or I might blast her with my bad breath.

"Would you care for something to eat?" Her lilting British accent makes my chest ache, and I realize it's because she reminds me of a version of my mother I knew a lifetime ago. "Some fruit? A croissant, maybe?"

"Do you have any coffee?" When she nods, I go on. "I'd

love some. And yeah, croissant, please."

The flight attendant beams. "Give me a few minutes and I'll bring it to you. You should be able to eat before we finish taxiing."

My stomach growls the moment she mentions eating. I will most definitely be able to get it down before we finish taxiing.

Once I get caffeine coursing through my veins and some carbs in my gut, I feel a little more alert. By the time the door opens and the flight attendant leads me out of the plane, I'm almost able to convince myself this whole charade isn't going to be an abject disaster.

A sleek black car sits on the tarmac, the engine purring and the windows tinted so dark, I can't see who's inside. My pulse races and my hands start to shake as I wonder if Peter is waiting for me in the back seat. I haven't seen him in almost twelve years, and I'll admit—I'm not looking forward to a reunion. As I head for the car, the wind whips my hideous hair across my face, and I peel it away from my eyes, shivering from the chill in the air. I come to a stop when the driver's side door opens and a tall, lanky man in a black suit climbs out.

My shoulders sag with relief.

"Miss Belinda Winters?" His voice is deep, and his accent is different from the flight attendant's. More polished somehow.

"Yes." I nod. My backpack nearly slips off my shoulder, and I readjust it, ignoring the way he's staring at me. Well, staring at my hair. It must look atrocious. "That's me."

"We have a stop to make first." His smile is pleasant, though it doesn't quite reach his eyes. "Before we head to Wickham Academy."

I frown. "Where are we going?"

He doesn't say a word, just holds his hand out for my backpack. I shake my head, because no way am I letting Lurch abscond with all my worldly goods. He nods, somehow managing to convey both acceptance and judgment at the same time. He holds the back passenger door open for me, and I slide inside. During the thirty seconds it takes him to round the front of the limo and get behind the wheel, I entertain a fantasy about sneaking back on the plane, barricading myself in the bathroom, and refusing to come out until we touch down again in the States. But with the press of a button, the engine roars to life and the opportunity to escape fades like exhaust from a rusty tailpipe.

We slog through city streets crowded with cars, all of them driving on the wrong side of the road, and I can't get over how weird it looks. There are classic red double-decker buses and black taxicabs, and I feel like a little kid with my face pressed to the window, watching it all go by. At one point, I spot the giant London Eye wheel, Big Ben not too far past it, and I stare unabashedly. It's almost surreal, being here. Like something from a movie. When I catch the driver watching me in the rearview mirror with amusement in his eyes, I pull away from the window, pretending I'm too cool to act like such a tourist.

The drive is long because of traffic, and it feels like it takes us forever to get anywhere. Eventually the gentle rocking of the car makes me sleepy. I only fell asleep the last hour on the plane, unable to get comfortable enough in my chair to doze off. Though I noticed later there was a whole-ass bed in the back of the plane. I missed out.

Although honestly, I doubt I could have slept much, even in the bed. Seeing Peter has always been the least interesting part of this arrangement, but the prospect of coming face-to-face with the man who separated me from my baby sister and left me stranded halfway around the world with a mom struggling with addiction started to feel too real at thirty thousand feet up. I hate myself for wondering what he'll think of me. Probably not much.

By the time the car comes to a stop, I'm exhausted and my thoughts are fuzzy. The driver once again opens the door for me, and I step outside to find we're in front of a large hospital. This is when it hits me and my hands start to really shake.

He brought me here to see Isla.

My baby sister—who I haven't seen outside a phone screen since our parents split us down the middle like property in a divorce when I was six.

I follow the driver from the car through the sliding glass doors of the hospital, grateful he knows where to go because I don't have a clue. He stops to talk to the woman behind the reception desk, speaking in low tones I can't decipher. Within minutes, I'm being whisked down several narrow hallways and into an elevator, a nurse as my guide.

"We're taking the service elevator," she explains, talking slowly, like I might have trouble understanding her. "We're keeping her whereabouts private, as her father requested."

It takes everything inside me not to grimace in disgust at the words "her father."

"The media has been unrelenting since the news broke. The scandal surrounding what really happened on that cliff is just..." She clamps her lips shut and shakes her head. I'm getting more and more pissed with every word she says. I can't believe this woman is practically gossiping about my little sister to me.

Time to take Belinda Winters for a spin.

"Your discretion must be such a comfort to the family." My voice is sharp as I try to contain my anger. But my words are a reprimand, and the woman realizes it. She stands a little straighter, averting her gaze.

We don't say another word to each other. When the elevator comes to a stop and the doors slide open, I stride forward like I own the place.

"She's in room twenty-six," the nurse calls after me.

Still simmering with annoyance, I don't so much as acknowledge her. I keep my chin up, though my nerves want me to hunch my shoulders and cower. I can't remember the last time I was in the same room as Isla. Though whenever it was, at least she was conscious.

We've drifted apart over the last year—missed calls, half-written texts I never sent. My chest aches for all the almosts between us. Somewhere along the line, it got too hard to pretend my life was holding steady while hers kept shining. And yeah, I'll admit it—jealousy crept in. Dad fought to keep her. No one fought for me.

Now I'm on my way to see her again, and the irony burns. After all this time, I finally get to be reunited with my sister... and she won't even know I'm there.

And that just about breaks my heart.

I pull up short at the sight of the police officer standing outside Isla's room. For a second, I let myself believe this is just Peter being overprotective of the daughter he actually cares about. But the truth rushes in like a tidal wave, destroying all my illusions.

The officer isn't here to protect her.

He's here to arrest her if she ever wakes up.

I approach warily, but after checking my name—Belinda's name—against a list on a clipboard tucked into a holder on the door, he lets me in.

I creep into the cold, silent room, coming to a stop when I see Isla lying in the bed. She looks like an angel, her blond hair spread across the pillow, her lips softly parted. The blankets are tucked around her, and it feels like she could wake up at any moment. Could laugh and smile and greet me in that sunny way of hers, the one I ignored far too many times.

She's hooked up to a monitor, the subtle beep keeping time with the steady beat of her heart. My baby sister is in a coma, and the guilt nearly causes my knees to buckle.

Grabbing a nearby chair, I pull it close to her bedside and settle in so I can watch her, staring at her face like I could make her wake up with my thoughts. She doesn't move. She's like a perfect wax statue, a sleeping beauty unaware of all the trouble that surrounds her. The rumors and the lies and the accusations. Does she remember what happened? Who did this to her?

The sight of Isla so defenseless makes my heart crack, and I reach for her hand, cradling it between both of mine.

"Isla. I'm here. And I'm going to help you. I promise."

No response. Just the steady beep of the monitor. Her hand is frail, her skin chilled, and I clutch it tighter, desperate to warm her up.

"I know we haven't talked much and that was—that was

my fault. But I'm here now. We're reunited at last." I grimace at the last statement, hating how corny I sound. Worse, hating that she's not awake to give me shit for it. It's pointless, this one-sided conversation, but I don't know what else to do. Or how I'm going to actually manage this—my new life. But seeing my sister in this bed, knowing she's in a coma, that someone did this to her... It shores up my resolve to clear her name. To be the big sister I should have been all along.

"I don't know if I can do this," I whisper, the words more air than sound.

"You'd better," says a deep voice from behind me.

Dropping Isla's hand, I turn to find Peter Vale standing in the doorway of my sister's hospital room, his expression unreadable. His features are sharp, his eyes the darkest blue I've ever seen against his lightly tanned skin, and I'm breathless for a moment. Scared of my own father.

But then my anger comes roaring back to life. I rise from my chair, making my way toward him with measured steps. I cling to the rage, needing it to fuel me. I come to a stop directly in front of him, tilting my head back so I can stare into his eyes. Breathing the same air for the first time I can recall.

"I'm surprised you actually came." His voice is like ice. Sharp and bitterly cold.

"Some of us keep our promises," I say, and it brings him up short. The silence stretches so taut between us, it feels like the air itself might tear in two.

But then Peter breaks our eye contact to gesture toward the three shiny black suitcases to his right. "You'll find everything you need in these."

I stare at the luggage, wondering what the hell I could need that fills three huge suitcases, but I suppose he knows best.

"I'm sure I needn't remind you that my wife had to pull a number of strings and call in quite a few favors to get you into Wickham Academy. If you reveal yourself, or if anyone discovers that we're related, the entire plan will be ruined," he says. "And whoever did this to Isla will get away with it. Because of you."

I scoff. The nerve of this man. "Like I'd tell anyone we're related. I'd rather be in a coma myself than consider you family."

His gaze flickers with irritation, but that's his only reaction. The dude is ice-cold.

"Whitney wanted me to give you this." He hands over a matte black folder that practically begs to be called a *dossier*. Inside, I find a letter welcoming me to Wickham Academy, printed on heavy, textured paper. Nice to see my new school spares no expense on the details.

"Great." I rifle through the other documents inside, but I don't really read them. "Can't wait."

Peter's gaze has gone from assessing to penetrating, like he's trying to see through my skin to the blood and bones underneath. I resist the urge to squirm, because if someone in this room should feel uncomfortable, it definitely shouldn't be me. "There's something else," he says, his words cutting through the tension in the air like a hot knife through butter.

His eyes flick to Isla behind me, and the sight of her melts the stern disapproval right off his face. He keeps his gaze trained on her, and I don't know if it's because he's drinking in every second he can with her, or if he'd just rather look anywhere but at me. I don't usually celebrate how similar

Mom and I look, but if seeing her features on my face reminds my father of the woman he abandoned, I call it a win. Let him remember. I've never been able to forget.

A glimmer of smug satisfaction is just starting to warm me from the inside out when he clears his throat and hands me a large manila envelope.

"What's this?" I ask, when what I want to say is, *do you realize you've given me more things in the past minute than you have in the past dozen years?*

"Isla's Year 11 yearbook. Whitney and I thought it might help you understand who's who at Wickham. And..." He closes his eyes and heaves a heavy sigh, like what he has to say next might sting on the way out. I sure hope it does. "Isla was working on a project of sorts. About the history of the academy. She'd started asking questions about things she probably should have left alone. Some of her notes are in the back of the yearbook. You should probably ignore them."

When he shifts his attention from the envelope to my face, his stare is hardened, icy.

"You're here for one reason, and one reason only. I want to know who's responsible for this—for *all* of this," he says. "My network and Whitney's connections can only get us so far. But someone on the inside will have access we don't. Keep your eyes and ears open. Don't get distracted."

"One job, don't screw it up—got it. Anything else?"

His gaze narrows, composure clicking back into place like a suit of armor. "Yes. We learned today that Isla will be formally charged with the murder of Emily Wells in two weeks. At that time, she'll be moved to a facility in the north—not the kind of place you'd like to be if you were unconscious and unable to defend yourself. Two weeks, Belinda. After that, she'll be beyond my reach."

I fight to keep my expression neutral when inside, alarm bells are blaring and strobe lights are flashing, and is that a foghorn? Two weeks until my sister is officially charged with the murder of her best friend. And I'm just supposed to stay standing, like the ground is trying to swallow me up?

Peter clears his throat. "You're supposed to be the jewel of New York's next generation. Would it kill you to look the part?"

I almost roll my eyes, even though all I want to do is scream. "I tried to dye my hair on the plane. It...didn't go exactly to plan."

Shaking his head, he wanders toward the window at the side of the room, his phone already in his hand. "Wait outside for a moment," he says over his shoulder, pressing the phone to his ear.

I kiss my fingertips and press them to Isla's cheek, then shove the folder and yearbook in my backpack. I head back into the corridor and approach the gangly nurse who just sat down behind the counter across from Isla's room. "The person in room twenty-six is my—" I catch myself. I'm sure my father wouldn't want the hospital staff knowing we're related. "My dear school friend. Can I add my number to the call list if she wakes up?"

She runs a hand through her dark hair, her brown gaze bouncing between my father and me. "I'll need to get permission from her father—"

"No need. He's right over there," I say, a wide smile stretching my lips. "Talking to Tokyo. Some big business deal or other." I glance back at him and toss over my shoulder, "Almost done, Mr. Vale?"

He scowls in my direction. "Hurry up, Belinda," he barks, then goes back to his call.

I startle at my father's use of my full name. But only for a second. Then I channel my quick anger into my performance. He wanted a Belinda so badly, he can have one. I turn back to the nurse, putting on an over-the-top snooty accent I've heard Isla use a thousand times when she's imitating her teachers. "Sorry, dear. In a rush." I reach over the counter, grab a pen, and scrawl my number on the back of a notepad. I hold the paper out. "Here you go. Just give a ring if she wakes, yes? Thanks so much!"

The nurse blinks at me, then reaches for the number. I mean, what else was she going to do, leave my hand hanging in the air? Put people in an awkward position, and nine times out of ten, they'll take the path of least resistance.

I blow her a kiss and twirl around, bouncing up to Peter. Maybe it will be easier to fake rich-and-entitled than I expected. "Ready when you are, Mr. Vale."

He puts his phone away. "Whitney just arranged an emergency appointment for you at her salon."

I frown. I've never met my stepmother before, but I've heard stories. All from Isla.

"The state of my hair is an emergency?"

"You can't show up on campus looking like that. No one will believe you come from money."

I grit my teeth. "Gee, that's so crazy, considering I don't."

My father ignores me, snapping his fingers once. Two guys stride over from the waiting area nearby, their expressions expectant, like eager dogs. "Take the luggage to the car."

They do so immediately, leaving us alone with my father still just inside the room, me just outside. Like always.

"You'll get your hair fixed and then you'll head to campus. The drive is long, and the road is windy. You'll most likely become carsick. I recommend—"

"I'll be fine," I snap, cutting him off. I don't want any sort of fatherly concern or advice from this man. "I guess I'll be on my way."

I head for the elevator, my steps slowing when my father calls my name. His voice is soft. Almost paternal. The sound throws me for a total loop.

Stopping, I glance over my shoulder to find he's watching me, his expression a mask. Unreadable. No emotion whatsoever. "Two weeks, Belinda. Isla's counting on you."

Jaw clenched, I rip my gaze away, square my shoulders, and stride through the open elevator door. "No shit, Sherlock."

CHAPTER THREE

My father wasn't lying. The road to Wickham is windy as shit, and I'm clutching my stomach, eyes squeezed shut, praying I don't lose my lunch all over my new sweater. Or *jumper*, as the hair stylist called it, her eyes glowing when she took it in.

Peter texted to ask that I change into more "suitable clothing" for my arrival at Wickham. I threw on the first sweater I found in one of the suitcases, quietly marveling at how soft and luxurious it felt on my skin. The hair stylist told me it was cashmere, and I believed her because why would she lie?

The stylist was nice. Incredibly chatty and constantly trying to dig for information, but I remained tight-lipped. Not about to give away a thing. She fixed my hair like a miracle worker, the color now a soft, butter yellow she called "trust fund blond," instead of brassy streaks of orange and gold—like a stray ginger cat I once fed.

"You look just like Carolyn Kennedy," she told me as we

both stared into the mirror to check out the results, her hands on my shoulders making me uncomfortable. I don't like it when strangers touch me.

I don't like it when anybody touches me.

Other than JFK and Jackie O, I can't tell one rich, beautiful Kennedy from another. But I put on Belinda's voice and said, "Carolyn! I was thinking the same thing." The stylist beamed a too-white smile at me through the mirror.

My phone buzzes, and I check it to find another notification from Peter.

Peter Vale: *Read the dossier.*

Dossier. Called it. Snobs are so predictable. I scowl at the folder already open in my lap.

Me: Do *you mean all those papers you gave me? Sure. I'll read them soon.*

I'm lying. I read as much as I could before the road turned into nothing but nausea-inducing curves. I can't imagine why knowing the history of Wickham Academy is pertinent info when my goal is finding out who tried to unalive my sister, but maybe knowing this stuff is second nature to the students here. It's ABCs and 123s for us public school kids, while it's family trees stretching back to Queen Elizabeth I and obscure histories of private schools for kids to the manor born.

Whatever.

If Belinda needs to know that Wickham was founded in 1879 by the families of a few Harrow School dropouts whose sons kept getting "sent down" for misbehavior, so be it. My takeaway? Wickham Academy has always been a safe haven for kids whose families have too much money and way too much privilege.

Though to be fair, an article in the dossier claims the current headmaster, Percy Harrington, has done *the most* to solidify Wickham's reputation as "an institution for rigorous academic excellence." I guess being infamous for sheltering the children of the rich and lazy isn't good for long-term endowment.

My stomach twists as we take another hairpin turn, and I wrap one arm across my waist. How am I going to pull this off? I have no idea how to act like some fancy rich person, and no amount of reading school histories is going to help with that.

For a moment, I want to fling open the door and jump out of the car. No need to even slow down. The urge to run away is so strong, even a broken leg sounds appealing. At least I could get a room alongside Isla to recover in. But just thinking her name, remembering her helpless body in the hospital, has me squaring my shoulders.

Determination fills me, and I take a deep breath, holding it for a second before I exhale. I need to remain strong so I can figure out what happened and who might've done this to my little sister. The sweetest girl ever, who wouldn't harm a soul.

I glance down at the most recent news article Peter included in the dossier. The headline reads MURDER-SUICIDE AT WICKHAM CLIFFS.

Two black-and-white pictures are framed on the left. One is Isla, smiling brightly with her blond hair in a thick ponytail, and the other is her best friend, Emily Wells, with dark hair cut just above her chin. I scan the article and frown. Nothing I haven't read before since the night my father called, but still, seeing my sister's name splashed throughout the article as an assumed murderer leaves a bitter coating on my tongue. The reporter claims police are investigating a theory that the two girls went up to a cliff near campus, got into a fight, and Isla pushed Emily. Isla allegedly jumped after her in an attempted suicide.

I read the whole article, though my stomach heaves at the words: "A source close to the investigation who asked to remain anonymous shared that the police had ruled out a suicide pact based on the position of Wells's body. 'She couldn't have fallen as far as she did if she jumped. She was thrown or pushed, no question.'"

But I don't believe it. I can't believe it.

Neither does Peter.

The car eventually comes to a stop, and I glance up from the papers to find we're idling in front of a closed gate. Tall, spindly wrought iron poles brace the name of the school stretched in an arc in fancy script, the letters rising toward the cloudy sky, gleaming wet from the drizzling rain.

The gates slowly open with a groan, and the driver accelerates, heading down the long drive. I sit up straighter, staring at the landscape, hating how...charming it is. Like something out of a movie or book.

Cobblestone paths wind their way through the sweeping, lush green lawns toward what I assume is the main building on campus. It appears ancient, as if it's stood here for centuries. A gothic monolith of crumbling brick, stained glass, and climbing ivy. Turrets crown each corner of the towering structure, the lead mullioned windows reminding me of watchful eyes that never sleep.

Behind the building looms a massive, brick bell tower, a tall black column against the darkening sky. I roll the window down and take a deep breath, savoring the cool breeze. The air is sharp with the scent of wet leaves and something I can't place. Dirt, maybe? The steady drizzle splats my face, and I immediately close the window, reaching for the door when the car comes to a stop. I'm conflicted. I want to both get this started and run away at the same time. I'm nervous. Scared. What if I mess this up?

"Hold on, miss. Let me help you."

I wait for the driver to open the door but bolt out the moment he does and run up the stone steps to large wooden double doors to get out of the rain. Under the relative shelter at the top of the stairs, I look back to find the driver still standing next to the car, holding an umbrella big enough to keep us and our five closest friends dry.

Oops.

The campus is eerily quiet, and I pause, checking my phone. It's almost noon. My hair appointment made me late, and I'm glad I can take in the school without hundreds of interested eyes watching me.

I slip into the building, glancing around until I find a door with a brass sign above it that says ADMINISTRATION. I slowly open the door to find a matronly receptionist sitting behind a desk, a reserved smile on her face.

"Hello. You must be Belinda," the woman says.

I blink at her, surprised she already knows my name. That she's expecting me. But then remember they had to open the gates for me. "Um, yes. I am."

"Right. A little late, aren't you? Never mind." The woman

shakes her head, shuffling through some papers on her desk. "You're here now, and that's what's important. Mrs. Vale has been waiting for you."

I frown. The only Mrs. Vale I know is in New York in a rehab facility. Which means—

"Belinda. Darling." A door swings open, and a slender, raven-haired woman with the most precise bob haircut I've ever seen in my life sweeps in, a cloud of expensive perfume filling the room and making my nose twitch. "There you are. We're *so* delighted you've chosen to attend Wickham. Please step into my office so we can discuss a few things before Mrs. Brown gives you your room assignment and class schedule."

I'm as stiff as a board when Whitney Ashbourne-Vale pulls me in for a hug, her hands barely touching me when she presses her soft, acacia-brown cheek to mine. She pulls away quickly, a bright smile curling her perfectly pink lips, and she waves me toward an open doorway, which I assume is her office.

I look back over my shoulder to see the driver rolling my bags into the reception area as I follow her. I jump when she slams the door shut. When I turn to face her, all remnants of the overly friendly woman are gone, replaced by a sour expression and a narrowed gaze.

"You're late."

"Thanks for the reminder, *Mom*." My stepmother is the worst. I don't actually know her at all, but I've heard stories. Isla regularly complained about Whitney and her constant demands for perfection.

She "works" at Wickham, according to my father and

the brochure I read in the limo. She is head of the board of trustees and is deeply connected to the administration and Headmaster Harrington. Isla told me Mommy Dearest rarely comes into the office for a regular nine-to-five, but I guess she's here today to greet me.

I'm so lucky.

Whitney glances around the room as if she expects to find someone lurking in a corner before she stalks toward me. She comes way too close, but I refuse to take a step back as she thrusts her finger in my face. "Don't ever call me that. No one is supposed to know we're…related."

I press my lips together so I don't say something I'll regret, staring at the finger in my face like it's a snake about to bite me. She eventually drops it, resting her hands on her hips, showcasing the elegant cut of her simple navy dress. It looks expensive. As do the giant diamond earrings she's wearing and the thin gold bangles on her wrist.

She studies me for a moment, something almost tender flickering in her eyes. "You look like your mother."

"Don't worry," I say, forcing a thin smile. What she really means is that I don't have Isla's classic good looks. I'm no troll, but I'm not the piping hot slice of all-American apple pie that Isla's always been with her blond hair, big blue eyes, straight white teeth, and natural pink blush. "Looking nothing like my sister will be an asset here. No one will suspect we're related."

She blinks, and the iciness is back.

"At least your hair looks decent," she finally says with a sniff. "My stylist let me know it was quite the botched job."

"I didn't have much to work with." I shrug, purposely

trying to annoy her. From the look on her face, I'd say it's working.

Ignoring my response, she begins pacing the length of the small room. "Did you look over the dossier we created for you? I hope so. You don't have much time to learn the information, and you won't have much privacy, since you're sharing a room."

My jaw drops. "Sharing a room? That was never a part of the plan."

She stops mid-step, turning to face me. "*Everyone* shares a room at Wickham. No exceptions."

Well, that's just freaking great.

"As I'm sure you read in the documents I prepared for you, our Big-Little program helps younger students acclimate to Wickham's culture by pairing them with a roommate from an upper year. This is hardly your first year, so you'll be exempt from Big-Little social events, but as a transfer student, you'll need all the guidance you can get if you hope to fit in. You're lucky—Priya Shah is an excellent student. Very smart. Part of a group you should be keen to infiltrate." She sends a pointed look my way.

Dammit. I'd been banking on having a safe haven to shrug off Belinda and just be Billie, but it looks like that's not in the cards. I hate that Whitney knows I didn't read the entire dossier, but I was a little busy learning the whole history of Wickham and oh, yeah—not puking my guts out all over the back of her nice, clean limo.

I clear my throat, determined to treat this woman like she's on my side and not an enemy. "Anyone else you think I should talk to?"

She taps a perfectly manicured finger against her pursed lips, thinking. "I'm sure the boys will come sniffing around without any prompting. A new girl on campus always sends them into a froth."

I do my best to keep a straight face, disgusted by her description. Doesn't matter what age they are: boys, men, whatever you want to call them, always end up disappointing me. I'm sure the ones here are no exception. "Anyone I should watch out for?"

"Priya." She laughs, the sound soft and lilting. "Oh, she's ruthless. But if you stay on her good side, you'll be fine."

Sleep with one eye open. Got it. She sounds like a joy.

"Abigail Roth, Priya's best friend, is extremely territorial. Don't try to get too close to Priya. If Abigail views you as a threat, she'll make your life miserable," Whitney adds.

She steps around her desk and settles into the creaking chair, leaning back to consider me. "Perhaps I should warn you about one boy in particular…"

"Who?" I love a good warning against someone. Makes me want to get that much closer to them.

"Connor Wells." She sighs and stares off into the distance, slowly shaking her head. "Emily's older brother."

Any urge to be contrary I might have felt comes crashing down around me at hearing the name from the article again. Emily Wells. Isla's best friend in the whole world. They were inseparable. Hot shame rises up the back of my throat when I think about all the times I felt jealous of Emily's closeness to Isla. Every time Isla told me stories about their antics, I wished Emily would disappear—wished I could take her place.

I never meant for it to happen like this.

I can't blame myself for wishing I had a best friend like that. Someone I could tell all my secrets to. Laugh and giggle and stay up late with, talking about the boys we crushed on or the teachers who made our lives miserable. The girls who didn't get it like we did.

Laid out like that, it sounds like all I ever really wanted was a sister across the hall instead of across the Atlantic.

"Connor hates Isla." Whitney's voice drips with genuine sadness for my sister, her lips trembling as if she's holding back tears. Isla always described her stepmom as cold, so I startle at seeing real emotion on her face. But then again, Whitney basically raised Isla as her own since my sister was four years old.

"Did he hate her before he thought she shoved his sister off a cliff, or is this a recent development?"

Whitney lifts one eyebrow, clearly unimpressed with the charming way I manage to cut to the heart of the matter. "Unclear," she says. "I confess I didn't take much of an interest in the social politics of the student body before…well, before all of this."

"Sounds like a douche," I mutter.

"Just…be careful." Her voice is tight, like she's holding back something heavier, but then she clears her throat, and the concern falls away.

She pulls a key from the top drawer of her desk and hands it to me.

"Your room key. See Mrs. Brown on your way out for a printed schedule and a map."

I know a dismissal when I hear one, so I retrace my steps to the receptionist's desk and wordlessly accept the papers she hands me, along with an umbrella she promises I'll need regularly. But as I follow Mrs. Brown's directions to my residence hall, Whitney's words echo in my brain.

Then it hits me.

Connor Wells wasn't mentioned once in any of the articles I read about his sister's death.

A small thing to notice.

But small things have a way of mattering later.

CHAPTER FOUR

My dorm room is in East House, the farthest building on the east side of the campus. It's three stories, and I'm on the third floor. Room 312. The one I'll be sharing with the very smart, very ruthless Priya. The girl with the overbearing bestie.

Can't wait to meet them all. They sound so fun.

When I shake the rain off my umbrella and enter the building, I spot a dark-haired white girl sitting behind a heavy, old-fashioned-looking desk, talking on an equally dated landline phone. The moment she notices me, she pulls the receiver away from her face and sets it on the desk.

"Do you need any help?"

"Yeah, hey. Hi." I shuffle my feet, suddenly awkward. But then I remember who I'm supposed to be and stand a little straighter. "I'm Belinda Winters."

"Oh, the new student, yes! I'm Ruth, the resident assistant." We're both distracted by a tinny-sounding voice coming from the phone. It sounds like someone shouting

Ruth, are you still there?

"My mom," Ruth mouths, rolling her eyes.

"It's fine. I know which room I'm in," I reassure her. I don't tell her how lucky she is to have a mom who wants to talk to her. Who *can* talk to her, whenever she wants.

"You'll be all right, then? Stairs are around the corner." Before I can answer, she's picking up the phone again. I head in the direction she indicated while she resumes her conversation like I never interrupted at all.

No problem, I want to tell her. I've done everything else on my own. I don't need a tour of the building.

I trudge my way up the winding staircase, gripping the worn wooden railing so tight I swear I'm going to get a splinter in my palm. The building is quiet and damp, and the hallway smells faintly of lemon-scented cleaner and musty old wood. My shoes squeak on the bare floor, my backpack bumping against my side as I reach the third landing and head down the hall. I pause in front of the door to my room, staring at the slightly tarnished brass sign with the room number etched into it.

I yank the key from my jeans pocket, but before I can slide it into the lock, the door swings open, startling me.

"Who the hell are you?"

I rear back slightly, surprised by the girl's hostile tone. "Uh, hi. I'm your new roomie."

The girl I'm assuming is Priya rolls her dark-brown eyes, gripping the handle like she plans on slamming the door in my face. "I begged Harrington to let me have this room to myself for the rest of the semester, but I guess that didn't work. Ugh. Don't you just *abhor* the administration?" She gives a theatrical sigh, then adds, "I'm Priya."

She thrusts her hand toward me, and I take it, giving it a firm shake. "Belinda."

The name sounds foreign on my tongue. I hate it. It's the name that appears on my birth certificate, but I don't recall anyone ever calling me that with the exception of teachers on the first day of school before I corrected them. Mom started calling me Billie the moment we moved to the U.S., like I needed a new name to go with my new persona, "child of a single mother." Maybe I did.

"Nice to meet you." Priya opens the door wider, her gaze zooming in on my ratty backpack. "Is that all you brought with you?"

"Oh, uh, no. The driver has my luggage. Is there an elevator in this building?"

"You mean a lift?" Priya's brows shoot up. "You're in our territory now, American. You'll have to learn what we call things."

"Right. A lift." I pause a beat, pushing down my annoyance. "Is there one?"

"Nope." She pops the *p*, appearing very satisfied with her answer. "Guess your little servant will have to drag your suitcases up the stairs."

"Oh." I laugh, trying to sound carefree as I wave my fingers in the air. "He'll be fine. He's used to this sort of thing."

I have no idea if he is or not, but I feel bad for him either way. I've heaved a week's worth of groceries up three flights of stairs enough times to commiserate. Priya doesn't need to know I was raised in shitty apartments in shitty neighborhoods, where a working elevator was a luxury and someone to help with heavy bags was a pipe dream. Belinda wouldn't think twice about someone carrying her bags up fifty flights of stairs, so I shrug like the insolent snob I'm supposed to be.

"Well, aren't you lucky," Priya mutters as we both head into the room. She closes the door, then leans against it. "Why are you here, anyway?"

"What do you mean, why am I here? I was assigned this room." I'm playing dumb on purpose, but I'm not sure if she realizes it.

Another roll of her eyes. "I mean at Wickham. We're almost six weeks into term, meaning you'll need to catch up. The curriculum is rigorous here. It's not for the weak."

I lift my chin, not about to let this girl tear me down or fill me with doubt. "Aw, aren't you sweet? Thanks for your concern, but I'm sure I'll be fine."

Priya goes quiet, watching me, and I blatantly stare at her in return. She has expressive eyebrows and beautiful long, black hair that cascades down her back in natural waves. Brown eyes look into mine as if she can reach into my soul. She touches her tongue to the corner of her full lips before sinking her teeth into the bottom one like she's trying to draw blood.

"You remind me of someone," she finally says, and alarm flares inside of me. If she says Isla, I might lose it.

"Maybe you've seen me on Page Six." I laugh again, the sound so fake it might be swinging all the way around to believable.

"I don't have time to keep track of gossip pages. Not here and definitely not in America. Where are you from, anyway?"

"Manhattan."

"Nice," she murmurs. "What school did you attend?"

"Oh, you wouldn't know it." I wave, dismissing her question. "A ghastly little boarding school with, like, one hundred students, all of us feral young women who ended up hating one another."

I don't know where I'm coming up with this nonsense, but I'd bet five hundred bucks it's not in my father and Whitney's dossier. They're going to want to kill me if this gets out.

"Feral young women? That sounds...illicit." Priya smirks like I'm alluding to something scandalous and dirty. I lean into this version of Belinda's backstory, because why not? If I have to be a stuck-up brat, I might as well be a stuck-up brat who knows how to have a good time.

"Let's just say I'm not welcome there any longer, so here I am. The newest student at Wickham Academy. My parents thought sending me to the English countryside would turn me into a dignified young lady." I smile prettily, batting my eyelashes. If Priya falls for this bullshit, she might not be as smart as everyone thinks.

"Uh-huh." Priya shakes her head, her doubt obvious. My grudging respect for her grows. "Keep up the mystery, Belinda. I'm sure the boys will love it."

"Ooh, really?" I rest my hands on my hips, feigning interest. Why not play it up like I'm a silly, boy-crazy American? "Anyone I should watch out for?"

"All of them. They're seriously the worst." Priya moves about the room, trailing her fingers along the edge of her desk, drawing closer until she's on my side of the small room. She pauses in front of the empty desk—the one I assume will be mine—and turns to face me, leaning against it.

"Well, save for Freddie Pembroke. He's an absolute doll and wickedly smart. Though he can say the most cutting things. Some people never recover from a Freddie insult. Oh, I also love Arlo Davies. Arlo is one of my favorites. Such a flirt. Everyone loves him."

"So the boys aren't all rotten," I point out.

"I suppose not." Priya's face falls, disappointment filling her gaze. "Though truly, the rest of them are mostly horrid. Typical, boring males who don't care about anything but their next sexual conquest."

"Hmm. Sounds interesting." I raise my brows.

"They're all pigs," she practically spits out. "Look, I need to get to my next class. Do you have your schedule yet?"

Panic fills me. I do, but I don't want her to try and convince me to go to class with her. Not yet. I need to prepare first. "They're still putting it together. I won't be starting class until tomorrow."

"Hmm, well good luck with that. I'll see you later tonight." Within seconds, Priya leaves, and the room goes deathly quiet.

She left the door half open. I let it stay like that. Not sure I'm ready for the full prison-cell aesthetic just yet.

Releasing a ragged breath, I glance around my new room, taking it all in. There are two beds, two desks, and a large window overlooking the quad. Priya's side of the room is immaculate. Neatly made bed, fluffy pillows, and a deep-red throw draped across the foot. Her desk is clean, a black notebook sitting in the center of it and an expensive looking silver pen resting on top. There's a corkboard hanging slightly askew on the wall above the desk, with a color-coded weekly planner pinned to it.

Even if I hadn't just met her, Priya's space would reveal her as the organized, type A overachiever I know she is. She's the sort who only respects those who are as smart as her. Everyone else is trash.

She probably thinks I'm epic garbage with my pretend interest in boys and getting kicked out of my previous school.

The other side of the room, my side, is completely bare. As I drop my backpack on the desk chair and sink onto the plastic-coated mattress, a realization hits me: Could this have been Isla's room? Why else would Priya be short a roommate? Unless her former roommate was Emily.

I swallow and run my fingers along the seam of the mattress. If it's the dead girl's old room, Priya didn't mention it. Shouldn't she still be upset about what happened here? Losing her roommate to either death or a coma is tragic—and traumatic.

A sour twist grips my gut. Shouldn't everyone at this school be devastated? Or are they all moving on like nothing happened?

Peter called me a week ago. Isla has been in a coma since a week before that... I guess fourteen days is all the time the rich allow for grieving. *If* they grieved.

Who knew I could loathe so many people I've never even met?

I unzip my backpack and check the schedule Mrs. Brown printed for me. If all class blocks are the same length, I should have the room to myself for at least the next fifty-five minutes. That should give me enough time to look through Isla's yearbook and start matching faces to names. Belinda needs to have the kind of confidence that comes from knowing everyone and caring about no one, which means I have some studying to do.

I click the switch on the desk lamp, but nothing happens—which is when I realize the plug is coiled around the base, rather than plugged in. I unwind it and pull the desk a little away from the wall, looking for an outlet. To reach it, I have to wedge my arm down the back of the desk at an angle that forces my head to the side. But I feel around and manage to plug in the lamp without electrocuting myself. As I pull my hand back, I feel the sharp edge of...something. It's flimsy and slick—a photo, if I had to guess. It's stuck between the desk frame and the back of the bottom drawer. I wiggle it side to side, careful not to tear it.

My prize comes loose. A Polaroid, bent at one corner and a little dusty from being wedged so close to the floor. I flick on the lamp and bring the photo under the circle of light to inspect it.

Isla. She's wearing a Wickham uniform—velvety hunter green jacket with the school crest stitched in gold on the right side. A green-and-black tartan pleated skirt to match. Isla's head is thrown back, a giant smile stretching across her face, and I can't help but smile as well.

But the expression quickly melts off my face when I take in the figure beside my sister. It's another girl, based on the cut of her uniform. But I can't make out her face because someone took a pen and scribbled over it, drawing endless circles and Xs until the person's features are nothing but ink. I can't even make out the color of her hair.

What's the likelihood that it's Emily? And if it is...who would deface her image this way?

I turn the photo over, and I'm shocked when I see the words written there, scratched in faint blue ink.

FUCKING BITCH!

Whoever wrote this clearly had a problem with Emily Wells. But did they hate her enough to push her off a cliff, and my sister with her?

Despite the fact that I know this picture can't be more than a year old—in it, Isla is wearing the diamond-and-garnet earrings Whitney gave her for Christmas last year—it feels like I'm holding a relic from another era.

And why was this picture stuck in Emily or Isla's desk? It's not something either of them would want to keep, unless...

Unless they knew who defaced the photo and needed evidence.

Girls, what the hell were you up to?

I've watched enough *Law & Order: SVU* to know the handwriting on the back of the photo is my smoking gun. I reach for my backpack, mentally crossing my fingers that Isla passed her yearbook around for signatures at the end of last year. I pull the book out of the manila envelope and center it on the desk. The front has the same gold embossed lettering as the dossier. Rich people love glitzy shit, apparently.

I flip through the pages, skimming for signatures or messages I can compare to the caption on the back of the photo. But I pause at a two-page layout with candid shots around campus. One photo in particular draws my eye, with the faces of each student circled in red. Their names are listed in the caption below.

Abigail Roth. Priya Shah. Arlo Davies. Freddie Pembroke.

Julian Ashworth. Connor Wells.

In the margins, scribbled in loopy cursive, are the letters "LL" with a question mark.

I press my lips together, swallowing down the sudden lump that forms in my throat. I feel like a little kid dressed up as a detective for Halloween. But the stakes are so much higher than seeing how much candy I can collect in a single night. If I can't figure out what all this means, the world is going to think my sister is a murderer.

And the world *can't* think Isla is anything but the incredible human she is.

My shoulders sag, and I blink back tears. If I fail Isla now, I'll never be able to apologize to her or tell her how badly I screwed up our relationship. I've seen the way losing my father's love has destroyed my mother's life. What will losing Isla's do to mine?

I reach back into the bag to pull out the picture from home next—the four of us standing underneath a tree blossoming with new growth, oblivious to the family rotting from the root in its shade. Even the knowledge that this is the last picture we took together as a family doesn't dull the peace I get from seeing Isla cradled in Mom's arms, full of life and vigor.

Does she feel that same loss of a parent like I do, when I let myself think of who Peter should have been to me? Missing what we could have been runs deep inside me, like a wound that can never heal. So while I'm tempted to put the frame on my desk as a reminder of why I'm here and who I'm doing this for, in the end, I decide to drop the frame into a drawer and slam it shut. The photo could invite questions from Priya—questions I don't know how to answer.

"You're sitting at a ghost's desk, you know."

Heart hammering, I slam the yearbook closed and whirl around at the deep voice, shocked to find a boy standing in front of me, in *my room*. And not just any boy, either. He's tall and broad, his body filling out the Wickham uniform to perfection. Inky black hair flops over his forehead, brushing the tops of brows that frame piercing eyes more grayish than blue. Almost silver, they're so light. His high cheekbones and sharp jaw make his face look like a work of art, which is not typically the phrase I'd use to describe someone who sneaks up on me in my personal space.

But this guy didn't sneak up on Billie.

He crept up on Belinda.

I paste on a bright smile and tilt my head to the side, like I'm confused. "Oh, but a good haunting can be so invigorating. Don't you think?"

His expression remains impassive, though his gaze roves over my body, taking in every inch of me, leaving me flushed. "Where's Priya?"

He doesn't acknowledge my question. As a matter of fact, his entire demeanor is dismissive. Like I don't matter. This type of attitude is something I've dealt with my entire life, and I thankfully stopped caring what people think a long time ago. Doesn't mean I go down quietly.

"She just left." I keep my smile pinned in place, even as my tone sharpens. Irritation buzzes under my skin. "Who are you? And who gave you permission to waltz into my room?"

He holds my gaze, his eyes sharpening at my tone like he's not used to being questioned. *Well, get used to it, buddy.*

"At Wickham, door open means come on in," he says eventually, then turns, giving me his back. He leaves, pulling the door shut with a loud slam that has me jumping.

I've met two students at Wickham so far—and both are assholes. Lovely.

...

Priya doesn't return to our room until long after dark, a large satchel hanging from her shoulder and exhaustion hooding her eyes. She barely acknowledges me, doesn't even speak to me as I watch her from where I'm perched on my freshly made bed, my laptop balanced on my bent knees.

Not long after Mystery Boy left, Lurch delivered my bags to my room. He then awkwardly handed me a sack with a sandwich and bag of chips inside. I don't know how he knew I was hungry or where he got the food, and he left before I could ask. Or say thanks.

I scarfed the food down and spent the rest of the afternoon putting my things away and rereading the dossier, paying close attention to the details of the fictional past life Peter and Whitney created for me. The story I made up for Priya was way off base, but it's too late to change it now. Looks like I'll have to retrofit my newest lies to match up with the totally separate set of lies I'm supposed to be peddling.

I had the good sense to store the entire folder under my mattress before Priya returned. And because only dumbasses keep their whole stash in one place, I tucked the yearbook into the back of a throw pillow shaped like a bottle of hot sauce. Not totally sure what Whitney was thinking with that one, but maybe she assumes Americans naturally gravitate toward fast-food icons. As much as I wish I could spend more time with the book—including the notes Isla wrote in the back about the secret project Peter warned me away from—Priya finds me casually looking at cat videos on my laptop like a totally normal human teenager, and not at all like someone assuming a whole-ass fake identity in order to prove her sister's innocence in the face of alleged murder. She doesn't need to know these videos are my one and only guilty pleasure in the world.

No one needs to know that.

Once Priya tosses her bag on the bed, she grabs her bathroom caddy and heads out again. Fifteen minutes later, she returns from the hall bathroom, face scrubbed clean and hair piled on top of her head, wearing a pale-pink pajama set. She tosses her uniform in a hamper, puts the caddy away, and falls into bed, her eyes tightly closed.

"I'm exhausted," she declares, eyes still shut.

I'm guessing this means she wants to chat. "Long day?"

"The longest. I'm president of the debate club. The meeting went on for almost two hours, and then I had to finish an essay." She remains quiet for a moment, and I start to think she's fallen asleep when she speaks again. "I don't know how rigorous your American school for feral girls was, but don't expect to ace classes at Wickham without putting in the work."

Why the concern for my academic performance? I get the sense she cares about school and nothing else.

"I'm not worried." My tone is easy breezy. I couldn't care less about my so-called studies. I've already graduated high school in the States, and enrolling at a university, even one in the city, is nothing but a faraway dream for me. The grades I receive at Wickham won't matter.

"Must be nice."

I say nothing because I don't know how to reply.

"Good night, Belinda," she murmurs.

"Good night." Leaning over, I set my laptop on the floor and slide it half under my bed, then turn off the lamp on my nightstand, plummeting the room into darkness. Within minutes, Priya's deep, even breathing fills the room, and I close my eyes, wishing I could fall asleep as easily as she does.

But I don't. My mind is racing with too many questions, all of them without answers.

Rolling over onto my back, I open my eyes, watching the play of shadows and light that dance across the ceiling from the glimmering moon through the thin curtains. It's cold in this room, a lingering dampness in the air making me shiver. I reach for my phone, tugging the covers over my head so I won't disturb Priya.

I open Instagram, using the new Belinda Winters account Peter linked me to this afternoon. I didn't ask questions about how he got this set up so quickly, because frankly, I don't want to know. But my new profile is filled with pictures of New York cityscapes and artful-looking lattes. Peppered among the stills are videos of dark club interiors full of pulsing lights and dancing bodies, and concerts at the Garden or across the river in Jersey City. There are also a few moody-looking selfies with enough filter magic applied that I doubt anyone will question why none of them show off my entire face. Whatever tech wizard put this together for Peter was smart enough to hedge their bet on AI-generated images of Belinda Winters.

It's good work. Scary good.

Most of the Wickham Academy kids have their profiles locked down with privacy settings. I send a follow request to Priya, then spend a few minutes studying the profile pictures of the students Instagram thinks I should follow next. Freddie Pembroke. Abigail Roth. Arlo Davies. Julian Ashworth. These must be the people Priya interacts with most on the platform, through likes and shares and comments. When I scroll to reveal more of the suggested follows, I suck in a breath.

Isla.

I swap from my Belinda account to my Billie one. I'm a nameless, faceless avatar on this profile, which is exactly what I need to be to safely engage with my sister's page.

She posted a lot, and I recognize plenty of the scenery on campus after just half a day spent on the property. Her subjects are fairly predictable: fit checks, selfies with and without smiling friends crowded into the frame, photo bursts of random birds in trees, all captioned #WickhamBirbs, #BirbsOfWickham, and #birdwatching. I can't help smiling at my sister, the bird nerd.

There's one image I keep circling back to, a selfie of Isla and Emily standing together in their uniforms, their heads close as they face the camera. Isla's eyes are closed, but Emily is looking at her, adoration in her gaze.

Zooming in, I see someone standing in the background, glaring at them. Two someones. Their arms are crossed defensively, disgusted expressions on their faces. One of them is Priya. The other I don't recognize. Probably the best friend

Whitney warned me about. Abigail.

Coincidence? Maybe.

But I can't help seeing an eerie contrast between Isla and Emily, radiating joy in the foreground, while Priya and her mystery friend seethe in the background. What else was going on behind the scenes that Isla didn't know about? Unless...

I pull the phone away from my face, taking a wider view of the shot. From the angle of the camera, it's clear Isla was holding the phone. She framed this shot with her and Emily slightly off-center. Are they the real subject of this picture, or was Isla purposefully capturing Priya and her friend behind them?

I stare at the picture for another minute, but the balance of what I don't know versus what I do doesn't shift.

"I'll find out who did this to you," I whisper, my heart aching.

I log out of my Billie account, then quietly set my phone on the nightstand. Rolling to my side, I face the wall and close my eyes, practically forcing myself to fall asleep.

Across campus, the old iron bell in the tower rings once. Long and low, the ominous sound drifts through the air.

Like a warning.

Like a promise.

CHAPTER FIVE

I wake with a jolt thanks to the loud bang of a door. Jerking into a sitting position, I glance about the room and realize Priya is nowhere to be found. She must've left and slammed the door behind her. Did she do that on purpose to be an asshole? Well, it worked. Guess I won't need to set an alarm if that's how she leaves every morning.

It's when I check my phone that I realize if I don't get ready soon, I'm going to be late to my first day of classes at Wickham. I scramble out of bed and grab my clothes before I head for the communal bathroom to take a quick shower. Lucky me, no one's in here, since I woke up late. As I stand under the lukewarm water, I think about how shitty it is that Priya didn't even bother trying to wake me up. Not that it's her job or anything, but wouldn't she show some common courtesy to her new roomie?

When I reenter my dorm room a minute later, I freeze when I see what's lying on top of my bed. My heart rate skyrockets, beating in my chest like a wild thing. I hurriedly close the door and lock it. No way can it be what I think it is, could it?

But when I approach the bed, I realize that yes, it is. Isla's yearbook from last year—the one I hid in the back of a throw pillow—is on top of my thin comforter and wide open. I tug it closer, squinting at the list scribbled on the page. AUTOGRAPHS is printed in the gold script Wickham seems to love so much. The rest of the glossy white page was left blank, presumably for Isla's classmates to cover in variations of "Have a great summer!"

But that's not what's written on this page.

Instead, it's a list of names, a few dates, and lots of question marks. All in my sister's loopy, lopsided script.

What does it all mean?

I slam the book shut and slip it into my backpack. Since there's apparently no such thing as a safe place to hide anything in this room, I'll have to keep it with me until I find somewhere else for it. I grab the dossier while I'm at it, grateful that it seems undisturbed. Leaving the yearbook wide open for me to see is some kind of message. And I'm guessing it's most likely Priya who's sending it to me.

Well, that's just fucking great. I have one job here, and I'm already messing up big time. How could I let this happen? Priya must realize I'm connected to Isla in some way, but did she figure that out before or after she decided to snoop through my stuff?

I thought I was being careful, but I'm going to have to do better. I can't trust anyone here. Not a single soul.

Isla's life may depend on it.

The realization leaves me cold, my skin like ice. Dread settles heavily onto my shoulders, and I hang my head. The truth is, there's no way I can manage this. I'm not qualified to help my sister. I'm not qualified to help *anyone*. Why do Peter and Whitney think I'm capable of figuring out who might've hurt Isla and killed Emily? Look at me—I'm on campus less than twenty-four hours and someone has already found the yearbook and most likely figured out that I'm somehow connected to Isla.

Meaning I fucked everything up. All of it. I've probably just set a new record for fastest failure in the history of covert operations.

There's only one thing left to do: I need to get out of here. Now.

I grab my backpack and leave the room, forgetting about all of my other belongings. I don't need anything—what I *do* need is to get the hell out of here. If all I get out of this brief trip to England is my rich-girl blond hair, then so be it.

The moment I'm outside, I'm shivering. Maybe I was a little quick to abandon the new wardrobe? But I can't worry about that. I keep my head bent against the cold wind, my hurried steps taking me straight to the administration building. I can feel the curious stares of other students as I speed past them, but they say nothing to me. I remain quiet, too, not wanting to bring attention to myself. If I'm lucky, my time at Wickham will be nothing but a distant memory for all of us. No one will remember my name or that I was even here.

I barge into the admin building, ignoring Mrs. Brown when she calls out a panicked greeting. She even gets up from her chair like she's going to try and body-block me, but I'm too quick for her. Whitney's office door is shut, but I throw it open without knocking and march inside, coming to a stop in front of the desk where she's currently sitting.

"I can't do this," I blurt, my voice, my entire body shaking from a mixture of nerves and fear.

Whitney remains quiet, gently setting her phone down before she stands. She goes to the wide-open door and shuts it, the snick of the lock sliding into place loud in the otherwise silent room. I grip the back of the chair that's directly in front of me and lock my trembling knees so I don't slither to the ground.

"Sit down," Whitney says as she rounds her desk once more and settles into the massive leather chair. "Please, Billie."

It's Whitney calling me Billie in that calm tone that has me automatically sitting in the chair. Hearing my actual name grounds me. Helps me realize that she sees me for who I really am, and not the poseur I'm already failing to be.

"What happened?" she asks once our gazes meet. Her eyes are full of sympathy, which brings me up short. "You seem quite...rattled."

"I can't do this." I'm repeating myself, but I don't care. There's no point in beating around the bush. "I want to go home. This campus sucks. Everyone here sucks, and no one is going to believe I'm some Manhattan socialite who only cares about parties and boys. They're going to see right through me. And I'm definitely not equipped to figure out who did this to Isla."

Whitney clasps her hands together and rests them on the desk, her expression solemn. "Why do you believe you're not equipped?"

"Because I'm not, okay? I'm just—I'm just a kid." I slouch in the chair and cross my arms, pouting like the sullen teen that I am. "Why can't you hire a private detective to do this? Peter has more money than God. I'm guessing he can employ an entire team of detectives to find out what happened to his precious daughter."

I squeeze my eyes shut and force the tears back. I hate how I sound, like a jealous asshole. Which I so am. Isla got everything, and I've got nothing, but who actually wins in the end? This isn't a competition, but hey. At least I'm not in a coma.

That thought makes me feel even worse, and I despise myself for it.

"Look, Billie. There's no one else who can do this. No detective would be able to penetrate the campus in time or get an insider's view of the culture here. You're just a kid? Lucky for you, that's exactly what we need here. No one's going to talk to a professional detective, especially if"—she lowers her voice here, even though the thick, oak-paneled walls seem to deaden sound from the outside—"a Wickham student is responsible. Besides, we are on an extremely limited timeframe. And we must figure out who did this to her before it's too late. You're our only hope."

"But I can't—"

"You must." Whitney's voice is firm. Thunderous, even. When I meet her gaze once more, I see the fury in her eyes. And the despair. It's a swirling mix of emotions that breaks my heart.

She jumps to her feet, and I do the same. "Can't you see? We need you, Billie. Isla needs you. Everyone is whispering about her, how she did this to Emily, and it's not true. She would never harm a soul. I may not be her birth mother, but

I've been a mother to her in every other way, and I know in my heart that Isla would never push her best friend off a cliff and then jump right after her. It makes no sense. Not with the girl I know and love and adore."

Whitney stops in front of me and reaches out, settling her hands on my shoulders. "Help me, Billie. Help your sister. We need you. Please don't leave."

The crack in her voice undoes me, and I step toward her, wrapping my arms around her waist. There's not a single moment of hesitation before she returns the embrace. We cling to each other for a few seconds, like letting go would send us both falling into an abyss we could never climb out of. My tears make a wet patch on her sweater, but I don't think she cares. The realization smacks me in the chest, making it hard for me to breathe.

Whitney's love for my sister is all I've ever wanted from my own mother. And it's the one thing Mom can't seem to give me. Unconditional love and total belief in her own child.

Eventually I pull away and wipe underneath both of my eyes with the back of my hand, sniffing loudly. Whitney doesn't say anything, though I hear her soft sniff as well. We're both emotional wrecks. But that's what makes my decision easier.

"Okay." I nod, swallowing past the lump in my throat. "I'll do it. I'll stay for two weeks."

Her relief is obvious when she jerks me back into a quick embrace before letting me go again. "Thank you, Billie. You don't know how much this means to me."

"I think I do." I offer her a pitiful smile but let it fade. I'm not just doing this for Isla. I'm doing it for Whitney as well. She loves my sister. Maybe even more than I do. The realization fills me with equal parts shame and hope. I should be the one who loves Isla more than anyone in the world, but the very fact that I'm here and no one knows who I am—no one knows that Isla has a sister—means my love wasn't strong enough. A sister who loved Isla as strongly as Whitney clearly does wouldn't be a secret. Every unanswered text and missed call in the past year stabs into me like shards of glass.

Isla deserved better than what I've given her the past year. But I think she had everything either of us could have wanted in Whitney.

"Where is your coat? You're not even wearing a jumper, and it's quite cold out there." Whitney marches over to a large armoire on the other side of the room and swings the doors open. Inside are a bunch of uniform jackets, and she pulls out a cardigan that looks like the one hanging in the closet back at my dorm. "Here. Put this on."

I do as she says and button it up, hating how long it is, but there's not much I can do about that. Whitney brushes off my shoulders and holds me at arm's length, like she's preparing me to walk into a board room instead of a dining hall.

I reach for my backpack but then remember the yearbook and dossier are inside. I think about stashing them here, not only because they'd be beyond the reach of whatever rat went through my stuff, but because I want Whitney to know that I trust her. But safeguarding things here means I won't be able to access them easily—and something tells me I'm going to want to spend more time with Isla's notes in her yearbook.

In the end, I offer Whitney a quick wave and get the hell out of there, desperate to escape before it gets awkward. *More awkward.* I leave the admin building, Mrs. Brown's irritated gaze burning a hole in my back. I only take a deep, cleansing breath once I'm outside on the front steps. The chilly wind cools my heated cheeks, and a hint of determination fills me, reminding me why I'm doing this.

This is what I came for, right? A different life and a different me. Shedding my old skin and becoming someone new. I'm no longer Billie Vale. I'm Belinda Winters now.

And I need to start acting like it.

...

I enter the stiflingly hot dining hall, the scent of food making my stomach growl. I've only had an airplane pastry and a soggy sandwich in the last day, and I'm starving. I head for the hot breakfast line, my skin prickling with awareness when it feels like a thousand pairs of eyes are watching my every move. Ignoring them, I toss my hair over my shoulder before I grab an egg sandwich and a coffee. Trying my best to act like I don't have a care in the world, despite my being the new girl.

I spot Priya grabbing a banana from a table covered in plates of fruit. I head toward her, putting on an easygoing smile the moment our gazes lock.

"Thanks for the wakeup today." From the flicker of irritation in Priya's brown eyes, I can tell my easy-breezy tone is grating on her last nerve. *Mission accomplished.* "Appreciate it."

"What in the world are you talking about?" Her voice is flat, and her fingers grip the banana tight enough that the fruit is bound to bruise. I wonder idly if she might throw it at me, but she doesn't. "Last time I saw you, you were soundly asleep. I'm not responsible for you."

"It's not Priya's fault you slept in." The snide comment comes from a voluptuous, redheaded bombshell who stops right beside Priya, lifting her chin in defiance. I recognize her from the photo in Isla's yearbook. Abigail Roth. "Need to get with the schedule, newbie."

Priya and Abigail laugh and turn away from me without another word. I follow as they head for an already crowded table, not about to let these two ice me out. I fall into the open chair on Priya's left, letting my tray land on the table with a clatter. Everybody lifts their head at my arrival, curious expressions on their faces.

"Everyone, this is Belinda Winters. American money and new resident bad girl." Priya laughs, and I know for sure she's making fun of me. "Belinda, this is…everyone."

"Everyone who matters, you mean." The droll baritone voice comes from my left, where a tall, thin white boy with dark-auburn hair sits beside me, a slight curl to his upper lip. "Freddie Pembroke."

"Hi." I offer him a dazzling smile, and he grins in return, his golden eyes dancing.

"Well, aren't you a gorgeous little thing. Tell us where you're from, Belinda." He props his elbow on the edge of the table, resting his chin on top of his curled fist.

This is going to be hard, getting used to anyone calling me Belinda, let alone everyone. "Manhattan, of course. The only borough that matters," I say, parroting his words back to him. Then I let the spirit of a lesser demon inhabit my body and *bat my eyelashes* at this boy. God help me, I may never recover.

"I can only imagine all the parties you've attended." Freddie's eyes sparkle, though they're slightly narrowed. I get the sense he's dying to figure me out.

Well, the feeling is mutual, Fred.

"I've attended my fair share." I play it coy. Mysterious. Not about to say too much. I'm positive everyone will go on the hunt for my social media, but they'll be sorely disappointed by the artfully bland profiles Peter set up for me. "Do you have parties here?"

Freddie's megawatt smile would probably put any normal person in a trance, but I can see right through him. "Of course. Though I prefer my parties a little more on the...intimate side."

"Isn't she a little too old for you, Fred?" An amused male voice, deeper than Freddie's, asks from over my shoulder.

I jerk my gaze up to find the source standing at the end of the table, his breakfast tray clutched in his hands. I suck in a sharp breath, because this boy? This boy I already know.

Devastatingly handsome is how Isla used to describe him, and I have to give the girl credit—she wasn't wrong. Dark-blond hair that he flicks out of his eyes with a quick toss of his head. Deep brown eyes the color of the earth after a heavy rain. A thick, cream-colored cable-knit sweater stretches over a crisp, white collared shirt with the Wickham emblem embroidered in gold thread at the tips of the collar. His white skin is richly tanned, giving *I just stepped off a yacht and all I got was this lousy golden glow.*

This is Julian Ashworth. In the flesh. And he's just as mesmerizing as Isla always thought he was.

Why he insisted Isla keep their relationship a secret is

something I plan to find out. Soon.

"Not too old. More like too *conscious*," one of the other boys sitting at the table mutters before he starts laughing. Because what's a little dub-con humor between friends?

These people are the actual worst.

Freddie glares at him before turning his attention toward Julian. "Oh, come on now, Julian. You're just mad you didn't get to meet the new girl first," Freddie taunts. That smile is still on his face, but there's a steel edge to his voice that tells me he doesn't like Julian much. If I didn't already mistrust Priya, her description of Freddie Pembroke as "a doll" would have made me question every word that comes out of her mouth.

"That's Julian Ashworth," Priya says to me. "And you're—"

"Sitting in my chair," Julian finishes for her. His expression remains friendly, and I don't know why, but I'm ready to bolt out of the seat and gladly give it to him. Something I wouldn't normally give a shit about.

"I'm sor—"

"Don't you dare apologize," Freddie interjects, smirking at Julian. "It'll be good for him to find a new group of friends. Maybe you can reconnect with your former bestie, J. Oh wait…she's not doing much talking these days."

The entire table goes silent at Freddie's knife-sharp words, and I return my gaze to Julian, noting the way his jaw clenches. The friendly exterior is gone, replaced by something cold and hard. I press my lips together and swallow the words I'm dying to say: *That's my sister you're talking about.*

Julian leaves without speaking, settling into a chair at a table clear across the room. Only once the proverbial dust settles does anyone at our table talk again.

"Way to make him feel like shit," says the dark-haired boy sitting on the other side of Freddie.

"Shut it, Ollie." Freddie begins to eat like nothing happened, and everyone eventually follows suit.

Especially me, because I'm starving. And while the egg sandwich doesn't taste as good as the ones I make at home, I still devour it while listening to the conversation happening around me. Until I notice someone familiar across the dining hall. It's the boy who came into my room yesterday. I can tell he spots Julian at the other table and changes direction, which has my curiosity piqued.

"Who is that?" I ask Priya, nodding in the boy's direction.

Priya scans the room, her upper lip curling with faint disdain when she realizes who I'm talking about. "That's Connor Wells."

"Stay away from him," Abigail interjects, her tone firm.

The boys say nothing. In fact, the table has fallen eerily silent.

"Oh, well he stopped by our room yesterday and asked where you were." I laugh, shaking my head. "Guess I forgot to mention that. Oops."

Priya's eyebrows shoot up. "He said he was looking for me?"

"You like 'em brooding and destitute, huh, Shah?" Freddie says, loud enough for everyone to hear him.

Priya's face turns red. "Fuck you, Freddie." She turns to Abigail, whose lips are pressed in a tight line. I'm not the only one at this table swallowing my words. She looks furious. "I would never."

Freddie guffaws and even slaps the edge of the table, but I

remain quiet. I might have set out to stir the pot by mentioning Connor's visit to our room yesterday, but Freddie has it bubbling over.

Priya and Abigail have their heads drawn close together, Priya executing a perfect pantomime of fervent apology. What does she have to say sorry for?

"Hi! Are you Belinda?"

I jerk my head up to find a girl standing behind Freddie. Her expression is open and friendly, and she's got a wide smile on her face, revealing perfectly straight teeth. "Um, yes?"

"I'm Sophia Harrington." She offers a friendly wave.

"The headmaster's daughter," Priya adds, her voice barely above a whisper.

Sophia's smile fades the slightest bit at Priya's comment. "You say it like it's a bad thing."

Priya shrugs but otherwise doesn't say another word.

"Well. I came over to ask if you wanted someone to walk you to your first class? Maybe even show you around campus, if you'd like." Sophia's attention never strays from me. "I know coming to a new school can be rough, especially when you don't know anyone."

"That would be great, thanks." And then, because it really was shitty of Priya not to wake me up this morning, I look directly at her when I add, "A warm welcome is so appreciated."

Before Priya can fire back a snarky remark, a shrill bell cuts through the din.

"That's the warning bell. We should go." Sophia waves a hand. "Come on, Belinda."

I do as she says and stand before I grab my tray. I head toward one of the trash bins near a set of double doors. Sophia keeps pace, chattering about the history of Wickham and how old the dining hall is. Quickly, I glance over my shoulder to see no one is watching us. They're still sitting at the table and leaning in, as if they're all having a whispered conversation.

About me?

Probably.

Though something tells me there's never been a shortage of gossip at Wickham.

CHAPTER SIX

Sophia's lush, dark-brown curls glisten in the autumn light as she leads us across the central courtyard. I'm momentarily mesmerized by the perfectly applied, pinkish-gold highlighter dusting her tawny cheeks. Have I ever been that put together in my life? Belinda Winters has a long way to go before she can believably play in the same league as Sophia Harrington, but standing next to her, I feel more than ever like Billie.

"It looked like things were getting a bit…intense in there," she says, her accent soft and melodic to my ear.

I have to take a moment to breathe in Belinda despite feeling so woefully inadequate next to this perfect specimen of private school polish. I paste a sheepish grin on my face and say, "You could say that. Thanks for the save, by the way. I may have dived into the deep end when I only meant to dip a toe."

"You couldn't possibly have known how dangerous those waters are," she answers. "To say the sharks are circling is probably a gross understatement."

Now *this* I recognize immediately. Sophia is in possession of tea, and she wants nothing more than to spill it. I raise an inquisitive eyebrow when she glances my way.

"Well, ever since the incident"—she pauses until I nod—"things have been strained to say the least. The girl who died, Emily Wells? She was Priya's roommate."

I suspected as much, but hearing it confirmed sends a shiver racing down my spine. "Should I feel some kind of way about taking a dead girl's room assignment?"

Sophia sends me a kind smile, though her too-white teeth have a wolfish gleam.

"The way I see it, almost all of us are sleeping in beds that used to be occupied by students who are dead now. Your bed is just on an accelerated timeline."

"Dark but logical," I say, pursing my lips like I'm really giving this some thought. "You're not wrong."

Sophia waves to a few students walking by and calls out to one about a study date later today. I'm not here to make snap judgments, and I know Peter wants me to keep an open mind, but my gut tells me Sophia is a genuinely good person—the kind of girl who sees a transfer student sitting at a table full of sharks and decides to rescue her before she's turned into chum.

"So...Harrington," I say, drawing Sophia's attention back to me. Her eyes are light brown, almost hazel, and accentuated by retro-looking black-framed glasses. "Is it tough being the headmaster's daughter? Like, socially I mean?"

She looks a bit taken aback, and it's only after I repeat the words in my head that I hear how nosy they sound.

"I just meant, you weren't sitting with that group, but it

seems like you know them?" I backpedal, turning statements into questions to soften my forwardness.

"I've known most of that crowd my whole life, but yeah, there's a little separation because of the role my dad plays here now. We all grew up together, of course—the Wickham circle is small, which is why a fresh face like yours garners so much interest. It's so rare for an outsider to just...find their way inside, I guess you could say."

I don't know if Peter and Whitney's paranoia is rubbing off on me or if I'm just waiting for the other shoe to drop, but I hear suspicion in her tone. Time for a subject change.

"Were Priya and Emily close? Is that why things are so weird in that group right now?"

"Friends? Hardly," Sophia says, punctuating the sentiment with a chuckle so dry, it's a fire hazard. "Priya was Emily's Big, but fulfilling the role properly would require her to give a shit about someone other than herself. Or Abigail. And between you and me, I don't see that happening any time soon. Even if Priya had wanted to care about her Little, Abigail would hardly have tolerated sharing her affections."

"Are they together?"

Sophia lets out a hard-edged bark of a laugh. "I think it would be more accurate to say that your roommate belongs to Abigail Roth. I don't know how much you know about the Roths, but they've never been famous for playing well with others."

Before I can ask what exactly that means, and find out if "not playing well with others" could possibly translate to "throwing others off a cliff," Sophia grabs my arm and pulls me over to a low wrought iron fence surrounding a stunningly beautiful garden.

"Daddy will blow a gasket if I tell him I walked you across campus and didn't point out the alumni garden. Green spaces are particularly dear to Mother, you see, so naturally Daddy and I are supposed to care about them just *endlessly*."

"In fairness, it's really pretty," I say, and I don't even have to pretend. The garden is beautiful, and I can tell it's been well tended, since everything is lush and green. There are so many willow trees, their long, sweeping branches blowing in the breeze. Rosebushes almost overwhelm the space, but not in a bad way. They're still blooming in a variety of colors, and I can smell their rich scent when the wind blows across my face. Gray and white crushed stone pathways meander in and out of the mossy green ground-cover foliage. I even spot a few wrought iron benches painted a crisp white, inviting anyone to sit down and enjoy their surroundings for a bit.

With a pang, I realize that Mom would know the name of every blooming flower and green shoot in this garden. I wish I could snap a picture and send it to her. I shake off the moment of melancholy by asking about the statue at the center of the square patch of greenery.

"He was a student in my dad's year, actually. I guess he died? Maybe he was sick or something, I don't know. Happened in the early aughts, so like…forever ago."

"Can I take a closer look?" My mom was here from 1996 to 1998. It might be nice to ask her about her years at Wickham next time we talk, and maybe she remembers this guy's story. He must have been something pretty special to warrant a six-foot-tall bronze statue in the middle of the alumni garden.

Sophia checks her watch, which looks like a sparklier,

sleeker version of the Cartier knockoffs I've seen around Chinatown. "I have to get to class a few minutes early to check in with my study group, but you've got time. When you're finished, head through that door," she says, pointing to a heavy, red-painted door in one of the buildings adjacent to the courtyard. "Our classroom is the third door on the right. Can't miss it. See you in a few minutes, and don't be late!" she warns, already walking away. By the time I remember to shout a thank-you—because Belinda may be fake as hell, but she's not inconsiderate—Sophia is too far away to hear me.

I check the time on my phone. Sophia's right. I only have a few minutes to spare here. But I feel drawn to the alumni garden. Maybe that's what gardens are designed to do—make you want to linger. Literally stop and smell the roses. I step onto the stone path and walk with purpose toward the statue. Pollen-drunk bees cling to purple flowers on my left, while a large, white-winged butterfly suns itself on milkweed to my right.

The statue has a friendly smile and swoopy hair. He's wearing a Wickham Academy uniform and cradling a book against his chest. At his feet lies sporting equipment that could be for croquet or polo or some other rich-people game I've only ever seen played on *Downton Abbey*. I spot a rectangular plaque on the statue's base. Shriveled white flower petals obscure the words engraved there, so I bend down to brush them aside and get a closer look.

"THE ONLY DANGER IN FRIENDSHIP IS THAT IT WILL END." – HENRY DAVID THOREAU

DEDICATED WITH LOVE BY THE CLASS OF 1998.

1998. The year Peter and Mom graduated from Wickham. I wonder if they knew this boy.

I spend another minute studying the statue and turning that epitaph over in my mind. Thoreau might have a point. Any relationship can be dangerous if you care about it too much, because when it inevitably ends, there goes your peace of mind. I never thought sisterhood would be a hazard, but—

I cut the thought off before it can fully form. Isla isn't dead. Nothing is over. I may not have a lot of time to figure out what happened to her, but I'll use every second I've got.

But first, class.

...

Sophia saves me a seat next to her in the back row. She keeps up a running commentary on the other students who trickle into class. Most of her intel is useless to me, but when a few familiar faces from the dining hall stroll in, I tune back in to her monologue.

"Freddie is absolutely awful," she declares, her voice firm. "Comes from an obscenely rich family. His father manages some kind of private equity fund whose investors are basically a who's who of Wickham alumni. And while yes, Freddie can be charming,"—she pauses here to give me *a look*, like maybe I've already fallen head over heels for the auburn-haired demon spawn after our brief dining hall interaction—"he has a terrible temper. Credit where it's due, he knows how to throw a good party. His parents have an estate not too far from campus where he hosts his infamous bashes. His parents are rarely there, and I guess they don't care what he does."

"They invite you to their parties, or is it just the inner circle?" My real question is, what's the likelihood I can score an invitation to see these creatures in their natural habitat?

"Sure. If I'm there, they figure I can't rat them out to my dad." Her smile is small. Downright victorious. "I'm not actually a snitch, but there's no convincing *them* of that."

"Hopefully you'll let me tag along." I bump my shoulder into hers, hoping my camaraderie isn't too forced. "I do love a good party."

"Of course! Though there haven't been many parties around here lately. Not much to celebrate, really." Her mood turns somber. "How much do you know about what happened?"

"Not much, I guess?" I say, swallowing a lump in my throat. "A girl died? Another one tried to kill herself?"

Sophia nods, her eyes extra wide. "It was tragic. Emily was *such* a sweet girl."

"What about the other girl?" I frown, trying to look like I can't remember my own sister's name. "Isabella?"

"Isla," she corrects. Sophia shrugs. "She was all right. I didn't know her very well. If she wasn't with Emily, she was following Julian around like a puppy. Bit of a try-hard, if I had to make a sweeping statement."

My frown deepens, and I tell myself not to get pissed about Sophia's feelings toward my sister. I need to focus on prying more information from her, starting with the guy my stepmom warned me about. Conveniently, Connor Wells just walked into the lecture hall. He takes a seat in the front row, all the way to the left. I pretend not to know his name. "Who's that?"

"Connor Wells." Sophia sighs as she stares off into the distance. "After his father's arrest, the family sort of fell apart and they lost all their money, save the trust fund for the children. Then his sister died, so now it's just Connor. Why he remains on campus, though, I'm not sure. No one really talks to him much anymore."

"His dad was arrested?"

I didn't even consider Emily's brother a suspect, but if his dad is in jail and his sister's dead... Does that mean their entire trust fund is now controlled by him? I once saw a guy stab someone for a pair of Nikes. Would killing your sister for millions be that wild a thought?

"Yeah. Embezzlement. It's all so tragic." Sophia's gaze meets mine as she leans toward me, her words softer now. "He's rather dreamy, Connor. A broken boy you can't help but want to fix."

"No, thank you." My voice is firm. My family is broken enough. I don't need to carry anyone else's burdens.

Sophia's face brightens as she quickly changes the subject. "What's the rest of your day like?"

I show her my course schedule, and she flags that I have to go to the counseling office during our next class block. Mrs. Brown will share my elective options, apparently, though Sophia's expression goes a bit grim when she explains this. When I ask her about it, she says, "Honestly, it's ridiculous for Wickham to have extracurriculars *at all* when we're meant to be studying for A-levels. Anything to be special, I suppose. And all the good options are gone by now, too. Coding, Modern Dance, Mock Court. Hard to say what you'll end up with, but it probably won't be good."

I'm saved from having to make up an excuse for why I have zero fucks to give about my elective assignment by the start of class. I let the teacher's monotone explanation of the Pythagorean theorem wash over me like a warm wave of sound.

I'm halfway to a daydream when a prickle of awareness climbs up my neck. When I turn toward the sensation, my eyes clash against the gray, penetrating gaze of Connor Wells.

He doesn't look away when I catch him watching me, and I'll be damned if I'm going to flinch first. A rush of heat moves from my cheeks to my neck, then spreads across my collar bones. I feel his stare like a physical touch, and it feels…

Dangerous.

...

I make my way to the administration building to check in with Mrs. Brown, who, in addition to playing guard dog for Whitney, is in charge of our schedules. I enter the building from the back this time and come to a stop when I notice all of the framed photos lining the walls. When I realize they're portraits of the graduating classes at Wickham over the last twenty-five years or so, I beeline for the class of 1998. Even though the pictures are here on the wall for anyone to see, my heart still pounds like I've unearthed some long-buried treasure. But maybe a picture of my mom before…well, before she became the woman she is today, *is* a precious artifact.

I search the faces for Mom, though my gaze snags on Peter first. He's standing in between who I assume are his friends, all of them grinning widely. They smile with the confidence of boys who know they're going to rule the world someday. I scowl back on principle.

When I finally find my mother, I only spend half a second looking at her beautiful, carefree, sober face before my attention snags on the boy next to her. Snags and holds.

It's kind of hard to tell, considering the first and only time I saw him, he was cast in bronze, but I'm fairly certain the boy standing beside my mother—with his arm around her shoulders in a move that could be affection or possession or equal parts of both—is the boy from the statue. Who is he? Mom's old boyfriend before she got with Peter?

If that's the case, she's never mentioned him to me at all.

I pull out my phone and snap a couple of photos of the class of 1998. Which reminds me that I need to take photos of some other things as well...

Dashing into a nearby bathroom, I hide away in a stall and hang my backpack from the hook on the door, unzipping it and pulling out Isla's yearbook. I flip the pages until I'm on the Autographs page in the back of the book, where Isla made her list. I take photos of it as well. What if I lose the book, or someone takes it? Whoever found it in the back of the pillow could have walked away with it, and I wouldn't have known right away. I need this list—need to figure out what Isla was working on and whether it was earth-shattering enough to get her and Emily in serious trouble. I just need more time to figure it out.

Time I don't have.

I flip through the articles in the dossier for good measure, to make sure I didn't miss anything. It looks like most of what's here falls into one of two categories: articles I managed to read in the car on the way to Wickham before I got motion sickness, and Wickham history Whitney filled me in on during our first meeting. But tucked in the back of the right-side pocket is a newspaper clipping I must have missed. At the top is a black-and-white photo of people dressed in cocktail attire. I recognize a younger version of Whitney, but Peter is nowhere in sight. A glance at the date on the article below the picture explains why. Peter was still married to Mom when this was published. In fact, she was pregnant with me at the time.

THE DAILY CUPPA: Society news and gossip from The London Ledger

14 December 2008

Last night's buzzy society soiree wasn't for a restaurant opening or charity fundraiser—it was to celebrate the Lumateg Group, the new private equity fund helmed by William Pembroke, formerly of Oakmont Capital Management. Champagne flowed as guests toasted Pembroke's leap from big-firm life to boutique power player. One partygoer who requested anonymity gushed that they admired 'the way Pembroke is turning his wife's inherited wealth into a legacy that will lift up the Group's core investors.'

In a short speech, Pembroke kept his remarks equal parts earnest and aspirational, thanking investors, family, and friends, and promising Lumateg 'will champion a diversified portfolio that values tried and true investment strategy alongside forward-thinking, calculated risk.' Party chatter noted the fund's name is a cheeky nod to posterity—'Lumateg' is an anagram of *legatum*, which is Latin for 'legacy.' Many of the fund's angel investors are Wickham Academy alumni, a designation Pembroke wears with pride. We expect big deals and bigger dinner invites from the Lumateg Group crowd, who knows a thing or two about building financial *and* social capital.

Why did Whitney include this in the dossier? She probably wants to make sure I understand the type of people I'm dealing with here at Wickham, but she doesn't realize that "too rich for their own good" is a population I interact with regularly. A good number of them manage to make their way into Doug's bar. Maybe there's some appeal in slumming it at a local NYC dive bar, or maybe we're just conveniently located next to the PATH train that shuttles white-collar professionals from their Manhattan offices to their New Jersey condos. If Whitney thinks I need this kind of preparation to sit in class…well, I'm sure she's just being overly cautious.

The warning bell rings, and it feels like a sign from the universe agreeing that time is not on my side. I snap the yearbook shut before I shove it into my backpack. I hide all of the photos I just took in my Notes app and slip my phone into the outside pocket of my bag. Within minutes, I'm wandering the corridor, entering the office like I'm out for a midday stroll. Like my impending mental breakdown from earlier this morning never happened. I smile brightly at Mrs. Brown, who frowns the second she spots me.

"Belinda." Mrs. Brown's voice is wary, and she's watching me like I'm a wild animal ready to strike out at any second. "Can I help you?"

Yeah, Mrs. Brown. I'd love to know who the boy is who's been immortalized forever as a bronze statue in the garden. You look like you've worked here for more than a few years. Do you remember the class of 1998? My mother? Or my—the word gets stuck in my brain like I'm actually trying to choke it out—*father?*

But I say none of that. Instead, I keep the smile pasted on my face and act like the concerned student I'm supposed to be. All the while, my brain is churning, churning, churning. Over and over again with the same questions.

Who's the boy? Who was he to my mother? Did Peter like him? Were they friends? Did he hate him? Were they rivals? I wish I could ask Mom about him, but she probably wouldn't tell me anything. She's got too many secrets.

Seems like everyone at this school does.

CHAPTER SEVEN

Mrs. Brown gave me three options for my elective class. Considering Advanced Mandarin would be impossible and Robotics sounded like my own personal nightmare, I went with Art. How hard can it be to paint and create stuff? Plus, Mom used to call herself an artist before she drowned her creativity in vodka. Taking this art class will make me feel closer to the best version of Mom. The one I adore and miss the most. The one I haven't seen in a long time.

I make my way to the arts building with hurried steps, though I'm not sure why. I'm already late to class, thanks to my meeting with Mrs. Brown. I shift my backpack strap on my shoulder as I head up the steps, wincing at how heavy it is. The yearbook and dossier add unnecessary weight, and I can't wait to get rid of them. Won't be until after class, though, and I have no idea where I'm going to hide them, considering I can't trust anyone around here.

The moment I make my way into the building, the door slams shut behind me, cutting off outdoor noise. The entire south wall is lined with massive windows, letting in plenty of early-afternoon light. After yesterday's drizzle, today's weather has been pleasant, though far from warm. It's cold around here, and I'm thankful for the cardigan Whitney loaned me this morning.

I stutter-step to a halt as realization washes over me. Why would Whitney have uniform pieces in the closet in her office? She certainly never has to wear them. But a mother whose daughter has to wear a uniform to school every day might very well stash a few spare items in her office on campus, just in case. My mind ricochets back to the moment earlier today when Whitney held me at arm's length and smoothed the cardigan over my shoulders. It was such a tender gesture...but I have to wonder if it was meant for me or Isla. Because I'd bet all the money Doug shoved into my hands the last time I saw him that this sweater belongs to my sister.

The fabric seems to grow warmer against my skin, like it's not just a poly-wool blend—it's a hug, too. If Isla and I had never been separated by divorce and an ocean, we probably would have shared clothes all the time. Maybe it would have become so commonplace to borrow without asking that I would have gotten annoyed with her—would have yelled at her to stay out of my closet. What does it say about my life that the thought of having a spat with my little sister over something as trivial as clothes feels like the stuff of daydreams? Because it's true—I'd give anything to hear Isla's voice again, let alone argue with her.

I've wasted so much time being jealous and letting the jealousy hide behind anger. What wouldn't I give to go back in time and tell myself to get my head out of my ass? To yell at myself to wake up and pay attention, cherish Isla at every opportunity, and stop being salty about our very different lives?

None of it was ever Isla's fault. Or mine.

Like most revelations, this one comes too late to be useful. There's no going back in time. All I can do is move forward. Find the truth. Bring Isla justice, even if she may never know I was here, fighting for her.

I swallow down the lump in my throat and run a finger under my eyes, expecting moisture but finding none. While my brain was spiraling into memory and regret, my body remained rock-steady. Maybe that's the secret to falling apart—you never let yourself go 100 percent. You hold back the pieces of yourself the world will see, and keep the devastation inside, where it can belong to you alone.

I pull the sleeve of Isla's cardigan over my hand until it covers my fingers, then curl the fabric into my palm. It's as close as I can get to holding her hand right now, so I'll take what I can get.

I come to a stop in front of room thirteen and peek inside the open doorway. There's no one in the classroom save for one boy with his back to me, sitting at an easel. In front of him, a large piece of paper is taped to a paint-splattered board. I can't really make out details from this distance, but the picture taking shape in front of him is dark and…lonely.

I clear my throat as I enter the room, not wanting to startle him, but I do anyway. His head jerks, and he glances over his shoulder. My breath catches in my throat.

Connor Wells.

He frowns the moment he spots me, then turns to face his

easel once more. His fingertips are smudged with charcoal, but when he touches the stick to the paper, the line he produces is slim and delicate. I force my eyes away from his confident hand and take a few steps forward so I have a better view of the picture taking shape. It's a dark forest with a lone cabin receding into the background. A gray curl of smoke rises from a chimney. Though the picture is entirely done in black and white, Connor has managed to capture warm light in the cabin's windows.

I approach slowly, stopping just behind him.

"You're...amazing." I sound breathless and a little starstruck, and I shake my head once, silently berating myself.

Connor grabs a short stick of what looks like tightly rolled paper. He smudges a shadow into the ground under the cabin. And he doesn't acknowledge me, the jerk.

I remain quiet, and so does he, as he adds highlights to the moonlit sides of trees and roughs in additional details around the cabin. The start of a woodpile, maybe. An overturned wheelbarrow.

"You don't belong here."

Alarm races down my spine, leaving me ice-cold. I want to stutter a defense—of course I belong at Wickham! Just another rich private school student, reporting for duty!—but I swallow down the panic and let Belinda's confidence take center stage. "You're always telling me where I shouldn't be," I say. "Any ideas about where I *should* be?" I raise my eyebrows in a way I hope looks suggestive. I don't have the backbone to eye his lap, like maybe that's where I should take a seat, but part of me wishes I did. I'd like to see Connor squirm.

"You don't belong in this class," he clarifies, and I exhale softly. I thought he could tell I don't belong at Wickham at all, and he'd be right. "As you can see, no one is in here."

I glance around the empty classroom before I return my gaze to his. "Art elective field trip day?"

He doesn't so much as crack a smile. "No. There are a few students who are actually enrolled, but no one sticks around. There's no supervision for this elective because the instructor was awarded a residency at the Louvre. It's almost always just me."

Once again, he turns his broad back to me as he reaches for another slim stick of charcoal.

"Mrs. Brown added me to the class," I tell him.

His shoulders slump. "This must be a joke."

"No joke." My voice is knife-sharp. Connor might be gorgeous, but he's annoying me in a way that renders his beauty moot. Almost. How dismissive he is, how freaking mysterious, feels like an act. One I want to rip down so I can call him out as a total fraud.

Takes one to know one.

"Are you an artist?" he asks, not bothering to turn around.

"I dabble," I hedge. The truth is, I don't have a fraction of the artistic talent my mother has in her pinkie finger. But like everything else in my life lately, I guess this is one more lie I'll have to spin into the truth.

"What's your preferred medium?"

I glance around the room, my brain spinning as I try to come up with an answer. Hanging on a wall labeled STUDENT GALLERY, I spot some abstract-looking blobs of sheer color on thick, creamy-looking paper. "Watercolor."

"Hmph." I never realized a single sound could capture so much disappointment.

"I guess I'll just…find some supplies," I say, turning toward the supply closet I spy in the corner.

"What's your name?"

"Billie." I wince at my mistake. "Well, Belinda."

This seems to pique his interest at last. He turns fully in my direction, his head cocked at an inquisitive angle. "Which is it? Billie or Belinda?"

Nice going, Billie. First the yearbook, now this. I can probably cross "undercover detective" off my list of potential careers. I feel my shoulders starting to hunch and force myself to stand ramrod straight. *Belinda Winters persona activated.*

"My friends back home call me Billie. *You* can call me Belinda," I tell him, infusing as much snobbery as possible into my tone.

A long beat of silence stretches between us. The cold steel of Connor's gray gaze melts a little, and he presses his lips together like…like he's trying not to laugh.

"Well, *Billie*, you can use that easel over there." He pulls his gaze away from mine, waving a hand toward an easel across the room. "And just to let you know, I prefer to work in complete silence."

He says nothing else, and for a moment I remain quiet, too. Is he for real right now?

His continuing silence tells me yes. Yes, he is.

"What are you, the artist in residence at Wickham?"

His expression doesn't shift at my sarcastic question. "Yes. As a matter of fact, I am."

When it's clear that this conversation is over, I straighten my shoulders and head toward the supply closet, which is much larger than I thought it would be. It's filled with shelves stacked high with art supplies, and there's a short countertop and cabinets with a sink to the right of the closet. I take stock of my options, deciding to grab a pad of watercolor paper and a set of paints, along with some brushes. I set all of my supplies on the counter, ready to fill a glass jar with water to dip the brushes in when I spot a stack of stretched canvases in the farthest corner of the room. An idea blooms.

Maybe that would be the perfect place to hide Isla's yearbook and the dossier.

After I fill the jar with water and leave it in the sink, I glance over my shoulder to watch Connor, but he's too busy creating his Dark Lord masterpiece. Chewing on my lower lip, I slowly unzip my backpack and pull the yearbook and dossier from within while continuously checking on what Connor is doing, but he's not paying attention to me.

Clutching both items to my chest, I slip over to the stack of canvases, testing one of them to see how heavy it is. I note the frame of the canvas and how it allows some space to stash something behind it. I slip both items between two canvases, where they fit perfectly. I check on Connor yet again, but he's either completely in the zone or his peripheral vision is seriously lacking.

I'm guessing it's the former.

Once I've got my backpack zipped back up, I sling it over my shoulder, the load and my heart both a little lighter now that the incriminating evidence connecting me to Isla is safely hidden. I reenter the art studio and drop my backpack on the ground by an empty easel before I start setting up my supplies.

As per usual, Connor doesn't bother looking in my direction.

I dig my earbuds out of my backpack and put them in, then grab my phone and bring up a playlist. The familiar song makes me feel normal. Almost like I'm back home, working at the bar and laughing with Doug about a weird customer. Feeling a little better, I dab a wide, stiff brush in water before pushing it into a moody dark-blue pigment.

Mom and I have never had premium cable or streaming at home, but we could usually get a few national networks and local channels to come through without too much static on our small countertop TV. Which is to say, I've seen my fair share of Bob Ross reruns—him dabbing "happy little trees" onto landscapes that always managed to look like fantasy lands to my city-kid eyes. I think of dear old Bob now as I sweep a diluted wash of paint all over the heavy paper. I press a little harder in some places, letting drips of colored water run down the length of my painting. The effect gives me a deep sense of satisfaction, like the paper is crying.

A few songs into my playlist, and I'm totally committed. Singing along with the lyrics, glancing over at Connor every few seconds like I can't help myself. Mentally willing him to pay attention to me.

Of course, he doesn't, though I swear I notice his broad shoulders tightening every time I sing, so I raise my voice, swirling the brush all over the paper and making an absolute mess.

It's when I'm practically singing at the top of my lungs "We Can't Be Friends" that he finally rises to his feet, his charcoal stick hitting the ground with a clatter. I pause, the words dying in my throat when he stomps his way over to me. He's scowling, his brows lowered, his lips thin, and he comes to a stop behind me.

Turning off the music, I hold my breath while he checks out my painting. The silence lasts for so long that I finally dare to look over my shoulder at him to find that he's smiling. It disappears the moment our gazes meet.

"What is this?" He gestures toward the heavy paper.

I turn to face my work of art, tilting my head to the side. "Well...I suppose it's an abstract representation of my feelings at the moment."

It's nothing but blobs and drips of dark paint that have merged together until the color is unidentifiable.

"It appears you're feeling a...certain way." The faint amusement in his voice is obvious, and my traitorous heart trips over itself. He's hot. It feels like the air between us crackles and snaps, and I banish the idea. I can't think like this about him. He is most definitely the enemy.

Crap, they all are so far, save for Sophia. And even she makes me nervous.

"Oh, definitely." I nod, pretending I'm confident in my talents. "Do you like it?"

Our gazes meet once more, and his eyes are lighter. Like quicksilver. "Let's just say you're a better painter than singer."

My jaw drops at his insult, though it feels more like he's teasing. "Seriously?"

He nods, his lush mouth stern. "Most definitely."

I leave him where he stands and head over to the student gallery, desperate to gather my agitated thoughts. I keep my gaze focused on the wall, taking it all in. While most of the pieces scream *students trying hard!*, my eye is drawn to a particular abstract painting that feels oddly…familiar.

It takes me a few minutes of studying the painting for it to finally come clear. It's the tree and cliff from the photo Mom is obsessed with. The one she forced me to bring here. But the sense that I've seen this painting before goes beyond the subject. The style of painting, the treatment of light and color…I actually recognize it.

It's my mother. She painted this. I'm sure of it.

"That one gets to me, too." Connor's deep voice pulls me from my melancholy thoughts, and I turn to find him standing beside me, his head tilted back as he contemplates the painting. "Considering it's the exact spot where Isla Vale murdered my sister."

A ripple of cold apprehension slithers down my spine, and it takes everything inside of me to keep my voice even. "How do you know she murdered your sister? Weren't they best friends or something?"

"I never trusted Isla. She was sneaky, especially those last few weeks before Emily—*died*." He swallows hard, and I feel bad for challenging him with my callous question. "No one ever knew where Isla was, not even my sister half the time, and that's just odd considering that yes, they were best friends. 'Up to no good' is what I always told Emily, but she defended Isla to the end."

I'm thinking Isla was probably sneaking around with Julian, not that I can tell Connor. I'm not supposed to know anything about anyone at Wickham.

The bell rings, and Connor takes that as his cue to gather his belongings and exit the studio without another word to me.

The door thumps shut before I can make it over to my easel and grab my dirty brushes to rinse them clear of paint.

It's when I'm standing at the sink, letting the cold water turn my fingers to icicles, that I realize I need to go find Julian. See if I can get him to talk to me about Isla without blowing my cover.

But how the hell am I supposed to do that?

CHAPTER EIGHT

After I've gathered my things, I leave the art building, surprised by how quiet the campus is despite the bell ringing not even five minutes ago. Or maybe it was ten? It took me a while to clean up after myself. Plus, I was halfway out the door when I decided to go back and check the stack of canvases again to ensure no one can tell there's anything hidden there. I have to keep reassuring myself that it's an excellent hiding place, but I'm still a little nervous that someone could discover them. The dossier especially will expose me as a complete fraud. If anyone finds it, I'll be ruined. More importantly, I'll have to leave Wickham a complete failure.

No way can I let that happen.

I'm heading for my dorm room when I end up detouring into the alumni garden. I don't stop walking until I'm standing in front of the bronze statue again. I study the boy's face. Pulling out my phone, I open up the photo I took earlier, and it's all the confirmation I need.

The statue is definitely the boy who had his arm around

my mother's shoulders.

Did Isla figure this out? I need to review her notes and that list as soon as possible. But how? I'm assuming Priya is in our room, and I'd prefer privacy to go over everything. Maybe I could sneak off to the library by myself for a couple of hours. Will I be able to look my fill at the photos and maybe even do a little research in the archives? Or will someone notice me? I have no clue.

I also need to talk to Julian and see what he might know. I feel like there are people all over this campus who know something, but it's not like I have time to interview every single student. This is why I need to focus on the key players. And speaking of key players...

I'm about to exit the garden when I spot Julian across the courtyard. Talk about perfect timing.

"Julian!" I wave my hand when he lifts his head, and he waits for me as I run across the grass to meet up with him. "Hey. Thanks for waiting."

"Anything for you." The mischievous grin on his face immediately makes me suspicious. His secret girlfriend is in a coma, and he's most definitely flirting with me. Talk about gross. But I can't let that bother me at the moment. "Were you just in the alumni garden?"

"I was." I laugh as if I haven't a care in the world. "Rather boring, though."

"I'll say." He chuckles. "Hot tip for the new girl: nothing fun ever happens in the alumni garden."

"Noted." We walk together in silence for only a few seconds before I decide to test him. "Tell me, then—where *do* fun things happen here?"

"Well, the Wickham campus is part of a sprawling estate. Acres and acres of land, as far as the eye can see." I lift my head to find he's already watching me. "There are plenty of places to get up to no good if you're creative enough."

I force my lips into a coquettish tilt, even when all I want to do is sneer at the audacity of this little twerp. He's supposed to be heartbroken, but he's flirting like his secret girlfriend *isn't* lying unconscious in a hospital bed. "What kind of trouble do you like to get into?" I scan the path ahead so I don't have to look him in the eye, wondering if I took it too far. But nope. Julian doesn't miss a beat, though his tone when he answers my question is a bit more…cautious.

"Depending on the weather, we usually light a bonfire out in one of the fields on Friday nights and sit around it for a couple of hours while we drink. Also, some of us have been known to have what we like to call 'secret house parties,' but they're always in someone's dorm room." He shrugs. "You know, the usual goings-on at a boarding school where we can let loose and relax for a bit. Get into a little trouble, even, though nothing too outrageous."

"Uh-huh." I nod, keeping my gaze on the dorm building looming up ahead. "What about the kind of trouble that doesn't include a crowd? Like…one-on-one trouble?"

"Are you asking where some of us might sneak off for a little shag, Belinda?" He makes a tsking noise, but I can tell from the look on his face he's eating this up. Ew. "Trust me, there are plenty of secret spots around campus. Old buildings that the school doesn't officially use any longer. The theater. Lots of mischief happens in the theater. There are so *many* dressing rooms."

"I'm guessing you've used a few of those dressing rooms before?" I pause for dramatic effect, then widen my eyes like I've just had a sudden thought. "Wait a minute. I'm not going to piss anyone off by asking you these questions, am I? Like maybe a girlfriend or…something?"

We come to a stop at the same time in front of my dorm. When I turn to face Julian, I can tell my question touched a nerve. His expression is blank, his eyes absent of the spark that was there only a moment ago. "You should be careful asking questions you might not want the answer to."

I frown, confused. "What do you—"

"Oh look, there's Arlo." Julian starts walking, his back already to me. "See you around, Belinda."

I watch him go, pissed at myself. I pushed too hard. I need to play it casual around these people, but it's difficult when all I want to do is catch everyone in a lie.

When I enter my room a few minutes later, it's an internal fight to hide my disappointment. Priya has company—Abigail. They're both hunched over Priya's desk, the two of them sharing the chair as they study an open textbook. The moment I shut the door, Priya leaps to her feet, her movements frantic, her eyes extra bright.

"Belinda! I didn't expect you."

"I live here." I drop my backpack on my bed before I face her. "You should expect me."

"Right, right. I don't know. I just thought—" Priya shakes her head. "I don't know what I thought. My brain cells are consumed with studying for the French exam tomorrow and nothing else."

"You're not in Advanced Mandarin?" I ask.

Abigail scoffs, stretching her arms above her head. "We want to live in Paris. I plan on studying fashion design."

"Yes. Fashion design." Priya nods, standing straighter. "Me too."

I watch them both, curious. I have a feeling Priya isn't interested in fashion design. And they're both acting a little twitchy. The energy in the room vibrates with a kind of manic tension. Are they…on something? If so, my mind is seriously blown. Priya is so damn uptight that I'm surprised she'd do something like this. And for what? To study?

That's no fun.

After I grab my phone out of my backpack, I flop onto my bed with an exaggerated sigh and start doomscrolling. Abigail and Priya resume their studying, reading out loud to each other from the textbook and trying to answer every question in French.

Ugh.

I pull up Sophia's number that she gave me earlier and send her a quick text.

Me: *What are you doing?*

It takes her a few minutes to respond.

Sophia: *In a meeting. I'm the president of the International Club, and it's our monthly meetup.*

Me: *Oh. Fun.*

I get the sense that Sophia is a total overachiever and is in lots of clubs. Probably to impress her dad and keep herself busy. My phone dings with another text from her.

Sophia: *Should be done in about fifteen minutes. Everything okay? Do you need something?*

Me: *Yeah, I need to get away from Priya and Abigail. They're talking to each other nonstop in French.*

Sophia: *That exam tomorrow is going to be brutal. Do you want to meet in my room?*

Me: *Where's your room?*

I didn't think she lived in a dorm room on campus. I assumed she lived with her parents.

Sophia: *Same building you're in but on the second floor. Room 222. The door is unlocked because I've been living at home the last couple of weeks.*

Sophia: *See you soon!*

Why has she been living at home the last few weeks? Why doesn't she just live at home always? I assume the headmaster has his own quarters on campus. And who just leaves their dorm room unlocked?

This is weird.

I quickly change out of my uniform and slip on a pair of dark-green sweatpants with the Wickham crest on the left front hip and a matching hoodie. It's thick and warm, and I'm about to leave the room without a word when Priya stops me.

"Where did you get that?"

I turn to face Priya and Abigail. They're both watching me with curiosity sparking their already bright gazes. "Where did I get what?"

"The matching sweats." Priya waves a hand toward me. "They're really nice."

Oh. I didn't expect her to compliment my outfit.

"My parents got them for me. I guess they were part of the

uniform package." I glance down at myself before returning my gaze to Priya's. I can feel Abigail studying me. Even spot the faintly disgusted curl to her upper lip. I wonder if being such a raging bitch is tiring, or if it gives her energy, like a succubus draining her victims.

"They're nice." Priya laughs, glancing over at Abigail. "We never got anything like that offered to us as part of *our* uniform package."

"Well, that was a few years ago," Abigail reminds her. "Maybe this is what they give the newbies now."

If they're trying to remind me of my lack of social status on this campus, they're doing a great job, I think to myself as I storm out of the room. The door slams on their laughter, cutting off all sound. I practically run down the hall, skipping down the steps as fast as possible.

I want out of here. I'm in desperate need of some peace and quiet, and listening to those two rattle on in French was only giving me a headache.

The second floor is laid out exactly like the third, and I find Sophia's room easily. I open the door and peek my head in, half expecting Sophia's roommate to be inside and pissed that I barged in like this, but I'm greeted by nothing but silence.

I enter the room fully, closing the door behind me. The quiet is like a balm to my frazzled nerves. For the first time today, I don't need to worry about being watched or judged or whispered about. I close my eyes and force myself to take a deep breath. I exhale in a slow, even stream, like I'm pushing the air through a straw. I do it again, and then once more, before I open my eyes and take stock of my surroundings.

I can tell which side of the room is Sophia's because of

the framed photo of her and her parents on the nightstand, but that's the only personal item in the room. I walk over to the desk on the other side and pull open the drawers to find most of them empty, save for a short stack of worksheets in the bottom drawer. All of them have the same name written in the top left corner.

Isla Vale.

Realization smacks me square in the chest, and I fall heavily onto the edge of the bed, my head spinning. This is—was—Isla's room. And the stack of school assignments is the only thing that remains of her. There's no computer, no laptop. The desk is bare, as is the nightstand save for a lamp. The bed is stripped, and the walls are empty. No inspirational quote posters or taped-up photos. Nothing. No wonder Sophia doesn't want to remain in this room. It's devoid of personality, of warmth, of *presence.*

Rising to my feet, I go to the closet on Isla's side and open the door, immobilized at what I see hanging in front of me. Some of her clothes are still inside. Mostly pieces of the Wickham uniform, but I spot a few colorful sweaters that are so Isla-like, tears spring to my eyes.

I should be digging around, looking for information or clues, but raw emotion swells in my chest, making it hard to breathe. I step into the closet and grab hold of the closest sweater, bringing it to my face and breathing deep. It smells like sweet perfume. Expensive. I tug the sweater off the hanger and clutch it. Bury my face in it as I cry. I let her scent surround me, let myself believe for a fraction of a second that this isn't a remnant of the girl but the girl herself. I imagine I'm embracing the sister I love so much but who isn't here.

The sister I'm afraid I might lose. The sister I ignored when I should have clung tighter, should have cherished and adored the one person in my family who loved me with a pure heart.

What if I fuck everything up? What if I can't prove what really happened to Emily and Isla on that cliff? I have to save Isla before she's taken out of reach, before she's formally charged and the course of her life shifts forever.

I must.

Taking a deep, shuddery breath, I wipe my tear-streaked face with the sleeve of the sweater before I slip it back onto the hanger. I thumb through everything else in the closet, coming to a stop when I see a hideous hoodie that doesn't fit in with the rest of the clothes. It's faded black with rips in it, and when I touch the fabric, it's rough. Feels cheap.

Not Isla's style at all.

I brush my fingers against the front of the hoodie pocket and go still. There's something inside. And when I pull it out, my mouth drops open in shock.

A wad of cash is held together by a rubber band. The money is colorful—something I'm not used to seeing, since it's British pounds. But I can tell that this is a lot of money. Why does Isla have it stashed inside an ugly-ass hoodie? Is it hers? Or does it belong to someone else?

The room door handle rattles, and I shove the money back into the hoodie pocket, practically leaping out of the closet when Sophia enters the room.

"Helloooo," she sing-songs, going quiet when she sees where I'm standing. We stare at each other in silence, my head spinning to come up with a proper, unsuspicious answer. "What are you doing in there?"

"I'm, uh, freezing. It's so cold in this building. I was trying to find a coat." I shrug, glancing down at myself. I'm already in a hoodie and sweatpants, but it's not necessarily a lie. It's pretty damn cold in this room. "No such luck, though."

"Oh." Sophia's delicate brows draw together. "That's not my closet."

"Shit. Yeah. I don't know what I was thinking." I laugh, but the sound is overly fake, and I clamp my lips shut. "Sorry. I just figured if you have a room to yourself, you'd take over both closets. I know that's what I would do!"

My overly bright voice and equally bright smile feel phony. *Calm the hell down*, I chastise myself.

"That's Isla Vale's side. You know, the girl who's in a coma." Sophia's voice is hushed, her expression solemn.

I mimic her, desperate to contain my own overwhelming emotions. "You were her roommate?"

Sophia nods. "It was hard staying in this room after—the incident. That's why I'm back at home. I don't like thinking I could've been sleeping next to a murderer. Oh, sorry—*alleged* murderer."

"I don't blame you." I glance over at Isla's bed, my chest tight. I rub at it absently, trying to ease the ache. "Do you think she did it? Killed Emily?"

Sophia is quiet for a moment. Just long enough to make my nerves rise. I didn't like how she called my sister an alleged murderer, but I can't hold that against her. Plenty of people think that.

"No," she finally says. "I can't imagine Isla killing someone, especially Emily. They were thicker than thieves—real 'ride or die' type stuff. Isla hurting Emily doesn't make any sense.

But I have no idea who did it, and being in this room, staying here alone after it happened...I didn't like it. So I stay out at my parents' house, and I leave things here just in case I need something quick and don't want to run back to the estate. A few changes of clothes. A box of tampons. A phone charger. The essentials."

"Right." I nod. "That's smart."

"I might move back in later in the term, but I'm not really in any rush. It feels so empty now." Her voice is hollow as she stares at Isla's bed.

"Maybe the both of us could stay the night here," I suggest. "Have a little slumber party?" At Sophia's frown, I forge on. "I just don't want to be in my room tonight. Not with Abigail there, too. Three's a crowd, you know?"

"Oh, I do. Abigail and Priya together is... Let's just say I understand." Sophia's smile is gentle. "If you need to stay the night here, you're more than welcome to."

"Really?" Relief makes my shoulders sag. "You don't mind?"

"Not at all, but I can't stay with you. Everything I use for my nightly skincare routine is at the house, and I can't skip it. I've finally got my acne somewhat under control." Sophia touches her chin, rubbing her index finger back and forth across a spot. "Come on, let's make the bed for you."

Sophia goes to her closet and throws the doors open, pulling a stack of neatly folded sheets out from the top shelf. I take it from her, and we both start to make Isla's old bed. My fingers tremble at the knowledge I'm going to be in the bed my sister last slept in, and it takes everything inside of me not to burst into tears again.

"I'll finish this." I grab the folded flat sheet and hold it to my chest. "You've already done so much for me, Sophia. Just by letting me stay here tonight."

"Are you sure? Well, it's no problem." Sophia glances at her phone. "I'm so sorry, but I need to get home. I have to study for the French exam as well, plus…my skincare regimen."

"Of course. I totally understand. See you tomorrow?" A gasp escapes me when Sophia pulls me in for a quick, tight hug, letting me go before I can return the embrace.

"See you tomorrow." She takes a step back, offers me a quick wave, and then she's gone.

Leaving me alone in the room.

Once I lock the door, I finish making the bed, letting the tears flow freely down my cheeks as I tuck the sheets tight beneath the corners. I grab the blanket draped across the foot of Sophia's bed and use it as a comforter, pulling it over my body. I bury my face in Isla's pillow and cry and cry. Big, heaving sobs rack my body, and when I finally fall asleep, it's deep. Dark. I dream of Isla. Falling.

Always falling.

CHAPTER NINE

I'm in the dining hall earlier than usual, eating my breakfast alone, thinking. I figured I would be an emotional wreck from spending the night in my sister's bed, but I woke up feeling refreshed despite the nightmares. Maybe being in the space Isla used to occupy every day inspired me, or maybe sleeping in a room by myself behind a locked door finally allowed me to catch up on deep sleep. Either way, I'm ready to tackle the day.

It's blessedly quiet in here, with hardly any students eating this early. I don't want to run into anyone who'll ruin my day before it's even begun. Just as I start to congratulate myself for discovering a brand-new life hack (eat early, avoid assholes), a certain someone spots me right away and heads in my direction with determined steps.

Connor Wells.

Nerves flutter at the intense expression on his face, and I brace myself for his approach. He drops his tray onto the table right next to mine before he pulls out the chair and settles in. I hide my shock under indifference, not so much as turning my head in his direction. The scent of his cologne wafts toward me, and I inhale as subtly as possible so he doesn't figure out I'm a complete freak who might grow addicted to his smell.

Ugh, I'm ridiculous.

Seriously, though, he is the last person I believed I'd start my day with, and I'm going to run with it.

"You figured out the secret," is how he greets me before he grabs a fruit-filled pastry on his plate and sinks his teeth into it.

"What's that?" My appetite vanishes at his question—and from having him so close. He leaves me breathless. Confused. Last time I saw him, he was a mixture of rude and flirtatious—heavy on the rude. I don't like how unsettled he makes me every time I'm in his presence. He's no one special.

"Eating in the dining hall early before all the arseholes come in." His words echo my own thoughts so closely that I can't help the laugh that escapes me.

He smiles, the sight of it making my head spin. I remind myself I can't read into this interaction. He'll probably treat me like shit the next time we're together, which I'm thinking is his usual mode of operation.

"The arseholes, huh?" I laugh, shaking my head as I tear my croissant to shreds.

"I think you Americans pronounce it *assholes*." His tone is flat, like he's trying to imitate me. "But yes. Beat them to the dining hall and you get to enjoy your breakfast in peace, stress-free."

"Do they stress you out? Your former friends?" I send him

a look, shoving a few torn pieces of pastry in my mouth.

"Everyone stresses me out." He scowls as he scans the mostly empty dining hall.

"Even me?"

"Especially you." He directs that scowl straight at me before his gaze drops to my plate. "What did that croissant ever do to you?"

I'm about to make some flippant remark when he grabs hold of my hand, shaking it a little to get me to release the torn pastry. His fingers smooth over mine. When he presses his big palm against my smaller one, I can't contain a quiet gasp.

He drops my hand like it's on fire, returning his attention to his breakfast. I reach for the steadying warmth of my coffee. "Are you enjoying your time at Wickham so far?"

I nearly choke on the bitter sip I just took. "Enjoying?" I manage to sputter after I swallow.

His smile returns. "Bad choice of words?"

"Terrible choice." I smile back, and his fades. "Let's just say my time at Wickham so far has been…interesting."

"I can only imagine." He scans the room before bringing his attention back to me. "Not too many friendly sorts here."

"But they used to be your friends, right?" I steer the conversation back in the direction I need it to go. Connor, once part of the inner circle and now an outsider, might be far enough beyond the circle of trust that he lets something slip. I'm sure he doesn't know exactly what happened, because he's still convinced Isla hurt Emily. If he had some idea of who was really responsible for his sister's death, there's no way he'd peddle a false assumption like it's the truth. He'd want justice for Emily.

Just like I want it for Isla.

Connor averts his gaze, lost in thought for a moment. "They were. Most of them still are. Somewhat."

"Then why do you seem to be on the outs? Why are you the brooding artist loner when you could be the brooding artist social butterfly?" That earns me the smallest upward tilt at the corner of his lips. I ignore the fizzy feeling in my chest at the sight. It feels like I'm wearing Belinda Winters like a costume as I force myself to take a calm, cavalier sip of coffee and pop another croissant fragment in my mouth.

Miracle of all miracles, he starts talking.

"Things got weird after what happened with my father. I'm sure someone's told you."

I slowly shake my head. No one needs to know about the half dozen articles in the dossier about the Lumateg Group scandal, or how I practically memorized their details. "I don't know much—just the basics."

"My father worked for the Lumateg Group. He was a fiduciary wealth manager, and his clients were mostly Wickham alumni. Parents of students who are currently enrolled, so many of them his friends. The Pembrokes started the company twenty years ago, and my father came on board almost immediately. He helped grow that company to what it is, until everything that happened," Connor explains, his voice hollow.

"You mean when he got arrested?"

He nods, swallowing hard.

"Pembroke? Any relation to Freddie?" I ask.

"His father. Our dads went to Wickham together. They're

close. Well, they used to be." Connor's expression is grim. "I understand why Freddie had to create a boundary with me. I felt the same way. I didn't expect everyone to swing to his side, though. My father may be the one behind bars, but it's not like I helped him embezzle money."

His tone and expression are bitter. I can't blame him, but also...*come on, guy*. Does he really think kids who have only ever eaten off silver spoons are going to excel at emotional nuance? Expecting his former friends to show him compassion is like expecting a hungry lion to spare a baby gazelle separated from the herd just because it's really cute.

"So tell me: Why do you stay here at Wickham? You're ostracized by your friends. And then everything that happened with your sister..." I press my lips together, not wanting to say anything else about Emily. It's a sensitive subject, and I understand his grief somewhat. At least my sister is still alive, even if she's in a coma.

"I'm on an arts merit scholarship at the moment. Someone in admin pulled that together after our family's assets were frozen. I've got nowhere else to go, so I stay here. My mother is an absolute wreck, and I told her I would come home and help her, but she wouldn't let me. I should 'stay here and complete my education' were her exact words. She even mentioned how I'd have to figure out my future on my own now that the money is all gone." His lips twist into a wry smile. "Think I can make it as an artist?"

"Maybe?" He chuckles at my response, and I feel like I insulted him. "From what I saw, you're very talented."

"Talent isn't worth shit if I can't manage to actually create anything. I've been blocked creatively since Emily died, which has brought my term project to a screeching halt. Not quite sure how I'll manage to qualify for the scholarship if I don't turn that in."

"I saw you working on something just yesterday," I remind him. "Doesn't that count?"

"Not really. I was just…messing around. My normal medium is hyper-realistic oil paintings, but ever since what happened to Emily, it's as if my fingers are detached from my body. Everything I try to paint becomes a mess. I keep my hands busy with the charcoal sketches, but that's not going to help my chances of maintaining my scholarship." He shrugs, and I can practically feel the hopelessness radiate off his body in waves.

I'm filled with sympathy at his plight. If anyone can understand what I'm going through, I think it's this boy. Everyone else I've met at this school seems like they have their shit together for the most part—or maybe it's more accurate to say that they operate with the certainty that their lives will be as easy as they've always been. Life hasn't given them a reason to question their luck, so they've started to believe it will last forever. If I was ever lucky, I don't remember it. And Connor's luck ran out big time this past year. The bubble he was in didn't just pop—it imploded.

"It'll come back." When he sends me a questioning look, I continue. "Your artistic…spirit." I grimace and shake my head. "You know what I mean."

"Right. Not so sure about that, though." A ragged exhale leaves him. "Guess it wasn't enough for Isla to kill my sister. Her actions also killed my creativity and my only chance at continuing my education."

"Are you serious?" I squeak. His remark has me instantly on the defensive. How dare he blame Isla for something she has no control over? And does he really believe Isla killed Emily?

From the serious expression on his too-handsome face, I'd have to wager yes. Yes, he does.

"Of course I'm serious," he snaps. "An unexpected tragedy has a way of affecting all aspects of your life. The grief counselor Mum made me talk to said tragedy is a rock thrown into a still lake. Its ripples keep multiplying all the way to the shore. Her advice was mostly useless, but that, at least, was true."

I know all about a tragedy affecting my life, though I wasn't necessarily close to Isla. And that's on me. That's the regret I'll live with for the rest of my life, especially if she never comes out of this coma. But that tragedy, should it ever come to pass, will have to get in line behind all the other rocks thrown into the lake of my life.

Connor's words and attitude fill me with simmering rage, and I clutch my fists in my lap. I feel like I might explode. And then, when I see the arrogant expression on his face, I do.

"Must be nice, not taking any responsibility for your shortcomings and blaming them all on a girl who's fighting for her life while in a coma," I retort, not caring that my annoyance is on full display. "She can't even defend herself against your accusations."

He jumps to his feet, the glower on his face making me shrink away from him. "But you can? You don't even know her, Billie. You don't know *anyone* at this school, which has me thinking you should keep your shitty opinions to yourself."

Before I can respond, Connor is walking away, his long strides taking him out of the dining hall in seconds. I sit in my feelings for a few minutes once he's gone, sipping my lukewarm coffee. A part of me is full of regret that I pushed him too far.

I shouldn't have said that about Isla, but my emotions have been on edge since last night, and I'm sure his have been all over the place since the night his sister died. I can't judge him. I shouldn't insult him, either.

But I also can't lie to myself—he infuriated me.

He's *so sure* Isla hurt Emily, even though none of the articles I've read have offered a single reason why that might have been true. Probably because it *isn't* true. It's like the whole world decided that the easiest way to process the tragedy of Emily's death was to blame Isla, who can't defend herself or offer an alternative explanation for what happened that night. No one seems to care that Isla and Emily were best friends—or maybe it's just that everyone has decided their friendship doesn't matter. If anyone bothered to consider that Isla and Emily were as close as sisters...

As close as sisters are supposed to be, I remind myself.

The thought grinds my runaway anger to a halt. The world may have failed Isla, but I failed her first. If I never get the chance to apologize to her, the least I can do is clear her name.

With a sigh, I grab my phone and pull up the photos of the Autographs page in the back of Isla's yearbook, looking for some sort of clue yet again. "LLAMAS '08" is written in my sister's loopy script above a list of names: Ashworth. Pembroke. Vale. Carmichael. Harrington. Canterbury. I don't get the "llamas" part. What does that even mean? Does Wickham have a mascot, and is it, inexplicably, a llama?

No way. That's too silly.

I study the names again, trying to connect dots. They make me think of the circled faces in last year's yearbook. Some of the surnames match, but not all of them. I need to find a yearbook from 1997-1998, but where? The library, maybe? In a place like Wickham, obsessed with its own legacy, surely there's an archive of them. I should ask the librarian.

Zooming in on the photo, I see there's a last name separated from all the rest, and I recognize it—Arnaud. My mother's maiden name. Acronyms are written beside it: "ACMER?" and "ARTSMER?" What does all of it mean? If I had to decipher the acronyms, I'd guess they could stand for some sort of academic or arts scholarship, like what Connor has. Maybe? I might be reaching, but it's possible.

I stare off into the distance, lost in thought. Remembering how cute Connor was when he smiled. When he said *arseholes*. And when he grabbed my hand and our palms connected? The touch was brief, but I felt it. A pulse of heat seemed to pass from my skin to his, and I can't explain what it was.

Chemistry? More like the zing of irritation. Though wouldn't Mom be thrilled that the boy I'm crushing on is into art like she used to be? They'd have something in common, a subject they could talk about passionately—

Wait. A. Second.

The boy I like? Please. I'm not *crushing on* Connor. I can't. And my mother will never have the opportunity to meet him, let alone have an entire conversation with him about art. What sort of delulu land am I living in, anyway?

It's obvious I need more coffee.

. . .

Halfway through the school day, I take a break from the grind, desperate to get away even if it's just for a few minutes. I hide out in my dorm room and eat a sandwich, enjoying the peace and quiet. No Priya and Abigail conversing in French. No ghosts lingering in the room as I cry myself to sleep. No professors droning on about a boring subject I don't give a damn about. Most everyone has left me alone today, and it's been nice. Not a single tear has been shed the entire day so far, either, and I consider that a win.

Once I finish my sandwich, I toss the wrapper in the tiny trash can by my desk and go to the closet to check my hair and make sure there's nothing in my teeth before I head back out. I throw open the door and gasp when I see the mirror hanging inside.

Someone took a berry-pink lipstick and drew circles over and over again in the center of the mirror. And written beneath the angry circles are the words *fucking bitch!*

Just like the Polaroid I found my first day here.

I whip out my phone and take a bunch of pictures of the damage. Then I proceed to grab a makeup wipe and get rid of the lipstick, scrubbing extra hard over the nasty words meant for me.

After I'm finished, I wrap the makeup wipe with a tissue and toss it in the trash, not wanting anyone like my roomie— or her toxic best friend—to see the evidence. Destruction-wise, using lipstick on a mirror is fairly harmless, but the words sting. And when I check the pictures I took, I realize the scribbled circles completely obliterate my face. Exactly like the photo I found.

Someone wants to make me disappear.

And I need to figure out who.

CHAPTER TEN

"Belinda! I'm *so* glad you're here." Sophia beams at me and opens the door wider for me to enter her house.

"I need as much help with this history exam as I can get," I tell her as I walk inside. I come to a stop in the foyer, tipping my head back to stare at the massive crystal chandelier hanging above us. The lights are on, and the crystals twinkle and shine. It's beautiful.

"Same." Sophia shuts the door. "Want a snack before we go to my room?"

"Sure." I follow her, reminding myself to act right. Belinda Winters isn't impressed with opulence and overt wealth. She's grown up with it, after all.

But damn, the Harrington house is something else. We pass through a living room with pristine white couches that look like clouds. There's a full wall of built-in shelves to the left, filled with knickknacks. Figurines of various sizes and colorful stuffed animals accent the room. At first it seems refreshingly whimsical, not the kind of thing I'd expect to find in a stately mansion, but why would I presume to know anything about the interior decorating habits of the obscenely wealthy? But then I take a second look. And a third. And that's when I realize that all this quirky charm is...llamas.

Any other time, I'd think it was some eccentric rich-person collector fetish, but not after seeing the word "llamas" written in Isla's yearbook. There's a connection, I just know it.

We enter the giant kitchen, and Sophia heads straight for a refrigerator paneled to look like a large cabinet door. I imagine Mom, drunk, standing in the middle of this room, trying to find the fridge so she can grab a diet soda. All these smooth, white surfaces, pristine and indistinguishable from one to the next, would have her absolutely floundering.

I fight back a hysterical giggle at the absurdity of it all, but only just. Here's Sophia, moving through a kitchen that could eat mine and Mom's entire apartment for breakfast, and she's just opening the fridge like it's no big thing. People really live this way—like their money and comfort is as natural as breathing. If I think about it too hard, I fear my brain will fracture into a million jagged pieces, unable to reconcile the life I've had with the one I'm living right now.

Without even realizing it, Sophia saves me from a thought spiral that could have gotten very dark, very fast. "Want a Coke?" she asks.

"Whatever caffeine you have on hand, I'll take." I offer a grateful smile. The one person I like spending time with is Sophia. Everyone else can suck it, even Connor, because that boy leaves me so on edge all the time.

Not Sophia, though. She's sweet and thoughtful and genuine. Which is a lot more than I can say about anyone else on Wickham's campus. Even myself.

I'm immediately swallowed up with guilt, and I put on a brave face when she hands me a frigid can of Coke. Not bothering to wait, I crack it open and take a few gulps while Sophia rummages around in what I assume is a pantry. Within seconds, she's approaching me with two bags of chips. She hands me one and grabs her own Coke. "Let's go to my room and get this over with."

We head up the stairs, and I quietly marvel at the smooth, polished wood railing. There's not a speck of dirt in the place, and I can't help but ask, "Do you have servants?"

"What? Servants?" Sophia laughs and shakes her head. "If you want to call my mother a servant, then yes. She's the one who keeps this place spotless. She's made the house her full-time project."

"Well, it's beautiful," I say, but inside, I'm wondering what it must be like to have a mother so devoted to home and family that just keeping the house pretty is a full-time gig. If Sophia weren't so nice, it would be too easy to let jealousy make me hate her.

She leads me to her bedroom, and I restrain myself from saying anything when we enter. It's done up in a tasteful mix of various pink shades, but it's not overbearing in its pinkness. An open door on the far wall reveals a walk-in closet stuffed full of clothes.

"Your room is beautiful. I see why you stay here instead of on campus." If I were Sophia, I would never set foot in my dorm room again. Compared to this, it's practically a box under a bridge.

"Thank you. I love my room, but I'm already a bit of an

outsider among the student population because of my father. I try to blend in as much as possible," she explains as she sets her soda can and the chip bag on top of her desk.

I do the same before I drop my backpack on the floor next to the desk. "Has it always been a struggle? Fitting in?"

"At Wickham? Yes. Once anyone finds out who I'm related to, everything changes. Their body language. The tone of their voice. At times they've even seemed…afraid? I can see it in their eyes." Her tinkling laugh is pleasant, but I see the pain flash in her gaze. She just wants to be accepted.

I can totally relate.

"It doesn't matter to me if your dad is the headmaster," I reassure her, and it's true. I actually prefer it because it's a good connection to potential information. Not that I'm using Sophia—okay, maybe I am a little bit—but I do like her. She's the most relatable person on this campus.

We spread out on the floor with our history books open to the latest chapter we're supposed to study, but through some unspoken mutual agreement, we totally ignore the task at hand. Instead, we crunch our chips and chat about meaningless stuff until I take my opportunity and ask her about what's on my mind.

"What's up with the llama collection downstairs?"

"Oh, you noticed that, huh?" She rolls her eyes, but she's also smiling, which she does a lot. "Everyone on the Legacy List calls themselves 'llamas' because of the double L. My father started a llama collection back when he went here, and now it has a life of its own. He receives llama gifts all the time. Birthdays. Christmas. Graduation. A class a few years ago even adopted a llama at a rescue center in the States. They named it Perceval Hairy-ngton."

That gets a genuine laugh out of me, but I can't lose sight of my purpose. "But like...what exactly is the Legacy List, anyway? Like a secret society thing?"

"Kind of? But also...it's a totally open secret. Probably more accurate to say it's an elite club of sorts, started ages ago. Students from royal lines are automatically in, of course. Super- wealthy families usually maintain their spots, too. It goes back generations. A spot is saved at every top uni and on every bank board of directors for a Legacy List member. Once you become a llama, your future is set," Sophia explains.

"So...what? You're either born onto the list or you're fucked?" I lift my brows.

"Of course not. You can marry in, too. Or, you know, earn your place. The top performer from each year gets on, so their kids get on, too, but in that case, it's more probationary than anything else. They have to be high performers for at least three generations before it's like, a foregone conclusion." Sophia munches on a chip.

"What about other kinds of scholarships? Like...art?" I think of my mother. Could she have been on the Legacy List thanks to her talent?

"Are you referring to Connor?" I nod at Sophia's question because obviously I can't tell her about Mom. "That's a tricky situation. He was a family legacy, but with his dad's *thing*... that sort of fell apart. Some folks at the top pulled strings to get Connor on an arts scholarship. It's the only reason he hasn't been turned out on the street. If Emily were alive...that would be a different story. But she's not. So I guess it doesn't really matter."

"What do you mean? Because Emily wasn't an artist?" I don't have to feign my confusion.

"More like Emily wasn't that great of a student." Sophia winces as if the thought pains her. "Though things did seem to be turning around for her right before the...incident. Isla was on her case all the time, reminding her she needed to keep up with her studies."

I revel in that bit of information because it's proof Isla was a good person who cared about her best friend's grades. What murderer would give a shit about GPA?

Sophia gently forces us to start studying, and for the next hour we go over our notes from class and ask each other questions. Sophia knows everything, so I'm not sure why she's studying, but I think it has more to do with helping me. It's obvious I need it.

"Thank you for going over everything with me," I tell her when she finally closes her textbook.

"You're helping me, too, you know."

"Not even. You get all the answers right," I point out.

Her expression turns contrite. "You're right. I might've offered to help you study, but...I have an ulterior motive." She drops her gaze to the floor, instantly shifty. Does Sophia have a secret she needs to confess? Wickham has no shortage of secrets, but I didn't think Sophia was sitting on something juicy. She takes a deep breath, and I brace myself. "Really, I just wanted to hang out. It gets lonely out here."

Relief gusts through me like a gale-force wind. I wasn't wrong about Sophia—she really is one of the good ones.

I give her what feels like my first real smile since I arrived in England. "Where's your mom?" I assume her father is still on campus.

"In London for a few days. She likes to go on little shopping sprees every few weeks," Sophia explains.

Must be nice. The Harringtons seem to have more money than they know what to do with.

But how?

"Headmaster" might sound fancy, but Sophia's dad is a glorified school principal. I guess they could have family money, but the fact that Sophia's mom cleans the house herself instead of employing a full-time housekeeper makes me think they're not so accustomed to wealth that they're willing to get careless with it.

"Want to stay and watch a movie?" Sophia suggests, filling the unintentionally long silence I've let hang between us.

"Yeah. That sounds fun." I glance around the room. "I need to use the bathroom first, though."

"Oh, the bathroom is right across the hall." She grabs her laptop and pops it open. "I'll search for something to watch while you go."

"Great." I don't have any trouble locating the spa-like bathroom. I decide that if things here don't work out, I might try to get the Harringtons to adopt me instead of heading back to the States. Actually, forget adoption—I'll work for free. Dusting the chandelier in the front hall is probably a full-time job, like cleaning the outside of the Statue of Liberty.

When I step back out into the hall and my feet sink into the plush carpet, I can't contain a little sigh of pleasure. I glance up and down the hall to make sure no one else is around before peeling off my socks and wiggling my toes into the velvety pile. I do a little twist with my hips, then skip a few steps, looking behind me to see if I've left footprints in the pristine carpet. I haven't, and I feel a little silly for thinking I might.

I roll my eyes at myself as I spin back toward Sophia's room. But my eyes snag on a set of open French doors halfway down the hall. Curious, I hover in the doorway. Looks like I've found an office or library.

The door is open, so I step inside. No surprise, the llama motif continues. I kind of love this side of the Harringtons; it's like finding out a stiff, tweed jacket is lined in bubblegum-pink silk. It's quirky and weirdly endearing. Endless rows of books occupy shelves that stretch from elegant wooden cabinets to the ceiling—including a long line of familiar, gold-embossed yearbooks.

Jackpot.

I beeline for the late nineties and pull the book I need off the shelf. Flipping it open, I thumb through the class photos until I find her, right on the front page for the graduating class that year.

Samantha Arnaud. My mother. Her expression is downright serene, with a barely-there smile curving her lips. She looks incredibly young. Even a little...sad?

Maybe Mom has always had that hint of sadness clinging to her.

Beneath her name, it says, "Arts Merit Scholarship," and it reminds me of the acronym Isla had in her notes. "ARTSMER." I'm sure that's what it stands for.

As much as I want to flip through the rest of the photos until I find Statue Boy, I'm wary of how long I've been away from Sophia. She deserves better than me sneaking around her house. If I want to see these yearbooks, I bet I could just ask her to show them to me.

I shove the yearbook back into its spot and exit the room. On my way back down the hall, I pause at a gold-framed mirror hanging above a pedestal table with a small flower arrangement in the center. I stare at my reflection, looking for any resemblance to my mother at the same age that I am now. I spot it immediately.

I have that same sadness clinging to me.

The source is easy to understand—it's Isla. But what was Mom's reason? I'm not sure.

I'm also not sure if Isla was able to figure out if Mom was ever a llama or not. Does that even matter? I assume it does. But is that part of the reason someone tried to take my sister out? It doesn't make any sense.

None of it does.

...

We end up watching the latest horror movie on Netflix downstairs in the living room with the white fluffy couches that are indeed as soft as a cloud. I'm snuggled under a thick faux fur blanket, a stack of pillows behind my back. Sophia is sitting on the opposite end of the couch in the same setup, the both of us content and barely moving except for the occasional yelp due to an on-screen jump scare. Mrs. Harrington arrives home around the halfway point of the movie, and she's perfectly pleasant when Sophia introduces us. Even a bit over the top, like she's thrilled Sophia is having a friend over.

Makes me think Sophia doesn't have guests to the house much.

Her mom putters around in the kitchen while Sophia and I continue watching the movie and I revel in the complete normalcy of it all. A parent who seems to care about their child while living in a nice, clean home is not normal for me. Not even close. Mrs. Harrington keeps asking us if we need anything, and we keep saying no, and I make sure to add "thank you" every time. This is just…unreal.

Must be nice to live with parents who act like parents and let their kid be a kid. I wonder how Mom is doing back at the rehab center. I have no clue, and I hate to admit it, but… it's kind of nice, the not knowing. Not worrying about her whereabouts all the time. Since coming here, Mom doesn't occupy my headspace twenty-four seven like she does when we're at home.

Being at Wickham is stressful AF, but it's downright refreshing to stress about a murder investigation compared to parenting a parent and trying to survive day-to-day without tipping anyone off that I'm drowning in never-ending bills and constant worry. Then again, there is one adult who's actually helpful in my life…

I pull out my phone and pull up a new text to Doug. I promised I'd let him know I'm okay here in England, and I haven't done that yet. I think about what I want to tell him, because I can't reveal too much…

Cheerio from jolly old England! No. He'll want to throw up in his mouth if I send him that.

Hey. Flight was ok. Settled in. No, that won't work, either. He'll probably think it's code for, "I've been kidnapped, please send help."

In the end, I send him a simple text asking him how the bar is doing. The only thing I feel like I can chat about with him without revealing too many details about what I'm really doing over here.

I set my phone down and try to get back into the movie, but I'm hopelessly lost. The heroine's love interest is suddenly chasing her through the woods with an axe, and the guy I thought was the villain seems to be trying to save her? Sophia is captivated, her gaze never straying from the screen. Every once in a while, her mother peeks into the room, making a face when she catches a glimpse of the screen.

So nice. So normal.

A few minutes later, my phone buzzes, and I check it immediately, fully expecting a response from Doug, but it's not him. It's a text from an unknown number.

Unknown: *Hey. Wanted to apologize for how I lost it on you earlier. Didn't mean to blow up like that.*

I frown, rereading the message. But it only takes a second for me to understand who it's from. There's only one person whose shitty attitude earlier today warranted an apology. Connor. And now he's *apologizing* to me? What a novel concept.

Me: *How did you get my number?*

Probably should've acknowledged his apology, but I'm in a state of shock over it. Plus, I feel a perverse zing of pleasure at making him sweat it out, wondering if I'll forgive him.

Connor: *Mrs. Brown is susceptible to dimples and isn't above peeking inside a student's file to find contact info if you ask nicely enough.*

My brows shoot up. I didn't realize Connor had dimples, since he so rarely smiles. And is he implying he *flirted* with Mrs. Brown to get my number?

Interesting.

Connor: *Are you angry? Do you want me to forget this number and never reach out to you again? I can, you know. Just forget your number and your beautiful face like neither of you ever existed.*

Okay, is Connor Wells…flirting with me? I reread the text, but I had it right the first time: he totally just called me beautiful. It's out-of-character enough that a frisson of alarm shoots down my spine.

Me: *Are you all right? Where are you right now?*

"Belinda, dear, would you care to stay for supper?" Mrs. Harrington is standing in the doorway with a hopeful look on her face. When I glance over at Sophia, I see she's wearing a similar expression.

"Um, I wish I could, but I need to go back to my room after the movie and finish a paper." My frown matches Mrs. Harrington's. "Maybe another time?"

"Of course. Anytime, really. Don't you agree, Sophia?" Mrs. Harrington glances over at her daughter.

"Definitely." Sophia nods, the disappointment disappearing from her gaze like it was never there. "What paper are you working on?"

My brain scrambles for an answer as my phone buzzes

repeatedly with multiple notifications from Connor. "Uhh..."

"Is it the English lit one? That's not due until Sunday night," Sophia reminds me.

"I haven't even started the reading yet," I admit sheepishly. "That's what I need to do first. Read the book."

"Well, you have an entire weekend to do that, thank goodness. I've already finished mine." Sophia beams, and Mrs. Harrington looks on proudly.

My heart pangs at their little mother-daughter moment. Then yet another text notification comes from Connor, and I forget all about it as I check his messages.

Connor: *I'm great.*

Connor: *In top-notch condition actually.*

Connor: *Feeling inspired for the first time since my sister died.*

Connor: *Fuck, that's the first time I wrote those words out.*

Connor: *I don't like seeing them. My sister died.*

Connor: *There it is again.*

Connor: *Still feels like she's just away, you know? She'll be back on campus any minute now.*

Chatty Connor is a red flag. As little as I know this boy, I can say with confidence that this behavior seems out of character. I quickly type out a response, concern filling me. He seems off. Maybe he's drunk or high?

Me: *Drop a pin with your location.*

Connor: *So demanding.*

Me: *Please?*

He does as I ask, giving me his location. Looks like he's somewhere out on the cliffs near campus. That's not scary or anything, considering his current state.

Connor: *Going to come rescue me, Billie?*

My skin warms at him calling me by my actual name. He even spelled it correctly.

Me: *Do you need rescuing?*

He doesn't even hesitate.

Connor: *Perhaps.*

I push the blanket off of me and jump to my feet. There's no such thing as an unserious cry for help, and while I can't know for sure if Connor is really in danger, I get the sense he shouldn't be alone right now. I can always call Sophia for backup if something's really wrong—her mom seems like the kind of woman who wouldn't hesitate to help a Wickham student in need. "I should probably go."

"But the movie isn't over yet," Sophia protests as she watches me fold up the heavy blanket and leave it on the couch.

"I know, but it's stressing me out how I only have a couple of days to read that entire book." Sophia can fully understand being stressed about an assignment, right?

"Oh, I totally get it." She nods. "We'll finish next time?"

I nod and take a beat to give her a warm smile—because I really do hope there's a next time. I'm out of the house in minutes, shocked by the darkening sky and drop in temperature once I'm outside. Mrs. Harrington offered to drive me back to campus, but I declined, telling her a walk would help wake me up for all the reading I have to finish tonight. Now, cold and adrenaline send a shiver down my spine as I map my way to Connor's location and turn my phone's flashlight on, stumbling my way through the damp field that separates the Harrington estate from the rest of the Wickham campus. I turn a hard right just before I'm on official campus grounds, drawing closer and closer to where Connor is. I come to a stop when I see the massive tree looming ahead of me.

Realization hits me like a punch to the stomach. I know this place. Or at least I've seen it before.

It's the very tree that appears in my mother's favorite family photo.

Right by the cliffs where Emily died.

CHAPTER ELEVEN

I approach the tree with trepidation, my steps careful, the beam from my phone's flashlight trembling slightly thanks to my sudden case of nerves. I round the tree and come to a stop when I find Connor sitting beneath it, drinking from a bottle wrapped in a brown paper bag.

"Well, isn't that terribly American of you." My statement is flat, my apprehension high. I don't like seeing him drinking. Alcohol brings nothing but problems. Look at my poor, addicted mother. Add in grief, social upheaval, and an actual cliff a handful of yards away *where someone died recently*, and the optics on this situation go from bad to worse.

"Billie! You came." He pats the space beside him. "Join me."

With reluctance, I settle in beside him on the soft, damp ground. He leans into me as if he needs the support, then drinks from the bottle and smacks his lips after he swallows. "Want a taste?"

I shake my head. "No, thank you."

"More for me, then." He shrugs and tips his head back,

chugging from the bottle.

It takes everything I've got not to snag the bottle and hurl it over the cliff, though I'm positive I couldn't throw it that far. Satisfying imagery, though.

"What happened?" I ask him, keeping my voice gentle.

"What do you mean?"

"Well, something triggered…all of this." I gesture vaguely at him, the bottle, the scenery.

A ragged sigh leaves him. "Life is just so damn unfair, don't you think?"

Don't even get me started, is what I want to say, but I remain quiet.

"After everything that happened with my father, it's just been one shit show after the next." He sets the bottle down heavily on the ground, causing it to tip over, but not much runs out. Meaning the bottle is pretty much empty. "He's being framed."

"Who?"

"My father. He would never do something like this—steal from his friends." He shakes his head, his expression grim as he stares at nothing. It's getting darker by the minute out here. "Someone is trying to take him out."

I want to roll my eyes. Come on. More like a rich man got greedy and now has to pay the price for his crimes. Connor's life has been so charmed, he can't imagine a world where there are consequences for a person's actions. I guess it's hard when your life has been so good that you can't see someone's faults, especially your parents. The people you love and admire. Unless you've been raised by a trainwreck from minute one and all you can remember are the bad times. The selfishness and destruction. The disappointments and lies.

Ask me how I know.

"Maybe a llama is trying to take him out," I suggest to see how he might react.

"What the fuck are you talking about?" he snaps.

Oops.

"Never mind." I shake my head and offer him a smile. "I was being silly."

The irritation clears from his eyes, and he focuses all of his attention on me. His silvery gaze roves over my face, drinking me in, and my skin grows warmer the longer he stares. I forget all about the chilled ground beneath my butt. "That's one word I would never describe you as. Silly."

Why am I offended by his remark? "How would you describe me, then?"

"Interesting. Beautiful." Oh, there he goes, calling me beautiful again. A girl could get used to that. "Smart."

He reaches for my face, his fingers grazing my cheek, and I rear back. He drops his hand. "You don't even know me."

"I know enough." He grins, and I finally see those dimples he was talking about. Poor Mrs. Brown never stood a chance. "You don't seem to mind that I'm the son of a criminal."

"It doesn't bother me." Air stalls in my throat when he leans in, his face close to mine. "Why should it? You're not the one who stole the money."

"I like that you accept me for who I am and not what my name is. Or how much money my family has. *Had.*" He makes a "poof" gesture and chuckles, the sound coming from deep in his chest. My entire body tingles when he reaches for me. His hand settles on my waist, and he gives me a tug. "It's cold out here."

"You think things are dire enough that we need to share body heat?" I'm pointing out the obvious but realize I sound like I'm flirting. And from the way his eyes suddenly get heavy-lidded and his lips part, I can tell he believes I'm flirting, too.

"Definitely," he murmurs, tilting his head so our lips align.

I jerk back, not about to let him kiss me. Talk about distracting.

"Hey. You're really drunk." I press my hand against the solid wall of his chest and gently push him away from me. "And I'm not as easily swayed by a pair of dimples as some people are."

He smiles. "They always work."

"Not on me." I shake my head.

"Huh." Connor squints, like he's trying to see inside my brain. "I can't quite figure you out. You're like a misery wrapped in a stigma."

I burst out laughing. "Don't you mean a mystery wrapped in an enigma?"

He waves a dismissive hand. "Whatever. You know what I mean."

His somber words and equally somber expression tell me he's starting to sober up a bit. For all I know, he's been out here a long time, the bottle long empty. Without hesitation, he gets to his feet and holds out his hand for me to take, which I do. His strength and steadiness are a shock to my system, given how loose and languid he seemed just a moment ago. I brush off the seat of my pants and straighten.

We're standing in front of each other under the tree. Where his sister died and mine fell to her near death.

This place should terrify me, but being here with Connor, I'm not scared.

"You feel it, don't you?" Connor asks.

I frown, confused. "Feel what?"

"The connection between us. It's there. Here." He gestures in the space between us. "Don't try and tell me it's all one-sided, either."

I gape at him for a moment before pressing my lips together like that's going to contain my uncomfortable feelings for this boy. I'm about to respond, but he speaks over me instead.

"I don't trust it. The connection." He adds the words like he might want to hurt me, but all I see is brutal honesty etched into his face. He's trying to tell the truth. That's more than I can say for myself these days.

Frankly, it's more than I can say for almost everyone I've met since setting foot in this country.

"Maybe you feel connected to me because I'm brand-new here and I don't know your history," I suggest, proud of how calm I sound.

"Maybe." His voice is full of doubt. "Want to walk back to the dorm with me?"

"Um." I glance over my shoulder, my gaze snagging on the Harrington estate. "I was just at Sophia's. I kind of want to go back."

I need some distance to figure out why he's acting this way. All cute and drunk and…into me.

"You two are becoming close." He doesn't phrase it as a question.

"I like her. She's one of the only people at Wickham who's nice to me." I sound defensive, but maybe I have a right to be.

Until this little drunken escapade, Connor has been mostly standoffish and rude. Are there moments when the connection he feels—that I feel, too—flares up into something warm and welcome? Sure. But I wouldn't say that's been the predominant vibe here. No, that would be more easily categorized as *hostile*.

"She's a decent sort," Connor admits. "Want me to walk you back?"

"No. That might end up looking a little suspicious, don't you think?"

"You're right. Not like leaving their house, spending a not-insignificant amount of time outside in the cold—without a proper jacket, I might add—then going back to their house instead of returning to campus. That's not suspicious at all." He grins again, and I sort of want to melt at when those adorable dimples pop. "How about you go your way and I'll go mine?"

"Deal." I watch him go until he disappears into the darkening night sky. A sigh gusts out of me.

I shouldn't pay any attention to the connection between us, but I do. He makes me feel all fluttery inside with only a look, and while hardened Billie shouldn't let that affect her, soft and flighty Belinda can. Meaning...I'm doing it for the plot. For my cover. For this totally unhinged mission I'm on.

Give me a break.

I've never been good at lying to myself. Lying to everyone else? That's another thing entirely.

Connor has no idea how similar we are, and I can't tell him about my past or my problems. Nope, I get to continue lying to him about who I am and where I'm from.

And standing out here in the wind, close to the place where Isla's whole life changed, I still manage to hate myself for it.

"Belinda!" Sophia looks as shocked by my reappearance on her doorstep as I am that I returned. "What are you doing here?"

"I walked back to campus and couldn't stand the thought of eating dining hall food again and reading a boring book all night." It's true. Plus, I don't want to spend the evening in my room with Priya and her bitchy bestie. No thank you. "I'm hoping the dinner invitation still stands?"

"Of course it does! Come in, come in." I enter the house, and Sophia practically drags me into the kitchen. "Look who came back for dinner!"

"Wonderful! Glad you're joining us, Belinda." Mrs. Harrington's smile is so kind, the sight of it almost makes me weep. "Why don't you get cleaned up? The bathroom is just down that short hall. Sophia, be a dear and help me with the salad?"

I leave the kitchen and head in the direction Mrs. Harrington indicated, coming to a stop when I see a closed door and a light shining from beneath. I also hear a familiar voice talking. Rising, in frustration or anger, I can't tell. Sounds like Headmaster Harrington is on the phone. I take a step closer to the door, trying to listen in.

"I *know*. But you have to understand, William, keeping him close is best. I've discussed it with the others, and I won't—" He blows out a frustrated breath as whoever is on the other end of the line—William?—interrupts him. A loud bang sounds, and I jump, clamping my lips shut on the gasp that was about to spill. He must've slapped his hand on the edge of his desk or against the wall. He definitely hit something. Hard.

"Enough, I said! You listen to me. His sister is *dead*. His father is *in jail*. I won't have a repeat of what happened to Nigel, not during my tenure here. That family has been at Wickham since the damn founding, and I'm not going to throw some poor kid out on his ass when he needs us the most. That's my final word on the matter." Harrington ends the call, and I can hear him pouring something in a glass before the gentle *whoosh* of a body settling heavily onto a chair. I dart into the bathroom and close the door, then turn on the tap and run my shaking hands beneath the cold trickle of water while Harrington's words run through my head.

He's referring to Connor. That's a given. Who's William? And Nigel? What happened to poor Nigel, and how long ago?

Harrington definitely knows more than I originally thought. About Connor, but maybe about Isla, too. Maybe he's in on it.

But what is *it*, exactly?

I'm more determined than ever to find out.

· · ·

I spent the night at the Harringtons', which was the right choice. I can always work on that paper all day Sunday. Sophia even volunteered to help me with it, though I told her I had to do something on my own.

And I meant it.

We ate a delicious meal and stayed up way too late talking

while lying in the cozy haven of her pink bedroom. It was hard for me to stay awake, thanks to Sophia's extra comfortable bed. Not to mention it's huge. A far cry from the narrow, hard-as-a-board bed in my dorm room.

My phone buzzing on the nightstand where I left it (plugged in, thanks to an extra charger Mrs. Harrington offered me before bed) is what wakes me up, and I reach for it, pulling the covers over my head so I can check my notifications in peace and not disturb Sophia.

My heart squeezes when I see it's a text from Connor.

Connor: *I was insufferable last night, wasn't I?*

Me: *You weren't so bad.*

Connor: *Lies. I was a drunken fool. But you should know I'm paying the price this morning.*

Me: *Why are you up so early, Drunky McDrunkface?*

Connor: *It's past ten. And that's MISTER Drunky McDrunkface to you.*

Connor: *I want to make up for my boorish behavior by inviting you to a horrible party tonight.*

Me: *Why would I want to go to a party if it's going to be horrible?*

Me: *And why do you want to make up for your boorish behavior? Such a good word, by the way. Boorish.*

Connor: *First, because it's the only party happening, everyone will be there, and a true party girl probably won't discriminate.*

Connor: *And second, because in vino veritas. If you're the one I drunk-texted, it must mean I don't totally hate spending time with you.*

Connor: *As long as you're not singing.*

Me: *Please, Mr. McDrunkface, I can't take this many compliments at once.*

Connor: *I'm just stating facts.*

Isn't he cheerful today.

Me: *Where is this party anyway?*

Connor: *At the Pembroke residence, not too far from campus. Freddie always throws a good party, and this one is an annual gathering for the alumni to talk about fundraisers and the like.*

Fundraisers? That sounds boring.

Connor: *Really it's just an excuse to eat apps instead of real dinner and drink and gossip. Watch couples fight and break up.*

Connor: *Watch unexpected couples hookup.*

I raise my brows at the last line. Is he implying he might want to hook up with me?

I'd consider it. Or Belinda would.

Me: *So it's THAT kind of party.*

Connor: *No, no, no. That's just what always happens when the liquor flows and the feelings get a little too real.*

He's not wrong. And when the liquor flows, it tends to loosen lips, too. I'd love to hear what some of the other

Wickham students have to say about…things.

"Good morning!" Sophia sing-songs.

A scream leaves me, and I drop my phone directly on my face. I flip the comforter off my head and offer her a sheepish smile as I scooch into a sitting position. "Uh, good morning."

"Did I scare you?" She laughs when I nod. "Sorry. I'm abnormally cheerful in the morning. Even my mother complains about it."

I can't imagine that. Mrs. Harrington is the sweetest woman I've ever met.

"It's fine. Don't worry about it." I rub the bridge of my nose where I just took an iPhone to the face.

"How did you sleep?" Sophia chirps.

I push my hair away from my eyes. "Pretty great, actually. Your bed is so soft."

"Better than the mattress in the dorm rooms, right?" Sophia rests her hand on her mouth to cover the yawn. "I don't know why I think I should return to my room there."

"I don't know, either."

She falls back against the pile of pillows beneath her head, pulling her own phone off the nightstand. She must check her notifications, because the next words out of her mouth are, "There's a party tonight. I almost forgot."

I remain quiet, because that wasn't exactly an invitation. For all that Sophia is happy to hang with me at her house, she might not want me shadowing her at Freddie's party. She doesn't know Connor already invited me.

"You should stay here, and we can get ready together and then go. It's at Freddie's," Sophia explains. "You want to go, right? It'll be a great way to get to know everyone."

The icy cynicism around my heart melts a little.

"Yeah, um...Connor just asked me to go with him." I wince, bracing myself for a reaction.

"Seriously?" She sits up straight, her eyes wide. "He asked *you* to go with him?"

"He called it a horrible party." I don't want to hurt her feelings, but he did ask first. And she's been nothing but a good friend to me since the moment I met her. "Will it be awful?"

"Dreadful. But also...fun." She slowly shakes her head. "I'm just surprised he asked you."

Irritation and insecurity battle for dominance. I try to hide both when I ask, "Why?"

Sophia's voice and smile are gentle. "Because Connor doesn't ask any girl anywhere. Even before everything that happened, he kept mostly to himself."

Her revelation is way too reassuring.

"Don't I remember you saying something about how broken boys aren't your thing?" Her words aren't accusatory. In fact, she taps an index finger against her chin in exaggerated thoughtfulness. It feels more like a sweet reminder because she's worried about me, and I appreciate that.

More than she'll ever realize.

I shrug helplessly. I can't say anything to defend my choices. I mean, look at him. I had no idea I was such a sucker for a handsome face.

"But...the dimples?" I say, shrugging like I'm helpless in the face of their hot-guy power.

Sophia snorts a laugh but nods like she totally gets it. "Well, this should be interesting. Come on, then. Let's go downstairs and get some breakfast. I'm sure my mum has made a feast for us." Sophia hops out of bed, and I do the same, surprised when she links her arm through mine and leads me out of the bedroom.

I could get used to this—having a best friend and hanging out at her house all weekend. I just hope when everything comes out, Sophia doesn't hate me for all my lies.

That would break my heart.

CHAPTER TWELVE

The Pembroke estate is massive, with a long, curving road leading to the house that cuts through acres and acres of rolling green hills. Connor was thoughtful enough to offer to take both me and Sophia to the party in the rideshare he booked. I didn't even have to ask. Is it possible that chivalry isn't actually dead?

He's quiet during the drive, content to let Sophia share stories about parties of the past. And while she's full of good gossip that I enjoy hearing, part of me stays tuned into Connor.

He seems...keyed up. Anxious. Perhaps he's nervous? His father worked for Freddie's family. Is this the first time he's seeing them after everything that happened? If that's the case, I'd be nervous, too. Lines of tension seem to radiate off his body, like heat shimmer rising from a sunbaked sidewalk.

Once we arrive and exit the car, I put a hand on Connor's back and rise up on my toes to whisper, "Are you all right?"

He winces and ducks his head for a moment, as if he hates revealing any sort of emotion or weakness. "Feeling a bit awkward, but I'm sure it'll be fine."

"It will be." Caving to my impulses, I reach out and grab his hand, giving it a quick squeeze. "Just...act like nothing happened."

I know how to do that far too well. When you find your mom passed out in the bathroom for the umpteenth time, you learn how to cope by shoving unpleasant memories from your mind. *Survive*, I would tell Connor if I were allowed to be Billie in this moment. But Belinda has never had to learn about survival. In her world, thriving is a foregone conclusion.

We enter the house, Sophia directly behind us, still prattling on.

"You know this is the Pembroke summer estate, yes? They own multiple homes all over the world."

That little tidbit makes me pause. If Connor's father embezzled money from the Pembrokes' company, how are they able to live so lavishly? Maybe this place is all paid off. It's not like they're renters on a month-to-month like me and Mom.

"They have a flat in Manhattan, I believe. Could you have run into them back home, Belinda?" Sophia asks me.

"No. I don't remember them at all. We probably move in different social circles." I shrug and smile, pleased with the little slice of truth I've been able to squeeze into the deception sandwich I'm serving. It's 100 percent accurate to say that the Pembrokes and I have very different kinds of friends.

The crowd is a hodgepodge of adults and Wickham students, even a few I recognize from sightings in my classes or at the dining hall. Considering it's an alumni function, that makes sense. It blows my mind that people my age want to hang out with people their parents' ages and older, but who am I to judge? From what I can see, there's delicious-looking food everywhere and the alcohol is flowing. No one is stopping any of our fellow students from partaking, and I'm guessing the liquor is top-shelf.

"Connor! There you are." An older, handsome man with distinguished gray at his temples approaches us, accompanied by a woman I assume is his wife. "So pleased you could make it."

"Thank you for having me." The man wraps Connor into one of those typical male back-slapping hugs while the woman looks on with a pleased expression.

"You know," the man says, lowering his gruff voice to a less strident volume, "you're always welcome at our home, Connor. We don't hold what your father did against you. And such a horrible tragedy about your sister." He shakes his head. "We want to support you. In any way we can."

Connor's expression turns stoic. Almost blank. Makes me think he's struggling to hold his frayed emotions together. "I appreciate it."

The man glances over at me with curiosity. "Who's your friend?"

"Belinda, let me introduce you to Mr. and Mrs. Pembroke," Connor says. "This is Belinda Winters. She's a new transfer student at Wickham, joining us from New York."

I want to tease him about how formal and uptight he sounds, but then I hear myself say, "So lovely to meet you, Mr. and Mrs. Pembroke. You have a beautiful home," and I know I don't have any room to criticize. I bob my head a little, and *holy shit did I almost curtsy?* From the corner of my eye,

I catch Connor fighting to contain a smirk. It's a relief to see an expression on his face where a blank mask hid him just a moment ago. If his smile comes at the expense of my pride, so be it.

I shake Mr. Pembroke's hand when he extends it in my direction, then his wife's. She's beautiful, though I can't help noticing there seems to be a somewhat significant age gap between her and her husband. Though maybe she's just well-preserved, like so many wives of rich men. My poor mother looks far older than her years. For all I know, Mrs. Pembroke is what the average mom of a teenage kid is *supposed* to look like. Mom wears the years like an albatross; Mrs. Pembroke wears them like a silk cape.

As I continue studying her face, I realize there's something vaguely familiar about Mrs. Pembroke, too. It's laughable to think I'd ever have had an opportunity to meet her in the past. Not unless she got lost downtown, far from what I'm sure is her bona fide castle on the Upper West Side, and wandered into Doug's bar. She'd step one Manolo-ed foot on the sticky floor and think she'd fallen into hell.

Maybe she just has one of those faces.

"Welcome to our home, Belinda. How are you enjoying your time at Wickham so far?" Mr. Pembroke asks me.

I decide to tell the truth. "It's been…interesting."

That has the Pembrokes laughing—chuckling sensibly, more like. Connor meets my gaze, a pleased expression on his face.

They spot someone else they have to greet across the room and leave as fast as they approached us to begin with. The moment we're alone, I glance around the room but don't spot

Sophia anywhere.

"She's outside. Sophia." It's as if Connor can read my mind, or at the very least he's paying attention to me. And while normally I would be defensive about that, I can't deny that the consideration leaves me feeling warm and fuzzy inside.

I like that he pays attention. That he seems into me and wants to spend more time with me. I should probably stay far away from him, considering what an emotional wreck he is, but I can't help being drawn to him. He may have been tipsy when he mentioned our connection, but that doesn't make it less real.

"They seem nice. The Pembrokes." I'm trying to break the weird silence that has fallen between us.

"They are." He grabs hold of my hand. "Come on. Let's go find somewhere quiet so we can chat."

"Chat about what?"

Connor ignores my question and leads me through clusters of people. He walks as if he knows exactly where he's going, and he doesn't seem to notice the many curious stares directed our way as we pass. I feel each one, though, like dozens of tiny pinpricks on my skin. I'm sure they're wondering who I am, which is fine. I'm wondering who they are, too. Specifically, I'm wondering which one of them put my sister in the hospital.

Only after we slip into a quiet room that looks like a library (what's with rich British people and their over-the-top collections of books?) does Connor finally speak.

"Sorry. Couldn't think in that crowd." He scratches the back of his head. "I, uh, wanted to apologize to you."

"Again? For what?" What did he do now?

"For last night."

"You already did," I remind him.

"Right. I did. But an apology over text is hardly an apology at all." He takes a step closer, and I can smell his intoxicating cologne. His body heat radiates toward me, and I want to lean in. Press my body against his. "In person is more…genuine."

I blink hard to snap myself out of his spell, but it doesn't seem to work.

"You don't need to apologize again. I accepted it the first time." I smile, though it wilts when he takes another step toward me.

"Funny thing is, my memories from last night are still a little fuzzy. But I do recall telling you that I felt a…connection between us." He touches me. A barely-there graze of his fingers across the top of my hand, but I feel it everywhere, leaving tingles all over my body.

"Yes." I nod. Clear my throat. "You may have mentioned that. But you also said—"

"That I don't trust it." He scratches the back of his head again, and I wonder if it's a nervous tic. "Let's just say I haven't had many reasons to trust people lately. But I want to trust you. And I think, probably, the best way to figure out if I should…"

He crowds me against the wall, his body pressed against mine. Blocking me from escaping, not that I want to leave. The air between us crackles with tension, and he dips his head the slightest bit, aligning our mouths so we share breath. He leans in closer, pausing just shy of pressing his lips to mine. "Yes?"

"Yes." My lips brush against his when I whisper my reply. I can feel his breath ghost across my skin right before his mouth meets mine. Once. Twice.

And then he's kissing me. *Really* kissing me. His lips are warm and smooth and undoubtably persuasive. One big hand curves around my cheek, holding me in place. I tip my head back and return the kiss, my lips parting, his tongue teasing. Circling mine over and over.

With a sigh, I give in, sliding my hands up the firm wall of his chest until I'm gripping his broad shoulders. His hands land on my waist, and his fingers press into my flesh, keeping me pinned against the wall. He shifts closer, our bodies pressed so tight a piece of paper couldn't be slipped between us. I can feel him all over me, and I revel in it.

Want more of it.

Everything becomes a blur. His persuasive lips, the rhythmic slide of his tongue against mine. His fingers tease the hem of my sweater before slipping to the bare skin beneath. I gasp into his mouth, and he pulls away slightly. I open my eyes to find he's watching me, concern in his gray gaze. I offer the tiniest nod.

The dimples appear briefly before he ducks his head, his mouth finding my neck. I tilt my head back to give him better access while I stare up at the ceiling. All of my thoughts and worries disappear the moment his mouth is on my skin, licking and nibbling, and I close my eyes, desperate to escape my life for even a few minutes and lose myself in this.

I hear voices in the corridor, but I ignore them, which is a bad move on my part, since the door cracks open mere seconds later, letting in a sliver of light.

Connor rears back, the panic on his face obvious. I decide not to think too hard about why he'd panic if we were caught making out and instead grab his hand to drag him down behind the nearby couch. Whoever's coming into the room won't spot us unless they purposely walk behind the furniture. I rest my finger against my lips, and he nods, both of us remaining silent when someone begins to speak.

"Why did you drag me into this musty old room, anyway? God, it smells like the library in here."

Great. It's Abigail. I'd recognize her bitchy tone anywhere.

"It smells like the library because there are a ton of books in here. Are you dense, Abby?" Priya's snarky tone shocks me. She so very rarely talks back to her bulldog bestie.

"Are we in here so you can finally tell me what's crawled up your ass? You've been a complete bitch since we arrived." Abigail sounds totally put out. I'm sure she's not used to Priya flipping her attitude.

"I'm sick of how mean you are when you use the generic Ativan. You turn into an asshole and treat me like shit when you're on it. It's exhausting," Priya huffs.

Connor and I share a look, though he doesn't appear too surprised by this revelation. I *knew* they were on something when they were studying in our room that one night. This is the confirmation I needed, not that I know how it helps me at all when it comes to Isla and Emily. Priya seems too uptight for drugs, so I guess what this information actually reveals is that my stuck-up, academically obsessed roommate isn't exactly the good girl she seems to be. I've been operating under a number of assumptions about Priya, but has that kept me from seeing how she might be involved with what happened to the girls? Emily was Priya's roommate. Was Priya dealing to her? Could Emily's death be drug-related?

"Fine. I'll get the good stuff next time." Abigail sniffs.

"You usually don't complain."

"It's been long enough that I can tell the difference." Priya's tone is sulky.

"If that's what you want, I'll get it next time. But don't come crying to me when there's not enough Ritalin to get us through term." There's a pause in conversation, and Abigail's tone switches to a more supplicating, almost whiny tone. "Come on, P. Don't be mad at me."

"You didn't even say anything about my outfit, and I wore it just for you."

Connor and I exchange a look, and I know we're both desperate to peek around the edge of the couch to see what Priya is wearing. I shake my head once, because there's no way we're risking discovery for the sake of Priya's sartorial choices.

"Let me have a look at you," Abigail says. "Go on, do a little spin." A beat of silence practically echoes in the room, and then Abigail—I think?—sucks in a sharp inhale. "You know how I feel about thigh-highs, P. They look absolutely darling when you have your legs over my shoulders. Now come here and let me apologize properly..."

There's no more talking. Instead, I hear lips connecting and little whimpers. I relax back against the sturdy couch. Connor does the same because I'm sure he realizes we're stuck here for the long haul. Who knew this was the chosen make-out room at the Pembroke residence? Connor was right with his predictions, too. Couples fighting. Couples hooking up.

Look at us.

Connor nudges me in the ribs, and I turn my head to find he's crossing his eyes. He twists his lips, making a ridiculous face to try and make me crack, but I don't. I'm made of stronger stuff than that. I mime zipping my lips and point at him, but he just flashes that dopey grin of his, the one where the dimples pop, and my resistance melts.

I hear a little moan coming from the girls and send Connor a knowing glance before I focus my gaze straight ahead. The couch is close to a massive window, and the ledge is covered with framed photos in a variety of shapes and sizes. I study them in the dim light coming from outside, squinting to see them better. Some of the photos are in black and white, they're so old, while others are from more recent times. My gaze stops on one photo in particular, and I barely contain a gasp.

A teenage boy wearing the classic dark-green Wickham uniform jacket is standing beneath the too-familiar tree near the cliffs. There's a younger girl standing in front of him wearing an adorable blue dress, her hair in two ponytails topped with silky white bows. He's smiling, staring straight at the camera while the girl looks up at him. The realization hits me like a bolt of lightning.

It's the boy from the statue in the alumni garden. I know it is. He looks a little younger here, like the photo might've been taken when he first started at Wickham, but it's the same person who had his arm around my mother's shoulders in the class photo. Who's the girl? Are they both related to the Pembroke family somehow?

"HOT TUB!" someone screeches from the corridor, making me jump.

Priya and Abigail jump as well, presumably. They both squeal, and when I check on Connor, I have to cover my mouth again for fear I'll start giggling. He's making another goofy face, his eyes crossed so hard I'm afraid he's going to hurt himself. I try to shove him away, but he uses his strength to crowd me. I back away at the last second, averting my face from his seeking mouth.

"We should go join everyone at the hot tub," Abigail suggests, her tone lighter.

"It'll be full of people." Priya's voice is slightly grating. Either Abigail has a brat fetish or Priya really is the whiniest snob. "Let's just stay in here."

"It'll feel good to soak in the water, and then we can catch up on the good gossip. Plus, I want to see you in the pink bikini. You *did* bring the pink bikini, didn't you?" Priya must nod, because Abigail says, "Good girl. Come on. We can do this later."

Definitely a brat fetish.

Within seconds, the door clicks shut. Connor and I stare at each other for a moment before he finally speaks.

"Well, that was a close one."

"Generic Ativan?" I raise my brows.

"Probably helps them sleep after they pop all that Ritalin to stay awake and study." He shrugs like it's no big deal.

"Uh-huh." I let him kiss me this time, his soft yet firm lips working their magic within seconds. Everything in me screams to let him lean me back on the soft carpet, let him cover my body with his. When Connor kisses me, the low-level worry constantly humming under my skin goes quiet. With our eyes closed and our bodies doing all the talking, I can be Billie—I can be myself. It's all I want right now, to strip away the Belinda parts of me and give Connor the truth of who I am.

But instead, I press my hands against his chest to shove

him away.

I'm not here to be me or lose myself in a cute boy's hot caresses. I'm here to investigate a murder, and it's time to act like it. Peter warned me not to get distracted. If he could see me now...

Well, let's just be grateful he can't see me now.

"Maybe we should go to the hot tub, too."

He frowns. "It'll be crowded, like Abigail said."

"I don't mind. Especially if you brought the pink bikini I like so much," I say in a terrible imitation of Abigail's accent. Connor chokes out a laugh but backs off, adjusting himself as he stands and extends a hand toward me. When we're both upright again, I pull him in for one last kiss.

It's what Belinda would do. Probably.

"You should leave the room first, don't you think?" I say against his mouth.

"Why?" He pulls back, looking genuinely confused, which is adorable. I guess his panic at being caught before was more about being discovered in a private moment than it was about being discovered in a private moment *with me*.

I scoot closer so I can slip my fingers into his dark, soft hair. I sift through the silky strands once. Twice. I decide to test my hypothesis. "We don't want to get caught together, right?"

He frowns. Almost looks...hurt. "You don't want to be seen with me?"

"I don't want to be seen sneaking out of the darkened library with you," I clarify. "That's not the kind of impression I want to make the first time I'm at the Pembrokes' home, at an event full of alumni."

"I understand." He kisses me again, but it's brief. As if he understands the effect he has on my brain cells. "I'll leave now and you'll join me in a few minutes?"

I nod. Let him kiss me again because I'm weak. Then he turns and exits the room quickly. The door shuts behind him, and the only thing that lingers is the scent of his cologne.

Can't believe the girls didn't notice, but maybe they're not Connor-obsessed like I am.

Ugh. I need to stop thinking like that.

Taking my chance now that I'm alone, I grab the picture of the girl and boy under the tree, turn it over, undo the clasps that keep the stand connected to the frame, and pull the actual photo out. Written on the back in perfect cursive is: *George and Daphne, 1994.*

George and Daphne. Probably siblings, based on their similar features.

I stuff the photo back into the frame and reassemble everything before returning it to the crowded ledge. I would love to stay here and study all the pictures, maybe figure out who the girl is and, by proxy, who the boy is. But I have to swing back around to the foyer where we entered and grab my bag from the hall closet. Sophia made me pack a swimsuit, since she said the likelihood we'd end up in the Pembrokes' hot tub was high. She was right, which doesn't surprise me at all, and I vow to find her and ensure she's been invited to the hot tub, too. It's what a friend would do.

Within seconds of leaving the library, I spot Peter and Whitney in the hallway, heading straight toward me, though their heads are close together and their gazes are trained low. I freeze in place, irritated with myself that I didn't consider they would be attending an alumni party.

"...and half these people think our daughter is a *murderer*. If they're not whispering behind our backs, they're outright staring at us. Not sure why we bothered coming to this." Even though his voice is hushed, I can hear Peter's irritation come through like he's talking into a bullhorn.

"Daphne specifically said we should come tonight. She said there was no point in hiding because we have nothing to hide. Remember?"

"Hello, hi." I rush toward them, putting on a bright smile. The sperm donor also known as Peter seems startled by my appearance, as does Whitney. "Did you say Daphne?"

"Well, hello Belinda." Whitney's smile seems genuine, which helps me ignore the scowl on Peter's face. "So lovely to see you."

My manners fly out the window. I'm too focused on the name she just said. "Who's Daphne?"

"Daphne Pembroke. Freddie's mother? We were in the same graduating class," Whitney explains.

"And that was in…"

"2001. Three years after your father—I mean, your parents—graduated." Whitney blinks rapidly, and I swear Peter's scowl deepens.

What was that all about?

"HOT TUB!" someone screams. "Come on, everybody!"

"We can't be seen chatting like this, Belinda." Peter's dismissive words cut me to the bone. The next second, they're pushing past me—or rather, Peter is pulling Whitney past me, and she's offering me a small, apologetic smile as she lets herself get dragged away.

I'm too distracted by this new discovery to get as annoyed as I should be at Peter's shitty attitude. If I'm right and the two people in the photo I spotted are related, then Daphne Pembroke is a sister or cousin to the boy my mom was involved with during her time at Wickham.

I'm not entirely sure what to make of that, but maybe a soothing soak in the hot tub will help me figure it out.

CHAPTER THIRTEEN

I hide away in a small guest bathroom after my encounter with Peter and Whitney, hating how shaky they made me feel. Our interaction couldn't have lasted more than a minute or two, but it replays in my mind a dozen times while I'm changing into a black bathing suit I borrowed from Sophia. Whitney was perfectly lovely despite Peter acting like his normal, sour self. I guess I can understand why he was upset. His so-called friends are treating him differently after what happened with Isla and her best friend. And while that sucks, I get why people suspect Isla in Emily's murder. Right now, the evidence points to the two of them being alone on that cliffside before Emily died. Without any proof to the contrary, what are people supposed to believe?

Maybe if dear old Peter wasn't such an asshole all the time, people would be kinder to him. Though come to think of it, I have no idea how he treats other people. He might be a veritable Santa Claus to everyone who isn't his estranged daughter.

Pushing all thoughts of my father aside, I focus on the information Whitney provided. Daphne is related to George. George was involved with my mother. Daphne is Freddie Pembroke's mother. Both Mr. and Mrs. Pembroke seem to know Connor pretty well, maybe because Mr. Wells worked for the Lumateg Group? The Pembrokes seemed really supportive of Connor earlier tonight, but the call I overheard between Headmaster Harrington and the mysterious William proves that someone wants Connor out of the picture. I need to pump Connor for more information, but I can't be obvious about it. He went on the defensive when I mentioned the llamas last night, and he was drunk as a skunk then. Sober Connor might have an even lower tolerance for my snooping. And speaking of Connor...

He's an excellent kisser—and an excellent distraction. I should focus on the task at hand, and instead, I'm thinking about when we can find some alone time again.

Nice job, Billie. Instead of figuring out who tried to unalive Isla, you're worrying about the next time you get to shove your tongue down some hot boy's throat. A-plus sister behavior.

My conscience puts my hormones in a time-out to think about what they've done.

After I've washed my hands and run my fingers through my hair, I march out of the bathroom and walk through the house like I know where I'm going. I'm constantly searching everyone's faces in the hope that one of them will be Connor, but he's nowhere to be found.

"Belinda! There you are!" Sophia pops up in front of me as if by magic. Her eyes are a little glassy, and there's a flute of something bubbly in her hand. "Where have you been?

Having a snog with Connor?" My face gets hot, and Sophia gapes at me. "You were having a snog with him, weren't you?"

I grab hold of her arm and steer her away from the cluster of people who are probably listening in on our conversation. "Maybe."

"You are so bad." Sophia is grinning. I get the sense she doesn't think I'm bad at all. "How was it?"

"Magical." My smile is small, and I let myself forget what my real intentions are at Wickham. For this moment at least, I'm just going to be a regular teenage girl. "But don't tell anyone."

"I would never." She makes an X with her index finger across her chest before taking a sip from her glass. "I think I'm tipsy."

"Is your dad here?"

"Um." She presses her lips together and glances about the room, her eyes wide when they meet mine. "Probably?"

"Sophia!" I grab her arm again, my grip gentle. "We need to sober you up."

"What we *need*," she says, her voice sing-songing in a way that could only sound like music to the inebriated, "is to go to the hot tub. He'd never come out there." She grins and starts walking, leaving me no choice but to keep up with her. "I saw Connor outside, and I asked him where you were. He said he didn't know and requested that I go find you."

My skin warms. "Isn't that sweet?"

"Yes, it is. And Connor is *never* sweet, so lucky you." Sophia comes to a stop. "Oh no, there's my dad!"

We turn in the opposite direction and push through the crowd, Sophia squealing every time she bumps into someone and always offering a high-pitched, "So sorry!"

I thought she didn't want her father to see her, and instead she's making a complete spectacle of herself. I blame the alcohol. It's obvious she doesn't know how to manage her liquor, and there's something oddly reassuring about that. Somehow, while I'm trapped in the middle of the most important lie of my life, I've managed to find a genuinely good, sweet person to call my friend. It's like discovering a fluffy kitten in a den of vipers.

We eventually make our way outside, walking past a massive pool and slowing our pace as we approach the hot tub, which is currently filled to the brim with Wickham students.

Including Connor.

He spots me immediately, a slow smile curving his lips as he raises his hand. My eyes trace the parts of him I can see over the surface of the water, the skin of his shoulders and chest glistening with steam. An intrusive thought about running my tongue across his collar bones battles to take center stage in my brain.

"Belinda! Sophia! Over here." Connor's eyes crinkle a little at the corners, and I wonder if we're both thinking of how ridiculous it is for him to call me Belinda. Then again, on this side of the world, I'm only Billie to him. I refuse to admit how much I like the idea of that.

"Hey everyone." Sophia greets the crowd with a little wave when we come to a stop in front of the hot tub. The water bubbles and froths, the rush of it adding a layer of sound that thrums in my ears.

There's Connor, of course. Priya and Abigail, looking remarkably put together for two girls who were very recently attached at the mouth. Freddie, Julian, and Arlo.

"Join us, ladies." Freddie stretches his arms out alongside the edge of the hot tub, shoving Arlo and Julian away from him. "I've got spaces for you both."

Sophia and I share a look. I can feel Connor watching me, and when I catch his gaze, he looks annoyed. By Freddie?

Hopefully not by me.

"We need to change into our swimsuits first," Sophia announces.

What? "No we do—"

"Pool house is right over there." Freddie points. "Don't dawdle, girls."

Sophia drags me over to the pool house and locks the door once we're inside.

"We already have our swimsuits on," I remind her. How drunk is she?

"Oh, I know. I just didn't want to start stripping with everyone watching. So awkward. Did you see the way Abigail and Priya were glaring at us? We're clearly not welcome." Sophia giggles as she takes off her clothes, revealing the white bikini underneath.

Insecurity floats through me at seeing Sophia. Her skin is still golden from the recent "quick holiday to Ibiza" she mentioned last night, and her body is toned thanks to the personal trainer she and her mom meet with twice a week. The closest I get to personal training with Mom is when I haul her off the floor when she passes out. All to say, I'm super pale and a little flabby in places Sophia definitely is not and OMG, this feels like a moment of crisis.

"Belinda, what's wrong? Are you okay?"

I snap my lips shut and shake my head, desperate to act like nothing is bothering me. Belinda isn't the kind of girl who would compare herself to others. She would walk naked through a crowd with her head held high. Climbing into a hot tub in the dark should be no big deal. "Nothing. I'm fine."

"You don't look fine." Sophia frowns.

"Just the usual swimsuit insecurities." With a dramatic sigh, I tug off the borrowed skirt and sweater and fold them, then set the clothes on the nearby counter. "I mean, look at me."

"You look great."

That would be Sophia's automatic response no matter what. "If you say so."

"Seriously, Belinda." She grabs hold of my shoulders and gives them a gentle shake. Her tone is more sober than it was just minutes ago, and I wonder how much of her goofy drunkenness was just leaning into the fun of a little buzz. "There's no need for any self-pity at the moment. You were *kissing Connor Wells* not thirty minutes ago, and we all know he's the hottest boy at Wickham."

"Is he?" My voice is weak. There are plenty of good-looking guys at Wickham. Several of them are currently sitting in the hot tub.

But no one makes me feel fluttery and breathless like Connor.

"Yes. He is." Sophia's voice is firm. "Now let's go join them. And make sure you sit next to Connor."

I glance down at the black one-piece I'm wearing. It's not exciting, but maybe it's classic. Sophia is right. I don't look terrible.

Connor certainly didn't have any complaints.

We leave the pool house and practically run to the hot tub, desperate to get warm, since there's a chill in the air. The moment we're in the water, I feel a gentle tug on my hand under the surface.

It's Connor pulling me toward him, and I go willingly. Sophia is close behind me, and I end up sitting between them. My new bestie and my crush.

Yikes. Listen to me. I sound like I'm living out my every teen fantasy. Nothing like this would ever happen to me back home. For starters, no one I know owns a hot tub, and it's not like I was ever getting invited to parties. I always had to work.

"Nice suit, Belinda." Abigail's snide tone makes me want to smack her, but instead I flash her a petty smile.

"Gee thanks. It's Sophia's."

Abigail sneers, taking the three of us in. "What an odd little group you make. Is this what you've resorted to, Connor? Hanging out with the snitch and the new girl?"

I can feel both Sophia and Connor stiffen at Abigail's snide comment. "When the alternative is the diva and her bodyguard," I say, bobbing my head at Priya and Abigail respectively, "can you really blame him?" My voice is calm despite my inner City Kid wanting to launch herself at Abigail and pull her hair.

The boys laugh. Priya's worried expression is almost comical, but I restrain myself from joining in the laughter.

"Now come on, Abigail. Not sure why you want to pick on poor ol' Con here." Julian's good-natured attitude always throws me. There's something about him that's incredibly fake, and I don't understand how Isla couldn't see it.

"Give me a break, Julian." Abigail wobbles a little, and Priya reaches out to keep her steady. Looks like she's had something to drink along with her recreational meds. Great.

"You two do look cozy," Freddie observes, his gaze flitting between Connor and me. "You up to something new, Connor?"

Connor says nothing in response, but I can feel the anger radiating off him in waves.

"I thought the hot tub was supposed to be fun, guys." Sophia glances around, her brows drawn together. I'm sure she can feel the tension, too.

"Oh, it was loads of fun until you two showed up." Abigail checks on Priya. "Right, P?"

Priya remains quiet as well, sending Abigail a meaningful look. One that probably says, *watch yourself.*

Abigail ignores her. "Connor, I have to say it's great to have you back in the fold, but you should know that none of us can quite decide whether to hate you because your dad is a criminal or pity you because your sister is dead."

Sophia gasps. Priya's mouth hangs open. All the boys duck their heads, seemingly uncomfortable. Me?

I'm fuming. I can feel Connor next to me, shaking with rage and humiliation. I rest my hand on his thigh beneath the water, giving it a squeeze.

He sets his hand on top of mine, curling our fingers together, and I want to lean into him but I'm too fired up to get cuddly.

"It's funny, Abigail, because I can't decide whether you're an unbearable bitch because you're miserable, or if you're miserable because you're an unbearable bitch." I shake my head. "I just…can't figure it out."

"Yeah, Abigail. You need to learn how to keep your mouth shut." Freddie's comment feels like a warning.

Abigail glares at me for a long, quiet moment before she turns to Priya, muttering, "Fucking bitch."

My mind instantly flashes to the Polaroid I found and the vandalism on my closet mirror. Both included that particular phrase. Is it a signature Abigail set-down? Is she the culprit?

I'm leaning toward a big hell yes.

"Ignore her, Belinda." Arlo smiles, his entire body swaying to and fro, as if he's a slender tree in the wind. "Abigail gets off on bullying everyone at Wickham at some point or another. She's just power trippin' because you're new."

"New Yorkers have such a reputation for being harsh, but Wickham is by far the least friendly place I've ever been," I announce.

"I hate hearing that," Sophia murmurs, her disappointment thick.

"You make up for it." I pat her arm, and she beams at me.

Abigail pipes in again. "You two make me sick."

"You're just mad Sophia wouldn't help out your girlfriend," Connor says to Abigail. "She probably saw right through you two."

I frown, confused. What is Connor talking about?

"Mr. Art Merit Scholar over here doesn't have to worry about a thing, while other students who are far more deserving struggle to—" Priya jabs her elbow into Abigail's side, silencing her.

Interesting.

"Far more deserving," I parrot. "Gosh, Abigail, I didn't

know you cared. I assume you're talking about me?" I ask, resting my hand against my chest like a prim southern belle. I'm trying to bait her, and the spark in her eyes tells me it's working.

She rolls her eyes. "Your fancy American GPA is stellar. You have nothing to worry about."

Freddie changes the subject and starts talking about someone grabbing more drinks while I sit there, muddling over what Abigail revealed. Bringing up my GPA and calling it stellar. How does she know? Abigail has obviously had a look at my transcripts...which are completely fake. My real transcript shows my GED scores, which are pretty impressive if I do say so myself. I have no idea what Peter's identity-creating goons put in Belinda Winters's transcript, but it must be, ahem, *stellar*.

The more important takeaway here? Abigail has a penchant for a phrase used to deface both a picture and my bedroom mirror. And she has access to my records.

I don't like it. Not one bit.

• • •

Later, after everyone has left the hot tub, I remain outside by the pool, draped in a pile of thick towels and stretched out across a lounge chair. Connor, also covered in towels, is on the one next to mine. Sophia went into the pool house to change into her dress, and last I saw, she was back inside with everyone else.

Connor and I are the only ones by the pool.

"Can I ask you something?" My voice is soft in the otherwise still night. Strains of music drift from within the house, as well as the dull roar of a crowd in conversation with itself. Despite us being at a party, I feel like we're the only two people in the world.

"Depends." Connor reaches out and grabs hold of my lounger, pulling me closer to his. "Is it something dirty?"

I burst out laughing, shocked. "You wish."

"You're right. I do." He offers me a sly smile, and I return it.

"It's about your sister." His smile fades. "But I don't want to upset you."

"No. You won't." He blows out a harsh breath, staring straight ahead. "Ask away."

"Was Emily a good student?"

His exhale comes more slowly this time, like he's keeping a bubble afloat and doesn't want to pop it. Or maybe like he needs the time to answer. "Not particularly. She always struggled in school. And it didn't help that the curriculum at Wickham is so rigorous. But the last couple of months, she seemed to be doing better. I know Isla was helping her. They studied together constantly."

I touch his arm, and he turns to meet my gaze. "Why would someone who was trying to help Emily get good grades want to murder her?"

"Don't be so naive, Billie." He makes a dismissive noise, and I drop my hand from his arm. His words hurt. "Look at Abigail and Priya. Love can make people act unhinged. Isla was helping Emily, sure, but was she also controlling her? The two of them were inseparable, but was that Emily's choice?

The police think it was a crime of passion, and no one was more passionate about Emily than Isla."

His words fill me with dread. Could that be it? Were Isla and Emily more than best friends, like Priya and Abigail? What about Julian? Isla kept him a secret, but was that because it would've upset Emily to find out she was messing around with someone else? No one wants to be cheated on. Did they fight over Julian?

I wish I knew.

"I don't want to talk about Emily anymore." Connor reaches for me, hauling me onto his lounger. The towels fall away from me, and I squeal from the cold air touching my bare skin. "It should be a fun night, right? Like what Sophia said earlier?"

"Right." My voice is hollow. I don't want to ruin the mood, either, but I can't deny he gave me a perspective I hadn't thought of before. "But I fear it's difficult to have fun when I'm freezing my ass off."

"Lucky you, I've got this." He reaches down on the other side of the lounger and holds up a thick blanket.

I punch him in the upper arm, but it's like hitting a brick. My knuckles ache from the impact. "You've been holding out on me."

"I only just noticed it." He drapes the blanket across the both of us and then pulls me into his side. I rest my cheek against his chest, snuggling closer when he slips his arm around my shoulders. We lie like this for long, quiet minutes, and I swear I feel him brush his lips against the top of my head.

If it was possible, I'd stay like this with him all night. For the next week, even. Just the two of us. Forget all of our troubles and problems and just…be.

But I can't. Real life is rude and intrusive, and we'd never get away with it.

"I have another question," I eventually announce, and Connor groans.

"Not another one." I playfully pinch his side, and he grabs my hand, stopping me. "Fine, go ahead. Ask me all the questions."

I lift my head and rest my arm on his chest. We're face-to-face, and he's smiling faintly, his heavy-lidded gaze making me feel fluttery inside. "Who are you passionate about?"

I'm alluding to his earlier "crime of passion" remark. And while I'm probably reaching big time with this question and hoping his answer will be me, I couldn't help myself. Sometimes I say dumb stuff.

"Who do you want me to be passionate about?" He reaches for my face, brushing his fingers against my cheek as he tucks a few wayward strands of hair behind my ear. "If you're trying to ask if I'm seeing anyone else, the answer is a resounding no."

I already knew that, not that I've ever had any official confirmation. "There's no one else in my life, either."

"Good." His smile grows, and his fingers trace along my jaw. My chin. He rubs his thumb against my bottom lip, and I let my mouth open slightly, anticipation curling through me. "Now that we've got that dreadful conversation out of the way…"

Our mouths connect, soft and sweet until he deepens the kiss. His tongue sweeps the interior of my mouth, and I fall into him. My body is sprawled on top of his, and heat courses through me when he rests his hand on my butt.

Voices sound outside, but we ignore them, too into each other to care about who might be watching or what they might see. A loud *boom* sounds from above, and colorful fireworks burst and crackle in the sky, lighting up the entire backyard. Partygoers are standing on the other side of the hedge that cuts the pool off from the rest of the lawn, their faces angled toward the sky.

I break away from Connor's kiss and watch the fireworks for a few seconds. Until Connor's hand on my cheek guides me back to his always-seeking lips, and I lose myself in his kiss again. My entire body lights up from within, exactly like the sky.

Oh, how I wish this night would never end.

CHAPTER FOURTEEN

I hunkered down in the library all day Sunday to finish the paper I noped out of Friday night. I thought I'd have an easier time of it, since I read *Rebecca* by Daphne du Maurier last year for my GED, but apparently I forgot more than I remembered. Still, I finally finished just as the library was closing. I managed to sneak in a few texts to Doug, too, who kindly ignored the fact that it took me a week to reach out. He was chatty and filled me in on what the bar regulars are up to, and he didn't ask too many questions about how things are going here. It almost felt like he was reassuring me that life back home is waiting for me whenever I come back.

And...I don't know how to feel about that.

Doug's messages filled me with a surprising ache. On the one hand, I miss him and the bar and even the regulars. I miss Mom and our shitty apartment. I miss home, despite how hard life is there. I guess it's normal to miss what's familiar to us.

But on the other hand, I'm starting to wonder what it will be like to return to the life I've been living in New York. All these Wickham kids are going places after school—places beyond the local watering hole for slow shifts and bad tips. Belinda Winters is like the rest of them, a girl with nothing but potential stretching out ahead of her. Being me again after having a taste of being her is going to *suck*.

Today has been refreshingly uneventful. It might be wishful thinking, but some of the kids I saw at Freddie's party seem to be warming up to me. I heard more than one "Hey Belinda" while I was crossing the courtyard after lunch, where Arlo saved me a seat so he could recap what he called my "nuclear annihilation" of Abigail in the hot tub. I get the impression that the urge to tell that girl to go pound sand is one most of the student body shares. I should start a club.

I only have one more class before the academic part of my day is done—and the work I actually care about can begin. Julian and I are going to have a long overdue conversation this evening. He doesn't know it yet, but he's going to fess up to whatever he had going on with my sister.

I'm a bundle of nerves when I enter the art room, but I stop short when I realize I'm the only one here.

Where's Connor? He's always in the room first. Sometimes I wonder if he secretly sleeps here because seriously—he's *always* here. When he breezes in a few seconds later with a giant smile on his handsome face, I realize it's the first time I've ever seen him enter the space from the hall. The thoughts that run through my head come very close to melting me into a puddle of sentimental goo. Phrases like *wow, a person really* can *light up a room*, and *there's my guy* bubble up totally unbidden. It's cute and gross and really worrying, given Connor has no idea who I really am.

"Billie." He approaches, ducking to brush the briefest kiss on my lips. "Looking adorable as ever."

His unusually good mood leaves me in a state of shock. It's like I'm frozen in place as he drops his backpack on a nearby desk and unzips it. "Hello to you, too," I finally manage once I find my voice.

He grins. "We're going to create some *real* art today, so I hope you're ready."

"Real art?" I don't try to hide my skepticism. What does he mean by "real art"? The past week I've spent blobbing watercolor paint on thick paper has proved to us both that I'm not exactly brimming with natural talent. I can admit to feeling more than a little disappointed that Mom's considerable artistic gifts didn't get passed down genetically. It would have been nice to make something I could be proud of—that *she* could be proud of.

Stupid, I scold myself. What's she going to do, display my latest masterpiece on the communal fridge at the rehab center?

Maybe Connor won't care that I don't have any real talent in this area. Maybe he's so enamored of me, my lack of artistic skills won't matter to him. Fingers crossed.

"Yes. We're going to sketch croquis of each other. You ever done those?" He raises his brows.

I slowly shake my head. It sounds like he said croak-ee, which seriously...WTF. It's like he's speaking a foreign language, which I'm guessing he is, but anyway. "Um, no. I have no idea what that is."

"They're also sometimes called gesture drawings. Here, sit down." He points at a chair, and I do as he says. "Give me a minute and we'll get started."

He sets us both up with three sharpened art pencils and spiral notebooks of lightweight drawing paper, then settles into a chair across from mine.

"What are we supposed to do?"

"We draw each other for a minute at a time." He gestures to the sand timer sitting on the table between us. "Your pencil should never really leave the paper, and you shouldn't look down at what you're sketching, either."

"I'm not supposed to look at it?" My voice squeaks because *yikes*. The potential for this sketch to be awful is high enough, but I can't even look at my paper? Forget it.

This is going to be terrible.

Connor shakes his head, his mouth quirked up on one side. He appears amused by my panic. "When the minute is up, we share what we've done so far. Then we flip the timer and do it all over again."

"For how long?" My palms are starting to sweat.

"Until we're finished. Or until we run out of paper. Or as long as we like, really." He shrugs.

"So...once?" I ask hopefully. "I'm sure there are other, more interesting things we can be doing here. In this room where we're the only occupants. With a door that locks."

"Belinda Winters, you are scandalous." His droll tone makes me smile. "Okay, go!"

He flips the sand timer with a quick flick of his fingers and starts sketching while I sit here like an idiot. His eyes never leave my face, even as his hand moves in swift, smooth movements.

"Billie, start sketching. Time's running out."

Again, I do as he says, keeping my gaze locked on him as I draw a circle on the paper that's supposed to be his head. He's watching me, too, his eyes narrowed and lips pressed together while his hand flies across the paper.

I cheat and check my sketch, wincing when I see the mess I'm making. It's obvious I'm not an artist. Not even close.

"Time's up," Connor announces, flipping his sketch pad in my direction. It's a rough but passable outline of the shape of my face and hair, without any real details. Still, looking at it feels a bit like staring into a fogged mirror; I know my face is there, just hidden.

I show him my sketch, and he tries and fails to contain a bemused smile. "Nice."

"It's terrible."

"Let's keep going." He flips the sand timer to restart, and off we go.

I try to infuse a little more artistic talent into my sketch this time around, but I fear I'll look down to find an even more unholy mess than my first attempt. When the next minute is up and we share what we've done, Connor laughs so hard at my feeble attempt that he actually slides off his stool and has to hang on to the table for support.

Meanwhile, my jaw hangs open in unabashed awe at his sketch.

He's managed to capture the curve of my neck. The slope of my cheek. The shape of my eyes and the shadow under my bottom lip. I can tell that's me and not some random drawing of a girl. He's so good.

We do another round, and this time I lean into my terribleness. His eyes are exaggerated circles, and his nose is a triangle with aspirations of greatness. I don't care what my picture looks like as long as I get to see his drawing of me again.

"I look like a clown," he declares when I show him my progress.

"I'm capturing your inner child, obviously." I shrug, though I'm smiling. "You make me look better than I actually do."

It's true. He's added more fine detail to my face by shading in my quirked lips and fanning my eyelashes. My expression is flirtatious. Almost knowing.

"This is what you look like, Billie." His voice is soft, and when I meet his gaze, I see how serious he is.

My heart flutters, and I wave a hand at the sand timer. "Flip that thing. Let's keep this going."

I feel like a jerk as I continue to draw him because he looks more like a balloon animal than anything else. And when the last grain of sand falls and we're flipping our sketch pads toward each other, all the breath gathers in my throat at what I see.

It's a fresh page in his notebook, and it says "*Go out with me?*" in blocky script at the top. He added a quickly sketched and perfectly beautiful bouquet of flowers below.

I don't say anything at first. It's like all the words I've ever known turned into wispy white clouds and got blown away. Nothing but clear blue sky in my head.

I use the silence to study the face that has become so dear to me in the short time we've known each other. It's the first time today that I actually regret not having the ability to draw him. I wish I could capture this moment, this boy, *us*, on paper.

Maybe then I could keep them—this moment, this boy, *us*—for a little while, instead of giving it all up when Connor figures out who I really am.

I lean over and flip the sand timer, our gazes never straying from each other.

It's intense, the way he watches me. Waiting patiently for my response. I stare back, unable to look away, my heart pounding so hard I'm worried it might fly out of my chest. The rational side of my brain reminds me we're moving too fast. I barely know him. But the romantic part of my brain? Can't deny the connection. The attraction. The chemistry.

The problem?

I still don't trust it—the connection. Or him. Not fully. I don't think he's responsible for what happened to Emily and Isla, so it's not like that. More that I'm worried what might happen if I fully give myself to this boy. And how mad he'll be when he finds out I lied to him.

That's the worst part. The lies.

Swallowing hard, I finally tear my gaze from Connor's and flip to a new piece of paper, my pencil scratching across the pristine surface. And when the minute is up, I show him my new sketch. It's simple. One word. Three letters.

Yes.

. . .

I'm floating on air when I enter my dorm room and become even more buoyant with the discovery that I'm alone. I shut the door and lean against it for a full minute, letting myself bask in the memories of what happened last period.

Connor and I are officially a couple. We kissed for the rest of class to seal the deal. I like him so much. He's the only person I can be myself with here, even though I never fully let myself go. I hate that I have to watch what I say and do around him, but I can't expose myself completely. I've halfway convinced myself that it'll all work out in the end because the heart wants what it wants, right?

That's what I'm going to manifest, at least.

I'm about to push away from the door when my gaze snags on the bulletin board that hangs above Priya's desk. It's always crooked, which makes no sense. Her side of the room is always immaculate, so why is that board off-center? Doesn't she notice it?

Marching over to the wall, I nudge the bottom left edge of the corkboard, which sends it tipping over dramatically on the other side. I nudge it back into place, but it's still crooked.

What the hell?

I rise on tiptoe and pluck the board off the wall completely, flipping it over to find a dry erase board on the other side. It's covered with names and lines and arrows. Columns and what looks like code words and dollar amounts. Excuse me, *pound* amounts.

What is this? She's clearly keeping track of something, but I don't know what. Most of the names listed are unfamiliar to me, but two stand out: Emily and Isla. Someone—Priya, I guess—has drawn lines through their names. It can't be a coincidence that two girls who are no longer on campus have been removed from whatever record this is. But no, not removed—*crossed out*. There's something eerily violent about their names remaining here, but struck through.

Alarm races down my spine, raising goose bumps along my back and leaving me cold. What is going on with Priya? This is some serial killer–level recordkeeping, according to every thriller flick I've ever watched. She has questionable taste in girlfriends, for sure, but I've never thought of her as inherently dangerous.

Maybe I should have.

I grab my phone and take photos of the board. My brain is screaming *this is evidence!* But evidence of what? Priya's always seemed too uptight for a life of crime, but maybe I should've suspected her from the start.

The door swings open at the exact moment I'm dropping my phone on my nightstand. I whirl around to find Priya standing in the doorway. Her lips are parted, and her gaze zeroes in on the board currently on my bed.

"What are you doing?" She slams the door shut and stalks toward me.

"I have the same question." I raise a brow.

My words don't faze her. She pushes past me and grabs the bulletin board, flips it over, and hangs it on the hook before taking a step back. With a frown, she pushes it this way and that, trying to make the board hang straight, but it's hopeless. She's really out here trying to pretend I didn't see what we both know I saw.

"What I'm doing is none of your business," she finally says, her voice shaky. She doesn't sound mad. No, more like nervous.

"Now that I've found it, it kind of *is* my business." Priya glares, and I throw my hands up in the air, frustrated. "Come on, Priya! This looks pretty suspicious, don't you think? All the times and code words you've got next to a list of names. The prices. Oh, and nice touch with the lines through Emily and Isla's names. Like they're both already dead."

She shrugs one shoulder, averting her gaze. "They're both basically gone."

Her callousness leaves me reeling. "Are you such an unfeeling bitch that you don't care about anyone? You hang out with Abigail way too much, because her attitude is rubbing off on you big time."

I'm grasping at straws with my accusations. I have no idea if Priya's moods have to do with Abigail or if she was always this bitchy. Maybe that's what makes them such a good match. Though I always assumed it's better for two people to be different enough to balance each other out.

Or maybe that's just wishful thinking.

"Who the hell do you think you are? You don't even know me." Priya crosses her arms, shifting into pure defensive mode. "You don't know my struggles or the pressure I'm dealing with. It's so easy for you, coming to Wickham with your perfect grades and your New York pedigree."

Ooh, what do you know? My stellar transcripts are brought up again. "How do you and Abigail know what my transcripts look like?"

Priya waves a dismissive hand. "It doesn't matter. Just know I'm doing whatever it takes to maintain top status in our class. Whatever. It. Takes. I can't let anyone take it from me. I *need* that spot on the Legacy List, Belinda. It'll change everything."

"Whatever it takes, huh? What exactly does that mean?"

There's more to this than endless studying. She's doing something else—like popping pills, for one.

"And don't tell me it's simply keeping up your grades with studying, because you're hiding something, Priya. The list on that board is proof."

A ragged sigh leaves her, and she shakes her head. We stand there in a silent face-off for what feels like hours but is probably only a handful of seconds. I infuse my spine with steel and let her see the determination in my gaze. Today is a day for answers. I thought I was only going to get them from Julian, but I'm happy to add Priya Shah to my list. I won't be moved.

And as Priya gusts out a huge sigh and drops her shoulders away from her ears, I think she knows it, too. "Fine," she says. "But you have to keep this a secret."

I make an X on my chest like Sophia did at the party Saturday night. "I will."

I do everything in my power to keep the childhood vow we all know from running through my mind with the gesture: *Cross my heart, hope to die.* It would feel too much like tempting fate. And something tells me I've done enough of that today already.

I can see the cogs turning in her mind as she tries to come up with a proper explanation. After a minute, though, the tension tugging at her forehead and jaw dissolves, and I know she's decided to tell me the truth.

"I sell old exams and use the money to buy Ritalin and Ativan. Whatever I can get." She presses her lips together and stares at the floor. "It sounds terrible, but I need to do something to stay awake and study. With classes and all the clubs I'm in, plus…other things, I need as much time as I can get. And the meds help ease some of my anxiety. I barely sleep right now."

Using pills to stay awake definitely isn't helping her anxiety, and neither is the pressure she's clearly putting on herself to stay at the top of the class, but I don't bring that up.

"Who else knows that you do this? Besides the students who buy the exams from you. And Abigail, obviously."

"It's sort of anonymous, my exam business." Priya lifts her head, her gaze locking with mine. "I have a burner phone, and they pay me in cash. I know their names, but they don't know mine."

"So no one knows it's you." Pretty genius, I must admit.

"Well, Abigail knows." Priya lifts her chin, her expression turning defiant. "But she's the only one. That's why she's so protective of me. She keeps people at a distance so they don't figure out what I'm doing. I would be ruined if it ever came out. Absolutely ruined."

Priya's right. I could destroy her now that I know about her dirty dealings.

"I can keep a secret." I hesitate. "I've already been keeping a secret for you anyway."

"Like what?" Priya's brows draw together.

"I know about you. And Abigail. That you two are… together."

Priya's face crumples, and she collapses onto the edge of her bed, crying. She covers her face and sobs into her hands. "Please don't tell anyone. That'll destroy everything, if word gets out about us."

I almost want to tell her lots of people must've figured this out by now, and that maybe if it's a secret they shouldn't make out in unlocked rooms at house parties, but I keep my mouth shut. Instead, I go over to the bed and sit beside her, slipping my arm around her shoulders and giving her a one-sided hug. "I won't tell. I promise. Though I don't get it. Would your parents be upset that you're...gay?"

"No, of course not," Priya says, like the very thought of someone not being accepted for their sexuality has literally never occurred to her. "They wouldn't care. That's not the point. Not really. It's because Abigail is a fifth-generation Legacy and I have no family history at Wickham. I'm the first to make it in, though my older brothers each applied. Twice. But if I nail that top spot, my younger brother and sister will have easy entry to both Wickham and the Legacy List. This could set our future family—my kids, and my siblings' kids, and *their* kids—on a path to excellence. Opportunities like this don't come along often. That's why I need to do whatever it takes to ensure I'm number one. And why I need to keep certain parts of my life...quiet."

I give her another gentle squeeze, doing my best to hide my shock at her admission. There's a tremendous amount of pressure piled on Priya, and I don't know how she does it all. In her shoes, maybe I'd be taking illegal prescription drugs, too. No wonder she's stressed and anxious and bitchy all the time.

The longer I console Priya, the more my imagination goes into overdrive. Did Emily figure out what Priya was doing and confront her? Selling tests, taking drugs, her relationship with Abigail...a roommate wouldn't have to be *that* observant to figure out what Priya is doing. Could that have pushed Priya to commit...murder? Maybe that's why Priya's stressed. She's hiding a tell-tale heart in the wall, like in that Edgar Allan Poe story. Murder is an even bigger secret to keep than selling tests, and that already seems to be sending her anxiety into overdrive. Killing a person would get to anyone eventually, even if it was an accident.

I decide to broach the subject carefully.

"It must be really tough to keep this from everyone." I release my hold on Priya's shoulders, and she wipes the tears from her face, sniffing loudly. "Like your old roommate? Did she know about it?"

"Oh, Emily was oblivious. It was her best friend who figured me out first."

Wow. Okay. That's interesting. "You mean the girl in the coma? Isla?"

Priya nods. "Yeah, and she was kind of a slag about it, too. She threatened to out me to administration."

"Seriously?" My brows shoot up. Look at how principled my sister is. She was so offended by Priya's little side hustle, she was ready to destroy it without hesitation.

"Yes, seriously. Isla told me if I didn't give her a discount on the tests for Emily's classes, she would send Headmaster Harrington an anonymous tip about my *business*." Priya's voice drips with disgust. "She always had cash to pay for the tests, and sometimes she'd even pay me more than I'd charge her, so after a while I didn't much care what she said, but still. It was still shitty of her, you know?"

I think of the cash in that old hoodie pocket in Isla's closet. She must've kept it on hand for the sole purpose of purchasing those exams. But why would Isla be the one to buy them for

Emily? Up until her father was arrested, Emily should've had her own money.

"So wait a minute…Isla was buying tests for Emily? That doesn't make any sense."

"It does if you knew Emily. Little Miss Perfect." Priya scoffs. "She would have sooner failed out than cheated. But it's not like having the test means you don't need to study. You still have to. Having access to the old tests just makes things… easier. No. *Less hard*."

Priya's phone buzzes, but she ignores it. It's been buzzing with notifications for the last few minutes. I don't actually have to wonder who it is. Who else would text nonstop but Abigail?

"You should check your phone," I suggest when it buzzes yet again. "Someone really wants to talk to you."

A sigh leaves Priya, and she grabs her phone, frowning at the screen. "It's Abigail, of course."

"Of course." I try to keep the sarcasm out of my voice, but it's difficult.

"She's headed to the dining hall for dinner." Priya lifts her gaze to mine. "Want to join us?"

I'm taken aback by her invitation, and I wonder if she's adhering to the old standard, *keep your friends close and your enemies closer.*

I don't necessarily view Priya as an enemy, especially not after what she revealed to me. I have a better understanding of her now, though I still think she's kind of the worst.

"I need to do a few things first, but you go on ahead." I smile at her, not wanting her to feel uneasy about our conversation. "And I meant what I said earlier. Your secrets are safe with me."

Priya stands, the relief written all over her face. "Thank you, Belinda. I-I appreciate it." She takes the time to run a makeup wipe under her eyes, fluff her hair, and just generally put herself back together. With her fingers on the door handle, she stops and turns back to me. "I know we haven't exactly gotten off on the right foot. I suppose I'm...defensive. When it comes to new people. I think you can understand why. So I guess what I'm trying to say is...I hope we can be better acquainted going forward."

I give her a nod, confident that's as close to an apology as Priya can possibly get without bursting into flame. When she closes the door behind her, I throw myself across my narrow bed, rolling over so I'm staring up at the ceiling. Every day, more information is revealed, which is what I need to figure out who could've hurt Isla and Emily.

But I don't feel any closer to discovering the truth. Not really. Because it feels like everyone at Wickham is up to no good.

CHAPTER FIFTEEN

My phone dings with a notification—a text from Connor. I smile when I see his name.

Connor: *You coming to dinner?*

Me: *Give me a few and I'll meet you there.*

Connor: *I'll save you a seat.*

Still smiling, I sit up, and I'm tucking my phone into my backpack's front pocket when the door slams open, revealing Abigail.

Gee, great. More drama.

"Knock much?" I arch a brow.

Abigail storms into the room, standing above me with her hands on her hips. "Priya told me you two had quite the heart-to-heart."

"We painted each other's nails and had a pillow fight, too. So sorry you missed it." I lay the sarcasm on extra thick.

Abigail rolls her eyes, unbothered. "I just thought I'd stop by to make sure you understand that Priya is taking the top spot in our class this year. It belongs to her and no one else. Got it?"

My gaze drops to Abigail's glossy, dark pink mouth. That lipstick shade is awfully familiar. Pretty sure the last time I saw it, it was smeared all over my mirror.

"It's so cute, how you're Priya's guard dog. We both know you can bark, but do you bite? Or are you only tough enough to leave lipstick on mirrors and deface the occasional photo?" I stand up, prepared for a fight.

The knowing smirk on Abigail's face makes me want to smack her. She doesn't even care that I called her out. She's basically admitting what she did without saying a word. I decide to push her a little further.

I step closer, practically thrusting my face in hers. "I guess the real question is, does the chain Priya keeps you on leave enough slack for you to, say, push someone off a cliff?"

Abigail narrows her eyes, her entire expression going dark. "You better watch your fucking mouth, *Belinda*. That's a serious accusation."

"Is it?" I blink my eyelashes at her with exaggerated slowness, like I'm a dimwit.

Abigail shakes her head once, her lips firm. "If I have to, I'll be the biggest bitch the world has ever seen to keep Priya at Wickham. That's what you do when you love someone."

Her confession is a surprise, I'll give her that. But it's not going to be enough to throw me off her scent.

"But I'm definitely not a murderer." Abigail shifts close enough that I can feel her breath when she speaks. "Stay in your lane, Nancy Drew. And keep that old A-minus average exactly where it is, or we're going to have a problem."

With that, she turns her back on me and heads for the door, but right before she gets there, I remember we have unfinished business.

"Abigail?"

She heaves an enormous sigh, like I've just called her back from the brink of nirvana. "Yes, Belinda?"

"How'd you get my transcripts?"

"Mrs. Brown, of course."

As much as I'd love to hide my confusion, I fear it's written all over my face. "But you don't…have dimples."

Abigail looks at me like I have ten heads. "Dimples? Is that some American euphemism I don't know? Actually, don't tell me. I don't want to know. Mrs. Brown has a well-known online poker habit. If you pretend to find twenty quid on the floor of her office that she 'dropped' on her way in, she'll tell you anything you need to know."

With that, she exits the room, slamming the door behind her so hard, the walls rattle. I can't help but feel a tad impressed by Abigail standing up for Priya. But do I believe her when she says she's not a murderer? Could Isla's threat to out Priya's test-selling scheme to the administration have inspired Abigail to take truly drastic action? And if so, how did that lead to Emily's death?

My gut says they're not responsible. Abigail may be mean, but I don't think she's a killer. And Priya doesn't have enough open space in her calendar to schedule a homicidal rendezvous.

And I don't think my sister reported Priya to administration. She wasn't a snitch, and besides, Whitney would've informed me of that little tidbit. Right?

Time is running out. In less than a week, Isla will be

formally charged with murder and taken to a hospital god-knows-where, and all of Peter's money won't make a lick of difference if she's so far out of reach that none of us can see her, talk to her, or manage her care.

I may have eliminated two suspects from my list today, but the day is far from over. Like it or not, it's time for me to push harder for answers.

...

I leave the dorm building and come to a stop midway down the steps. I spot a familiar dark-blond head across the grounds. It's Julian, walking by himself with his hands in his pockets and his lips pursed like he's...what? *Whistling?*

This is my chance to talk to Mr. Happy-Go-Lucky and confront him about Isla and why he kept their relationship a secret. My brain is already spinning from my talks—confrontations?—with Priya and Abigail, but I can't let an opportunity like this pass me by.

Though my whole body pulls toward Connor waiting for me in the dining hall, the good luck of seeing the guy I need to talk to at the exact moment I need to talk to him is too fortuitous to ignore. Changing my course to aim for Julian is a physical effort, like pulling two magnets apart when all they want to do is stick together. Reluctantly, I whip out my phone and fire off a quick text to Connor.

Me: *Hey. Change of plans. I can't make it to the dining hall.*

He responds almost immediately.

Connor: *Everything okay?*

His concern makes my heart sing. Such a small thing, asking if everything is okay. It makes me realize how rare it is for someone to take an interest like this. And that's…super pathetic, so I shove the thought to the back of my brain, where I'll hopefully never have to look at it again.

Me: *Yes, everything's fine. Tell u everything when I see u in art.*

Another lie, of course, but they're getting easier and easier to tell. What would that conversation even look like, anyway? *Sorry I couldn't meet you for lunch, I had to interrogate one of your ex-friends about his possible involvement in your sister's murder and my sister's assault. Wanna make out?* I'm sure that would go over like a lead balloon. What will I tell Connor about why I was delayed? That's future Billie's lie to sort out. For now, I pocket my phone and jog over to Julian, pleased when he slows his pace to wait up for me. The expanse of lawn between us is bigger than it looks.

"Belinda." Julian smiles, his eyes twinkling. How can he flirt with just a look? I'd be impressed if I didn't know his girlfriend is in a coma. "What are you doing out here? I figured you'd be canoodling with Connor in the dining hall."

There's the slightest edge to his voice, which trips me up a bit. What, is he jealous? *Please.*

I ignore his remark and get straight to the point. "We need to talk."

"Talk?" He manages to put air quotes around the word with the slightest inflection of his voice. But he starts walking, and so do I. "Are you sure Connor will be okay with that? He can be quite the jealous type, you know."

I'm curious about that little tidbit—is there history there?—

but I don't let myself get distracted. "Save it, Julian. We need to talk about Isla."

He comes to a complete stop and takes a deep breath, exhaling through his flared nostrils. His agitation is obvious, and when he glances down at me, I note his furrowed brow and troubled gaze.

"What do you know about Isla? You only just started here," he so kindly reminds me. The edge in his voice is equal parts defensive and accusatory.

"I know enough." I glance around, noting the various students milling about. "Let's find somewhere more private to talk. Where no one will see us."

Julian leads me to the clock tower, which is on the opposite side of campus. We make the journey in total silence. He enters the building as if he owns it, the door swinging open for him easily. I scurry inside after him and gaze about the space. We're in a lobby with high ceilings and glass cabinets lining one wall. The shelves are filled with various old trophies and photos of sports teams from the past. I'm tempted to check them out, searching for familiar faces, but I've got limited time with Julian and a lot of questions.

"Why would you think I have anything to say to *you* about Isla?" Julian asks.

I appreciate him getting right to the point. "Because I know you were seeing her secretly. And I know it was a secret because *you* were the one who insisted she didn't tell anyone."

"Who told you this?"

Panic? Anger? I can't tell what emotion colors his question, so I have to tread carefully. He doesn't sound happy that I know his little secret. "It doesn't matter. What I want to know is, why keep your relationship with Isla under wraps?"

His deep frown pulls his whole face downward, causing a line to appear between his brows. "Doesn't much matter now, does it? If you know about us, our secret didn't exactly work out well for me."

The audacity. Most everyone at this school is incredibly selfish, but Julian Ashworth might have just taken the cake. "For *you*? What about Isla? Are you the reason she's in a coma?"

Julian rears his head back, and his eyes go wide. "Perhaps you should step away from the *Law & Order* marathon, Belinda, and retire your make-believe detective badge. I know it's easy to say 'the boyfriend did it' and congratulate yourself on a job well done, but I would never have hurt Isla. I wouldn't hurt *anyone*."

"Then why wouldn't you go public with your relationship?" There has to be a good reason he kept it concealed. Isla is someone he should have been proud to date. Gorgeous, smart, kind, funny...my sister is a prize.

Julian averts his gaze, and I spot a movement in his jaw that tells me he's clenching his teeth. I'm glad to have touched on a sore subject. Maybe I'll finally get closer to some answers.

"It's complicated," he bites out.

"Isn't it always? Let's see if I can keep up with this complex plot." I cross my arms, waiting. I'm sick and tired of being kept in the dark. Bullshit answers aren't gonna fly today.

Julian scrubs his hand over his face and keeps it resting over his mouth. He closes his eyes for the briefest moment and shakes his head once. As if coming up with a response is a struggle.

"Spit it out," I demand. I'm losing patience, but I also need to create some momentum here. If Julian slows down enough to wonder why he owes me any answers at all, I'm either going to have to tell him the truth—which I don't want to do—or walk away with my tail between my legs. Better to bully my way through than give him a chance to put up his defenses.

He blows out a harsh breath. "Look, I can admit now that it seems...less important than it once did. Especially after everything that's happened. But the truth is, my father absolutely *despises* Peter Vale. They competed for *everything* when they were at school together here at Wickham. Sports, academics, girls...eventually the friendly rivalry turned not-so-friendly. It should have been the kind of thing that ended after graduation, but it's like Peter could never let it go. Did you know that at their ten-year reunion, Peter started a rumor that my father had had an affair? Who *does* that, Belinda? The man is a monster."

"That's...horrible. I'm so sorry, Julian. I can understand why—"

"The two of them have been in direct competition with each other going on two decades," he says, interrupting what was going to be very heartfelt agreement that Peter Vale does indeed sound like a monster. Julian doesn't realize what a receptive audience he has in me, especially when it comes to dunking on Peter. Do you know what my father does for a living?"

"No." Why would I?

"He's the deputy head at Brookfield Academy—our rival school. But what people don't realize is that my father applied for the headmaster position *here* when it came open several years ago. My dad wanted that position so badly, and Peter Vale put a stop to it. He convinced the board that my father would be a terrible choice and campaigned hard for Harrington instead," Julian explains, his voice dripping with disgust. "One more thing my father wanted that Peter Vale took. Dad was distraught for weeks, and then he got...angry. So angry. He's not the same man he was before it happened."

If anyone can understand hating Peter Vale, it's me. But could Mr. Ashworth have decided to take his anger out on his nemesis's daughter? My gut says Julian was telling the truth when he said he wouldn't hurt Isla or anyone else. But what about his father? How far might he be willing to go in the name of a twenty-year-long grudge?

I've been assuming that whatever happened to Emily and Isla had something to do with the two of them—what they knew, or did, or said. But maybe I should have been thinking about Peter this whole time. Who else has he harmed? And who would want to harm him in return, maybe by hurting his daughter? I wouldn't be surprised to learn that the list of people Peter has pissed off is a mile long.

Is Isla in a coma because of our father?

Scrambling for a response that doesn't reveal I'm considering whether Julian's dad could be a murderer, I ask, "But wait—if your dad works at another private school, why do you even go here?"

Julian scoffs. "I'm a seventh-generation legacy. You don't just *give up* that kind of social capital."

I think I just experienced the living definition of "rich people problems," and I have to say...zero out of ten stars, would not recommend experiencing again.

I'm saved from having to respond to *all that* when Julian continues. "What Peter Vale did…it convinced me that every complaint and bad feeling Dad has been going on about my whole life was with reason. The Vales are terrible people. I firmly believed that." Another exhale leaves him, and he shakes his head. "And then I met Isla."

It's the reverent way he says my sister's name that has me perking up. "You hated her on sight?"

Julian sends me an incredulous look. "More like love at first sight, though I know that sounds unforgivably pedestrian of me. But she was so damn beautiful. Sweet and funny, with the best smile. She fell for me as hard as I fell for her, but we were destined to be nothing but Romeo and Juliet. Because no two houses at Wickham hated each other more than the Ashworths and the Vales. Well—at least not until the Wells-Pembroke feud unfolded in real time this year."

An aggravated sound leaves me. I do not want to talk about Connor and his problems right now. "Don't change the subject. Do you really expect me to believe you kept the girl you were madly in love with a secret because you were afraid Daddy might take your feelings as a personal betrayal? You know Shakespeare is fiction, right?"

"Of course I know!" Julian's cheeks are red, and his eyes flare wide. He looks angry. "And of course now, with twenty-twenty hindsight, I can see that I should've been open about my relationship with Isla from the start. Maybe then…"

His voice drifts, and he presses his lips together for a moment before he speaks in a hushed tone. "Maybe then someone would let me see her. Let me sit next to her and hold her hand and—"

Julian turns his back to me with a loud sniff. It's like he can't face me if he's showing any real emotion. A small part of me feels bad for pushing him to confess his feelings. His very big, obviously very real feelings for my sister.

When he turns to face me once more, he's got his hand clenched into a fist and resting against his mouth. His eyes are glassy, but I don't think he's shed any tears. I guess it's true what they say about the British and their stiff upper lips.

"I miss her terribly," he whispers when he drops his hand. My heart aches for him. *So do I*, I want to tell him. Neither of us should have to be alone in our grief, but missing Isla together would put finding the truth in jeopardy. So I keep my mouth shut, letting this boy believe he's suffering in solitude.

It's just one more way I'm lying to the world, but it feels like a brand-new low.

"I'm sorry, Julian. I'm so, so sorry." And I mean it. I am sorry that he's gone through this. Julian has never seemed as terrible as his peers at Wickham. Maybe a broken heart has softened him.

"It's been so difficult, not knowing how she's doing. I can't believe she still hasn't woken up. What if she never wakes up? I can't ask anyone about her, either. Can you imagine if I rang up her father and requested an update? My father would kill me, because you know Peter Vale would rush to tell him." Julian's voice breaks, and I can't hold back anymore—I close the distance between us and wrap him up in a big hug.

Julian returns it, the both of us clinging to each other. His shoulders shake, and maybe he is crying after all? I almost want to cry, too. We've both been suffering in silence, and it's just not fair.

I only realize someone else has entered the clock tower lobby when I hear the clang of a door slamming. I lift my head, and Julian does, too, both of us glancing toward the entrance to find…

Connor.

CHAPTER SIXTEEN

I spring away from Julian as if he's contagious with a deadly disease while my brain scrambles to come up with a proper explanation. Seeing the confused expression on Connor's face as he stares at us doesn't help. The flicker of irritation in his silvery gray eyes is more than obvious, and it sends my heart into free fall. My first impulse is to run to him and beg for forgiveness.

Forgiveness for...what, exactly? You haven't done anything wrong.

"Hey Connor." I offer him an awkward wave and immediately drop my hand because wow, I must look guilty.

He nods, his gaze shifting to Julian. "Julian. Are you all right?"

Connor's voice is hesitant. This is probably the last thing he expected to see, and my second impulse is to overexplain everything to him in painfully specific detail. Throw it all out into the open, though I can't. After all, most of this isn't my story to tell.

I glance over at Julian, who's got a contrite expression on his face as he runs a hand through his hair. "I'm…good, mate. Thank you for asking."

"I was just leaving the dining hall when I saw you walking and—anyway, it looks like you two need a minute, then. I'll be waiting outside for you, Belinda." Connor's gaze locks with mine, and I can sense he has so many questions, but he's being respectful. I'm guessing it's because he noticed the distraught look on Julian's face—his glassy eyes and flushed cheeks.

Connor leaves the lobby, and I want to collapse with relief. "I won't tell him anything, Julian. I promise."

"He's a right good friend. I can't deny it." Julian slowly shakes his head. "Better than I've ever been for him. You can go ahead and tell him, Belinda, if it makes things easier for you. I mean, you don't need to go into all the sordid details, but if you let it slip that Isla and I are in a relationship, I won't hold that against you."

The way he uses the present tense—*Isla and I are in a relationship*—makes me want to wrap him in another hug. She's not gone. Not yet. Maybe not ever. The hope I'm too afraid to look at directly shimmers on the edge of my awareness like a mirage. She could wake up and be okay. It seems impossible, and yet…

"Are you sure?" I'm shocked at how easily he gives me permission. "You can trust me. I know how to keep a secret."

"So does Connor. I doubt he'll tell anyone about this, either." Julian gives me a quick hug. "Thank you for letting me unload on you. I feel much better."

I don't bother reminding Julian that I came at him like he's a criminal I wanted to catch in a lie. If he feels better after revealing his secrets, maybe he won't even remember that I knew about him and Isla in the first place. I'm glad I could be there for him, even if the circumstances were less than friendly at first.

"Thank you for telling me." I offer him a small smile, and he returns it.

We exit the clock tower together, and I join Connor where he's waiting for me. The guys exchange a fist bump as Julian passes, but he doesn't stop—just keeps walking toward the dorms. His head is angled down, probably heavy with thoughts of Isla. Regrets he has about their time together. Hope that he'll have a chance to make it right.

Once Julian is out of hearing distance, I offer Connor a simple explanation. "He needed someone to talk to."

"So he chose to confess his deepest, darkest secrets to the new girl on campus?" Connor frowns. "Make it make sense for me, Billie. I'm not the jealous type, but I can admit I didn't love seeing the two of you together like that."

Guilt swamps me. "It was nothing, Connor. I promise. Sometimes...it's easier to confide in someone you haven't known since the day you were born."

"I suppose you're right." He scrubs his hand across his jaw, and I can practically feel the doubt radiating off him in subtle waves.

"I think he has a hard time talking to any of you about what he's going through because..." My voice drifts. I know Julian said it was okay if I told Connor about him and Isla, but it still doesn't feel like my story to tell. Then again, being truthful with Connor is starting to outweigh the importance of keeping anyone else's secrets. There's so much that I've kept from this boy that I care more and more about with each passing day. The need to tell him what we talked about makes my chest grow tight until it feels like my heart might burst. "It was about Isla."

Connor's frown deepens. "What about her?"

"They were seeing each other. Secretly. They had to keep it under wraps because of a…family feud, I guess? Seems like a bad reason to keep your girlfriend as classified information, but who am I to judge?"

"Ah, right. There's always been some tension between the Vales and the Ashworths," Connor says.

Hearing him say my last name throws me for a moment, but I brush it off. I put on a bright smile and curl my arm through his, shifting closer to his firm, warm body. "Will you walk me back to the dorms?"

"Like I can turn you down." He smiles at me, and we begin to walk in silence. After a minute or so, he says, "I think it was good of you. What you did for Julian."

"What do you mean?" I fight the nonstop guilt that wants to sweep over me like a wave and pull me to the bottom of the darkest part of the ocean. I was basically interrogating Julian until I broke him. That's not very good of me.

"Helping him out. Being someone he can count on." Connor sends me a knowing look. "That's hard to find around here."

"No kidding." The understatement of the year. You can't trust anyone on this campus. And everyone is keeping secrets.

Connor's phone dings with a notification, but he ignores it. "I think maybe that's why I was drawn to you at first. You seem steady in a way the rest of them aren't. Grounded. Like someone I could rely on."

"I'm stubborn." I lift my chin. It's an asset and a curse.

"Stubborn and beautiful." His smile is sly, and my heart skips a beat. "A winning combination, I might add."

"Ooh, you flatter me." I rest my free hand on my chest with a light laugh. I remember feeling like I'd found Belinda's laugh on the plane—a high, tinkling sound without any real warmth. But the sound I just made? It was…real. The happiness that's supposed to come with a genuine moment of lightness vibrates through me, nothing fake about it. Maybe there's a world where Billie Vale and Belinda Winters merge into someone who laughs like this all the time. In that fantasy, Isla and Mom are both hale and healthy, the boy next to me is as familiar to me as my own skin, and I…

I'm happy. Content.

I get pulled back to reality when Connor's phone dings again. And again. A cascade of alerts brings us to a halt in the middle of the path on the east side of the courtyard. One ding after the other sounds, all different pitches and tones. As if he's getting notifications from every app he's got.

"Something must be going—"Another notification interrupts him.

"Maybe you should check your phone?" I wince at the scowl that appears on his handsome face.

"Interruptions come at the worst time, I swear." With a little groan, he pulls his phone out of his pocket, then comes to a complete stop as he reads. "Holy shit."

Alarm streaks through me, and my skin goes cold. "What's wrong?"

I'm overwhelmed by instant, pervasive anxiety about what

kind of news could trigger so many alerts on Connor's phone. A headline about a student, perhaps? *Second Student Death at Wickham Academy...*

My fingers itch to reach for my own phone, to see if Peter or Whitney texted me. They *would* text me if something happened, right? Peter might not think to include me, but surely Whitney...

"I set up Google notifications for my father's name, so I know when he's mentioned somewhere online." He lifts his head, his gaze meeting mine. "An article about the case published not five minutes ago on a major news site." He pauses and glances at the phone again like he has to confirm what he just read. "Freddie's dad has been arrested, and my dad...it says he's the centerpiece of a sting operation orchestrated by the National Crime Agency."

"What?" My earlier alarm has been replaced by complete and utter shock. "Does this mean your father was never guilty in the first place?"

Connor grins. Oh, he looks pleased. "That's exactly what it means."

"Oh my God. Connor." I hug him, and he holds me close while burying his face in my neck. His entire body seems to relax against mine, and I tighten my arms around him. This changes everything for Connor and his family. "That's incredible. Like, legit not believable. And amazing! You must be so happy right now."

He pulls away so we can look at each other. "It's all such a relief."

His reaction is big, but not quite as big as I think it should be, considering the circumstances. How heavily his father's supposed crime has weighed on him. How it changed *everything* for him at school. "Did you know? About your father working with the NCA?"

He pulls his bottom lip under his top teeth, buying time. I lift a finger to his mouth and gently pull his lip free. Without saying a word, I want him to know that he can tell me anything. That a lie won't end what's between us—especially not one as important as this.

"I didn't have any idea at first. I couldn't believe it when my father was first arrested. That he would even *think* of stealing from his clients seemed totally ludicrous. It must have, for anyone who really knows him." His expression turns grim. "I felt it in my soul from the start that he could *never* have done what they said he did. He's the best man I know. He always has been."

"You said 'at first,'" I point out, curious. "Does that mean…"

A ragged exhale leaves him. "An agent from the NCA contacted Mum earlier this week. She told me there would be a break in the case soon and that it would be good news."

Smiling, I reach out and cradle his stubble-roughened cheek. "That's wonderful. You must be so happy."

He leans into my touch, his expression serious. His smile has faded, and even his eyes are dim. Troubled. "You're not angry at me, are you?"

"Angry?" I drop my hand from his face and rest it on his chest, right above his thrumming heart. "Why would I be?"

"I've kept this from you for days." He hangs his head. "I felt terrible about it, too. My mother made me swear I wouldn't tell a single soul until the news was announced, and

I promised her I'd stay quiet. But it killed me that I couldn't tell you, Billie."

It's downright laughable, thinking about all the secrets I'm keeping from Connor and here he is, overwhelmed with guilt for keeping a secret for actual legal purposes. His biggest sin is nothing but a small omission, while mine is an outright lie. Multiple lies. A whole identity's worth. His secret is a tiny pebble compared to the mountain of untruths I've built.

I touch his face again, forcing him to look at me. "Sometimes you have to hide the truth in order to protect the people you love. I could never be angry at you for that."

He smiles and drops a kiss on the tip of my nose. "You're the perfect girl, you know that? Always there for me. Always compassionate and understanding."

The corners of my eyes sting with tears, and I blink them away, not about to let him see me cry. I am far from the perfect girl. What is he going to think when he finds out my truth? How will he react? Eventually it'll all come out and he'll discover my connection to Isla. Will he be hurt? Furious? Will he refuse to talk to me ever again? I wouldn't blame him if he turned me away.

A cold gust of wind whips around us, and I shiver. "It's getting cold out here. Let's keep walking," I suggest.

Connor takes my hand, and it remains in his grasp for the rest of the walk to my building. He even escorts me inside, all the way up the three flights of stairs, and delivers me to the door of my room. Considering his own dorm is located on the west side of campus, in the complete opposite direction of mine, the chivalry seems especially sweet.

"Wow, such excellent service," I tease.

"When I said I'd walk you home, I meant it." He smiles and leans in, kissing me briefly. I reach for him before he can pull away, my hand against the back of his neck to keep him in place. He kisses me again. And again. Our lips parting. Our tongues tangling.

He rests his hands on my hips and presses me against the door while he devours me. The kiss becomes heated fast, and my mind starts to float. Contemplating if I should invite him inside. Hopefully Priya isn't in there...

His phone rings, but he ignores it, as do I, though the sound brings me back to reality. To the fact that we're making out in the hallway, where anyone can see us. Belinda wouldn't hesitate to make a private moment public, but this? I want this just for me.

The ringing stops, but only for a brief moment before it starts again. I try to pull away from him, needing the distance so I can gather my wits about me, but his grasp on my waist is too firm.

"What if that's your mom?" My breaths are coming heavy and fast, as are Connor's.

He quickly checks his phone. "It is. But she can wait." He dips his head again, and I rest my fingers against his mouth, stopping his descent.

"This is a big moment for your family," I remind him, my voice low. "Some of the best news you've received in a long time. You should talk to her, Connor. Celebrate with her."

"You're right." He presses his forehead against mine and stares into my eyes. "Always right."

"I'll never let you forget you said that." I poke him lightly in the chest, making him chuckle. "Text me later?"

"Absolutely." He kisses me one last time and pulls away, walking backward for a few steps, like he can't bear to tear his gaze from me. Then he flashes me a dopey, downright lovesick grin and turns, heading for the stairs.

I watch him go, marveling at how light he seems. I can't help but wonder if I'll ever get to experience that feeling. Will I find resolution for my family and justice for Isla? I hope so.

Once I unlock the door, I'm relieved to find my room empty. I collapse on top of my bed with my phone and go straight to Google, searching for the article. It pops up immediately, like the Internet can't wait to tell me what I want to know.

LUMATEG LUMINARY ARREST SHOCKS CITY

Juno Siegel, The London Ledger

LONDON – In a shocking development that has rattled the city's investment community, William Pembroke, long-time lead portfolio manager for private equity fund Lumateg Group, was arrested late last night on multiple counts of embezzlement, according to officials familiar with the case.

Pembroke, 46, has been widely regarded as the architect of Lumateg's sustained success over the past decade. The boutique asset management firm, famously founded in 2006 by inherited wealth from Pembroke's society marriage, has weathered market shocks and sector downturns with what many analysts have described as 'remarkable resilience'—a resilience frequently attributed to Pembroke's leadership and investment strategy.

That narrative was thrown into disarray on Tuesday when investigators confirmed that Pembroke is alleged to have siphoned off company and client funds over several years, using complex internal transfers and offshore structures to conceal the activity.

The arrest comes mere months after senior analyst Jonathan Wells was detained on similar charges. At the time, Wells's arrest raised questions about oversight within the firm but was widely viewed as the possible work of a single rogue employee.

However, sources close to the investigation have now revealed that Wells had in fact been working in conjunction with the National Crime Agency (NCA), acting as a critical set piece in an elaborate sting operation to uncover what is being described as a 'broader and more sophisticated scheme' allegedly orchestrated by Pembroke.

Internal documents obtained by *The London Ledger* appear to indicate reckless spending in Pembroke's personal portfolio. The records, which span the last three years, show that Pembroke made a series of substantial real estate acquisitions that seem incongruous with his disclosed compensation and declared assets.

Among the purchases are several high-value commercial properties in London's financial district and midtown Manhattan, along with a luxury bungalow on Laucala Island in Fiji, a private resort enclave known for its multimillion-dollar villas and strict confidentiality provisions for buyers. Property filings reviewed by this reporter indicate that the Laucala bungalow was acquired through a layered network of holding companies and trusts, obscuring the ultimate beneficial owner.

The Lumateg Group issued a brief statement immediately after the arrest, confirming Pembroke has been suspended from all duties pending the outcome of the investigation.

The headline has it right—this really is a shocking development. But what piques my interest isn't the way Freddie's dad defrauded the investors who put their trust and wealth in his hands. No, the detail rocking my world right now is way more basic.

William Pembroke. Is this the same William that Headmaster Harrington was arguing with on the phone?

My guess is a resounding yes.

CHAPTER SEVENTEEN

The news of William Pembroke's arrest has spread all over campus by the next morning. Everyone seems to be talking about it. In the dining hall and in classrooms. In the admin office and outside in the quad, where students hang out between classes. The name Pembroke is on everyone's lips, though Freddie is nowhere to be found, and I can't blame him. I wouldn't want to show my face around here, either.

And while yes, it's huge, what happened to William Pembroke, I can't help but get stuck on all the news *I* uncovered over the last twenty-four hours or so. Priya is a pill-popping, test-selling, anxiety-addled mess of an overachiever. Abigail would do anything for love, but a murder charge would separate her from Priya—a huge risk I suspect she wouldn't be willing to take. Julian's love for Isla is so all-consuming, he literally can't stop himself from referencing Shakespeare when he talks about their relationship. And the ultimate discovery: Connor's dad was innocent of the embezzlement charges all along.

What does any of this mean for Emily and Isla? Time is running out. It's Wednesday. My sister will be formally charged for Emily Wells's murder by the end of the day on Friday. I'm fairly certain I know who *didn't* hurt the girls, but I'm not any closer to figuring out who is responsible, and I'm frustrated.

So frustrated that I break down and contact Peter Vale. I need to know if his beef with *certain people* is a strong enough reason for them to have hurt Isla, as a way of getting at Peter.

When I pull up our text thread, the last message about reading the dossier feels like it was from another lifetime. How is it possible that little more than a week has passed since then?

Me: *Did you really try to convince people that Mr. Ashworth was having an affair?*

Satisfaction curls through me at my message. There's no need to hold back. We're getting down to the wire, and I need to look at new angles.

Peter: *Why are you asking about ancient history when Isla is days from being charged?*

Billie: *Answer the question.*

Ugh, I'm being a bitch, but come on! We don't have time to waste.

Peter: *It was a joke between friends. Nothing more.*

Huh. That's some joke. More like it's a serious accusation.

Billie: *Doesn't seem like Mr. Ashworth agrees with you.*

Peter: *What? That it was a joke?*

Billie: *That you two were friends.*

After waiting for a few minutes and receiving no response, I leave the library and head outside. The sky is clear and the air is crisp and cool, but most of the campus is quiet. Almost peaceful.

What a crock of shit. There is no peace on this campus. Too many people are keeping secrets and faking genuine friendships to maintain any sense of calm around here.

As I head for the dining hall, my gaze snags on the alumni garden. I remember the epitaph on the boy's statue: *The only danger in Friendship is that it will end.*

Is the real danger never knowing who's your friend or your enemy? I thought I was good at reading people. That I had solid common sense coupled with street smarts. But the people at Wickham—in every generation, it seems—are on another level. It's like you don't even know someone's stabbing you in the back until the blade is already sinking into your flesh. I'm always watching, always listening, but it feels like someone is lying in wait. Just dying to trip me up and call me out as the fraud that I am.

At least one person here on campus knows about my connection to Isla—they found the yearbook and left it out so I'd know my cover was blown. But I've been here long enough that if the culprit wanted me to know their identity, they could have approached me at any time. Hell, they all think I'm an American socialite with deep pockets; I would have expected an extortion attempt at the very least. But it's been crickets from whoever snooped through my stuff that first day.

The shrill ring of my phone startles me, and I pull it out of my sweater pocket, shock streaming through my blood and leaving me cold.

Peter Vale's name flashes across the screen.

This is only the second time he's voluntarily called me in my life, and it throws me completely off-balance. I slide the answer button and lift the phone to my ear, and he's already talking.

"You should know better than to put things like that in writing, Belinda." His tone reeks of frustration and annoyance.

"Well hello to you, too, Peter." I let my sarcasm fly because why not? We're way past niceties here.

"Why are you asking about Maximillian? Everything between us was so long ago, it's ancient history. You need to be focused on the present. On Isla. We're running out of time. I warned you not to become distracted."

Now I'm mad. "I *am* focused, Peter. In fact—"

He cuts me off. "Are you telling me you believe Max Ashworth could've...hurt Isla? Because so help me God, if he's responsible, I will rip him limb from limb and bury the pieces—"

"*Peter!* Calm down. I'm not saying he did or didn't. You brought me here so I could dig into the culture here, try to understand what was really going on with her life and who might've wanted to hurt her and Emily. But did you ever stop to consider that someone hurt her because they wanted to get to *you*?"

He goes silent, though I can still hear him breathing. It's possible that for the first time in his life, he's considering how his actions might have put his daughter in danger. God knows he didn't think about that when he shipped me to America with Mom. But now that his beloved youngest child might have suffered the consequences for *his* mistakes, he might suddenly care. If someone other than Isla was lying in a hospital bed as part of Peter's great awakening, I might be able to take some satisfaction in it.

But it's not someone else.

It's my sister.

And even Peter discovering he's not invincible isn't enough of a reason for her to be hurting.

When Peter begins to speak again, his voice is taut and hushed, like a rope so frayed it'll break with the next strong gust of wind. "You're asking if I've ever thought someone would hate me enough to throw my daughter off a cliff? No, Belinda. The thought never even crossed my mind. But..."

Maybe it should have goes unspoken. Does he have regrets? Does he feel foolish for not considering that everything happening to Isla could be because of him? He's a powerful man, and you don't become that powerful without making a few enemies along the way. Enemies who would do anything to take you down.

Like try and kill a beloved family member.

I notice that when Peter talks about Isla, he refers to her as "my daughter," and never "my youngest daughter" or "one of my daughters." Like I'm never on his mind at all. Even now that we're on the same continent and working together(ish) toward a common goal, he still talks as if he only has one child. And that hurts.

Oh, how I wish I could point out that little factoid, but now isn't the time. He'll just say I'm distracted. Ask me why I'm thinking of myself when I should be thinking of Isla.

And he'd be right.

"Look." I clutch my phone close to my face, my lips practically brushing the screen. "I have to go. I'll let you know if I discover anything else."

I end the call before he can respond and just stand there for a moment, replaying our conversation. What we said and, maybe more importantly, what we didn't say.

"Hey."

I whirl around at the sound of the familiar voice, almost dropping my phone. Sophia is standing in front of me, her normally happy-go-lucky expression gravely serious. "Hi." I try to smile at her, but the expression falls from my face almost instantly.

Her expression doesn't change, either. "We need to talk."

...

Peter might not have wanted text exchanges between us as potential evidence, but he clearly never considered that phone conversations in public spaces can be overheard. I'm a bundle of nerves while Sophia leads me back to the library, both of us silent. We walk through the back entrance, and she pulls me into a study room. The moment she has the door shut and locked, she's on me.

"What's going on?" Sophia's voice is surprisingly stern. "What are you, some sort of undercover detective snooping around the school?"

"No, of course not!" My response is too quick. I sound like a liar even to my own ears. I don't know if the exhaustion of living a double life finally breaks something in me, or if I was already too broken before I got here. Either way, I feel my defenses crumble under Sophia's earnest stare. "More like I'm an...undercover sibling."

I'm trembling. Full of immediate regret. I shouldn't have said that. My chest is so tight, it's hard for me to draw in air while Sophia studies me. Like, *really* looks at me. She narrows her eyes and tilts her head to the right, remaining silent for so long I feel as if I might scream just to make some noise.

"You're Isla's sister," she finally says.

The panic swells inside me. "We don't look anything alike."

"It's not about your face." Sophia thrusts her index finger in my direction. "It's about...you. And how you act. Like Isla."

A tide of overwhelming emotion crashes over me and sends me straight into Sophia's arms. I cling tightly, so grateful when she returns the hug. It's such a huge fucking relief to have told her, to have someone at Wickham know who I really am. And while it's also scary and huge and I'm not sure where to go from here, it's just so damn comforting to acknowledge and embrace the connection I have to Isla.

She's my baby sister. I've had to deny that fact since the moment I stepped off Peter's plane. But I've spent years fighting the connection at home, too. Pretending Isla doesn't exist. Mom would fall apart any time her other daughter was mentioned, to the point that I kept any of my thoughts or stories about Isla to myself. It became too painful to acknowledge our connection at all. But now that Sophia knows, I can be

Billie Vale, Isla's big sister, on this side of the world.

Still in secret, of course, but it feels like a move in the right direction.

"How did you end up here?" Sophia asks once I let her go.

I proceed to tell her *everything*. My mouth is a fountain of facts and impressions and experiences as I try my best to remember every single detail about my discoveries from day one until now. When I mention Priya popping pills, Sophia finally interrupts.

"I fucking knew it. No one studies that much without some sort of illegal substance helping her along."

I almost want to laugh, but it's not funny. None of this is funny. And when I finally finish my story, I fall into a nearby chair and lean forward, hanging my head, completely spent.

Sophia rubs the space between my shoulder blades, trying to soothe me, which I appreciate. "What happens now?"

Lifting my head, I meet her gaze. "I don't know. Are you going to tell your dad about Priya and Abigail?"

Her response is automatic. "No way. Everyone already believes I'm a snitch, but the truth is, I don't care enough about any of these twats to actually get them in trouble. What would be the point?"

I feel bad for her. That our fellow students are so dismissive of her feelings. Like she's not even a real person in their eyes, which is tragic. Sophia is one of the nicest girls I've ever known. "I'm sorry they don't see you for who you really are. Because you are one of the best people I've met here. They're all missing out on your greatness."

"Aw, I'm touched." Sophia ducks her head for a second before flashing me a knowing smile. "Are you saying I'm...

better than Connor Wells?"

"Well...maybe the both of you are tied for first." We laugh together and then both go quiet. Like, seriously quiet. Enough to make me nervous. "Are you...mad at me? For lying? I mean, you have every right to be. You've been so kind since my arrival. You even invited me into your home. I slept in your bed. I wore some of your clothes. I wore one of your *swimsuits*."

That feels like a level of intimacy that deserves the truth.

"It's true that I do prefer to know the real identity of someone *before* we share spandex." Sophia's droll voice and dancing gaze make me relax a little bit. Enough that I roll my eyes at her. "But Belinda, you're out here trying to solve a *literal* murder. Wait—was I ever a suspect?"

I start laughing again. "You sound a little excited by the idea. Do you *want* to be a suspect?"

"I guess not. As much as I want to be a certified baddie someday, murder is a bit rich for my blood. Though..."

Sophia goes quiet, and I send her a questioning look.

"I'd make a terrific Watson to your Sherlock," she suggests.

She's so right. Sophia would be a tremendous help with my investigation. "That sounds amazing, actually. I could use that big, beautiful brain of yours. Only, Sophia?"

"Yes, Belinda?" Sophia is beaming. I can tell she loves the idea, too.

"Can you please call me Billie?"

...

A THOUSAND PERFECT LIES

I'm in my dorm room, trying to figure out what to wear on my date with Connor. I asked him what attire would be most appropriate, but he only said I always look nice and I should wear whatever makes me the most comfortable. Cute but not super helpful.

Priya and Abigail are in the room with me, curled up together on Priya's bed and quizzing each other on French vocabulary. If I didn't already know them so well, I'd find this scenario downright adorable. Like two sweet kittens helping each other out. But these kittens have serious claws.

I open the closet door, then stand in front of the mirror and start applying makeup while thinking about the tail end of my conversation with Sophia. While I didn't confess to her that I eavesdropped on her dad's phone call that one night, I did ask if she could find out what happened to a student named Nigel who probably attended Wickham around the same time as our parents. There are a few surnames on Isla's 1998 Legacy List that I haven't figured out yet, and maybe one of them belongs to Nigel?

Just as I finish my makeup, my phone buzzes with a text.

Watson: *Found him! His name is Nigel Carmichael.*

Sophia insisted on the update to her contact details in my phone, and while initially I thought it was just a cute gag, I'm starting to wonder if it's not a well-deserved moniker. She sends me a picture of Nigel's yearbook photo, and I study it closely. He's fair-skinned and blond, with a tiny gap between his two front teeth and a pleasant smile. He gives boyish, charming vibes. Harmless, even.

Watson: *Oh no.*

Me: *????*

Sophia sends a link to an article from a local newspaper's archives. I click on it with dread, skimming the words as fast as I can. Nigel Carmichael...student at Wickham Academy... dead at seventeen...family lost everything in a Ponzi scheme...

Nigel's death was ruled an accidental overdose. The article states that after the family went bankrupt, he and his younger brother abruptly withdrew from Wickham in the middle of the academic term. According to "a close friend of the family," Nigel never recovered from the financial and social blow.

The article is dated June 1998. Nigel was a student when Peter and Samantha were at Wickham. So was Percy Harrington. I'm assuming the conversation I overheard the night of the sleepover was...Percy trying to *protect* Connor. Wanting to make sure a student under his care didn't suffer because of his father's crimes, the way Nigel did. That's so reassuring.

I realize that Sophia comes by her kindness honestly—that her dad is one of the good ones, too, and that brings me even more comfort. There are a lot of assholes at Wickham, but the Harringtons aren't among them.

Me: *This is awful.*

Watson: *I know. And before you ask, I already checked the yearbooks for 1999 to 2003. The brother never came back to campus.*

I'm impressed with Sophia's sleuthing.

Me: *Ur good at this. I should've tagged you in sooner. <3*

Watson: *Anything else, Sherlock?*

Me: *Actually, yeah. Is ur mom home?*

Watson: *Umm yeah???*

Me: *You mentioned she's really into the green spaces on campus, right? Can u ask her about the statue in the alumni garden for me, please? Find out the guy's name?*

Watson: *That's relevant how?*

Me: *Might not be. But there are still a couple of names on the LL Isla was working on in the back of her yearbook. If he was a student in our parents' class, maybe...??*

It's farfetched, what I'm asking.

Me: *I'm reaching. Sorry.*

Watson: *Literally do not apologize. I'll talk to Mom at dinner and text u after. x*

I receive another text notification from Connor saying he's downstairs waiting for me. I send him a quick response that I'll be down in a minute before I pocket my phone. Checking my reflection one last time, I slick on some lip gloss and then slip on my shoes, going over what I just learned.

Percy Harrington put his foot down to a board member because he refused to see Connor suffer. I'm assuming that board member was William Pembroke. And while our headmaster obviously wanted to be sure history wouldn't repeat itself, Mr. Pembroke seems to have been counting on it.

If Connor had advance warning about the break in his father's case, who's to say the Pembrokes haven't known the other shoe was bound to drop eventually? What if William wanted to be sure the man responsible for exposing his crimes—Jonathan Wells—would suffer the unthinkable hurt of losing not one child...but two?

Even if breaking the law is a slippery slope, it's a long way from embezzlement to murder.

Or...is it?

CHAPTER EIGHTEEN

Connor is waiting for me outside his dorm building as I approach, and my skin warms at the way his gaze slowly sweeps over me. I'm wearing a simple, long-sleeved black dress with a row of tiny buttons at the bodice. I worried I might not be dressed up enough for this date, but from the appreciative gleam in Connor's eyes, I think I chose well.

"Billie." His voice is lower than normal. "You look... gorgeous."

He dips his head, his mouth briefly brushing mine—just enough of a tease to leave me flustered. "Thank you. So do you."

His outfit is simple yet effective. He's wearing a black cashmere sweater and charcoal gray slacks that show off his powerful build. He's freshly shaved, and his dark-brown hair is a bit of a mess on top. As if he's run his fingers through it continuously. Was he nervous? If so, that's adorable.

"Do you play a sport?" I ask suddenly, and it's such a random question that we both set loose little laughs into the air between us. His smile sends a jolt of serotonin straight to my brain, so I add, "You're from the UK, so I assume rugby and…water polo?"

"Tsk, tsk, my American friend. One can't forget footy and horse racing. What would the King think of your oversight?"

"Yeah, yeah," I say with an exaggerated, old-timey accent. "Tell that guy I'll throw his tea straight into the Boston Harbor if he gives me any lip." I know the smile on my face is too wide and goofy, but I can't contain it when Connor closes his eyes and looks up to the sky, silently asking God for patience. "But seriously. You're like, really fit. What gives?"

Even in the half-light of dusk, I spot his cheeks darkening with a little blush. "Well, thanks for that," he says, interlacing our fingers and leading us down a dirt path branching off the courtyard. "I'm not a team sport kind of guy. Solitary pursuits only to achieve this god-tier physique."

"Wouldn't wanna make the other guys jealous."

"Precisely. I run and lift weights. The past few months, blasting my music and working up a sweat felt like survival techniques, you know?"

I give his hand a squeeze before rising up on tiptoes to plant a soft kiss on his cheek. "That's all over now. Let's not talk about problems tonight. Just enjoy the time together."

"You're right. It's been a good day." His eyes crinkle at the corners when he smiles, and I step away, though I keep our hands linked. "Let's go."

"Where are we going?" I let him lead me along the path, and he walks a little slower so I can keep up with him.

"You'll see." He smirks. I bet he looked just like that when he was a little boy. Full of mischief and trouble, no doubt. "It's a surprise."

"Oooh, I can't wait." My stomach jumps in anticipation.

We make idle chitchat as we head deeper into campus, catching each other up on today's gossip around Wickham. I bring up Abigail and Priya's dorm room study date, and he sends me a knowing look.

"Those two are never apart."

"They obviously care about each other."

"I don't know if Abigail Roth has enough of a heart to really care about anyone," he says. "But I 100 percent believe she's as horny as the rest of us. I would bet you two whole donuts that one or both of them is naked right now."

"I'm not taking that bet because I'm sure you're right. But *two whole donuts*? What kind of bet is that?" I haven't really seen this silly side of Connor before. The world has been weighing heavy on his shoulders, I guess, and now that the weight has been lifted, he's…different.

Still damn cute.

"One donut is low stakes. Two? You've got to have the courage of your convictions for a two-donut bet." Connor chuckles.

The realization that there's still so much to discover about him sends a hot thrill of curiosity down my spine. How wry is his humor? How dry is his wit? How salty is the skin just behind the waistband of his pants? Curiosity will make me an excellent student for my new favorite subject.

I haven't known Connor for long, but the feelings spinning through me? Tornado strong. The eye of the twister is the hope that our date will afford me the opportunity to get my hands (and lips…and tongue) on him. I sip in a breath of cool night air in an effort to quench my thirsty thoughts.

We end up at one of the last buildings on campus. It looks like it's been here since the dawn of time. Constructed of faded, crumbling brick, the three-story structure is covered in a thick layer of ivy.

"We're going in here?" I gesture toward the building.

"Just wait until you see it." The promise in his voice has me excited, and I'm practically giddy as we run up the two flights of stairs. By the time we're at the top of the building, standing in front of a large metal door, I'm a little breathless from the climb and my entire body is tingling.

"Here we are." Connor opens the door, and I walk onto the rooftop, which has been transformed into a greenhouse. There are plants and flowers everywhere, with the walls and roof constructed of steel beams and glass. The air is humid, and it smells like fresh dirt mixed with sweet, green, floral scents. "What do you think?"

I turn to him, noting the smile on his face. The nervous flicker in his gaze. He wants me to love this—and I do.

I so do.

"It's beautiful." I throw myself at him, and he catches me, his arms tight around my waist. "I love it."

"Good," he murmurs against my temple, his lips brushing my skin. "I wanted to share this with you because I've always loved it, too."

I pull away from him so I can stare into his eyes. "How do you even know about this place?"

"My first year here, my art teacher suggested I take horticulture fundamentals. I thought it was a complete waste of time, but eventually the professor brought us up here to do some hands-on work with the plants and flowers, and I thoroughly enjoyed it. She explained the importance of 'budding artists' spending as much time in nature as possible. I've come here almost weekly ever since, save for when Emily…" He clamps his lips shut and shakes his head once. "This rooftop has become my sanctuary. It feels like I'm in another world."

"Almost like a jungle." I glance about the room, wondering if Mrs. Harrington spends time up here, what with her love of plants and flowers. "It's truly magical. There are even fairy lights."

Twinkling white lights have been strung up haphazardly all over the greenhouse, adding a whimsical element to the space.

"I added those." His cheeks turn ruddy as if he's embarrassed, and it's the cutest thing. "I wanted to make the night special."

I press myself into his side like a magnet, helpless against his pull. And it's true—I can't help myself. I need to touch him, to feel his solid heat beneath my hands. "It's already special."

When he kisses me, we get lost in each other for long, wet-hot minutes. Our hands wander and our breaths quicken until he finally pulls away, taking a step back as if he needs the distance. "We're getting ahead of ourselves."

My body sways, and he grabs my elbow, steadying me. "I don't mind."

"Well, I do." He chuckles. "We need to eat dinner."

"We're having dinner up here?"

Connor leads me to a small table covered in a pristine

white tablecloth with two silver dome plate covers at each setting. He holds my chair out for me, and I settle in, leaning over to breathe in the scent of the single white rose sitting in a glass vase in the center of the table.

"Was this grown in here?" I gesture to the rose.

"Actually, no. It came from the alumni garden." He sits across from me. "Ready to eat?"

I nod. "I'm starving."

"Let's see what we're having for dinner, then." The mysterious look on his face tells me he already knows.

On the count of three, we lift the domes off our plates and I gasp in surprise. There's a giant cheeseburger sitting on my plate, accompanied by a pile of skinny fries. I lift the sesame seed bun off the burger to find there are two strips of bacon crisscrossing the cheese and barbecue sauce slathered on the bun. "Oh my gosh, this is like a western bacon cheeseburger!"

Connor can barely contain his smile. "I heard that's what you miss the most, being here in the UK now."

"From who?" It dawns on me almost immediately. I complained to Sophia at one point that I was sorely missing cheeseburgers. American cheeseburgers. The dining hall serves them, but the buns are always soggy and the meat is too thin. Being stuck out here in the middle of nowhere means we can't go out to eat anywhere, either. "Sophia."

"She's a valuable source of information." He unwraps the cloth napkin from his silverware and sets it in his lap. I do the same. "I've never had a western bacon cheeseburger, as you call it."

"Well get ready to have your world rocked," I tease.

We start to eat, and the moment I sink my teeth into my

burger, I groan so loud I embarrass myself. It's too delicious to hold back, though, and within minutes I've devoured half of the burger while Connor has only taken a couple of bites.

"You like it?" he asks.

"It's delicious." I pour some ketchup onto my plate and dunk in a couple of fries. They're salty and crispy, and I immediately grab a couple more. "Where did you get all this?"

"I have my ways." His sly tone makes my stomach flutter. He most definitely has his ways. He only has to say a few words and I turn into a puddle. "I'm glad you're enjoying it."

"Are you?" I watch as he opens the tiny jar of mayo and pours some on his plate, then dips a fry in it. "I don't get the fries-in-mayo thing."

"Have you tried it?"

I shake my head. "It sounds disgusting."

"It's quite good." He swipes a couple of fries from my plate and dunks them in the mayo before holding them out toward me. "Try it."

Warily, I lean across the table and wrap my lips around the fries, our gazes locking. Holding. His intense stare has goose bumps breaking out all over my flesh as I chew slowly, then swallow hard. "Meh."

He bursts out laughing, shaking his head. "Meh? That's your response?"

I start laughing as well. The entire moment is a little absurd. Feeding me mayo-covered fries and getting all sexy with it. "It's kind of bland. That's what your country's cuisine is known for, right? Flavorlessness?"

"Ha. Ha," he deadpans. But a smile quirks the side of his mouth when he says, "Is that why I'm so drawn to you?

Because you bring flavor and texture and spice to my bland existence? You make me want to taste every moment we're together. Savor it."

Hot damn.

I love it when he talks like this, so open with his feelings. I'm always on guard, worried I might reveal too much, but this boy has been an open book with me lately, and it fills me with guilt. I want to share more with him. Tell him everything, though I know that's not possible. But revealing little, inconsequential personal facts about myself here and there—that's okay, right?

"I have my own reason for being drawn to you," I start, going silent when I see the light in his eyes. He definitely wants to hear those reasons, though I don't want to list the obvious ones. "For one, I like that you're an artist."

Connor tilts his head, appearing confused. "Why is that?"

"Well, my mother is an incredible artist. Not that I inherited any of her talent." I laugh softly. "I'm probably a disappointment in that area."

Not that my mother has encouraged me to create any art in the last few years. She hasn't painted for so long, I wonder if she's forgotten how.

"Your mother is an artist? Has she shown her pieces anywhere?"

I shake my head, my appetite disappearing when I think about Mom. "She doesn't paint anymore. She's…sick. And it's not the kind of sick that gets better, at least so far. Though I have hopes she'll recover soon and rediscover her artistic abilities. It gave her so much peace and joy, being able to paint. I miss that for her."

"I'm sure you do," Connor murmurs. "Is it hard, being so

far away from her?"

"Part of the reason I'm here is to give her time to get well." It's partially true, isn't it? Part of my agreement with Peter was to get Mom into the best rehabilitation center money can buy. I know she has to want to recover, and I'm hoping this time it works. For her.

And for me.

"I hope she does." The warmth in Connor's tone makes my shoulders relax. I reach for another fry and pop it into my mouth.

"I do too." A sigh leaves me, and I lean back in my chair. "I don't want to talk about depressing stuff."

"Me neither. Let's change the subject." He does exactly that, launching into a story about his father. "I spoke to him on the phone earlier. He sounds great, like the weight of an entire world has been lifted off his shoulders."

"I'm sure that's exactly how he feels." I reach across the table and tangle our fingers together. "I'm so happy for you, Connor. That your father has been exonerated. I'm sure your parents are glad it's all over."

"It's not quite over." He curls his fingers around mine. "There will be all sorts of legal depositions and a trial. My father believes there's plenty of evidence against William Pembroke, but he's a powerful man with strong ties to even more powerful people. What if he gets away with this?"

"He won't." My voice is firm. "I have a feeling he's not going to get away with this. I'm guessing he'll get serious prison time."

"He might, and then again, he might not." Connor keeps his head bent, his focus on our connected hands. "I don't know."

"Hey." He lifts his head at my strong tone. "Don't let the

doubts in. You've stood by your father through all of this. Have some faith and believe that justice will be served."

I need to take my own advice. I have to keep believing there will be justice for Emily and Isla. We're less than forty-eight hours away from Isla's potential arrest, and I can't let it happen.

"You're right." He lets go of my hand and pushes away from the table, rising to his feet. "Are you finished with your dinner?"

"Definitely." I stand as well, and he takes my hand again, leading me across the greenhouse to a makeshift tent created out of white cotton sheets, with more white fairy lights strung inside. A pile of blankets and pillows spills across the floor. The cozy setup has me squealing and throwing my arms around Connor. "You've gone all out tonight."

"I wanted to." His arms slide around my waist, pulling me in close. "I know we've only known each other a short time, but I—I care about you, Billie."

I stare up at him, getting lost in his dark-gray gaze for a few seconds. It's too fast for us to have feelings this big for each other. Logically, I know this, but I also know that being in a pressure cooker of drama and emotion, secrets and lies, life and death…it can change a person's perspective. Reveal what's really important. Make impossible intensity feel totally grounded in reality. I try not to overthink the words on the tip of my tongue. I just let myself feel. "I care about you, too, Connor."

"I felt so hopeless before," he admits, bending down so he can press his forehead against mine. "What happened to my dad. My sister. I didn't understand why you'd want to be around me at all. I felt like a disease that would infect anyone who got too close. But now, after my father's been cleared, I feel more…whole. Even before that, though, you were starting to bring me back to myself. You made me feel needed. Wanted. Like an actual normal human being instead of the empty shell I'd been for the last few months. I thought I wouldn't be able to feel anything anymore, but you convinced me otherwise, and I can't thank you enough for that."

You've done the same for me. The words crawl up my throat, demanding to be released. But they come dangerously close to revealing what I can't, so instead of saying anything, I press my mouth to his, cutting myself off. He returns the kiss but pulls back too soon to stare into my face, concern overpowering the lustful haze in his eyes that must be a mirror of my own. Can he sense my uneasiness? My need to forget my problems for the next few hours and just be? Does he understand that feeling?

He has to.

His mouth returns to mine, and he slides his hands into my hair, gently tugging, holding me in place. I absorb him, wishing he would swallow me whole. I run my hands up and down his back before pulling him closer. He presses his big body close to mine, and I lean into his heat, his strength, letting him guide me backward until we're both on the floor, lying on the pile of blankets he made just for me. For us.

He's consuming me, and I match his hunger with an incessant, almost desperate need that beats like a drum in my chest. Between my legs. It pushes me to yank on his shirt and pull it from where it was tucked into his trousers. He doesn't stop me, just urges me on with the low groan that sounds deep in his chest when I touch his bare skin. I skim my fingernails along the smooth skin of his back, his side, his flat stomach, my touch making him shudder. I spread my thighs, and he nestles his hips between them, slowly pushing against me as we kiss and kiss, letting me feel him. He's hard. Big. I'm not scared, though. I want it.

I want him.

We're a scrambling mess as we strip off each other's clothes. I marvel at the sight of his firm chest, and he traces the edge of my pale pink bra, his fingers making my exposed skin pebble with goose bumps.

It's too much and not enough until eventually we've discarded our clothes and our legs get tangled up as we reach for each other, hungry mouths clashing, tongues tangling. Breaths panting in time to the beat of our hearts. He's hot, his skin slick with a faint sheen of sweat, and he pauses at one point, reaching under one of the pillows for the condom he clearly stashed there earlier. He wordlessly holds it up to show me, and I nod, afraid he might say something to ruin the moment, but he doesn't.

I reach for him, our mouths connecting, chests pressed together, heartbeats matching time. He works his way down my body, his mouth touching me in places that make me shiver. Make me moan. His fingers explore between my legs, then begin to stroke, ratcheting my need for him higher and higher still, until I'm falling apart with his name on my lips, my entire body engulfed in shivery flames.

When he rolls on the condom and finally works his way inside me, I close my eyes, my body going tense. His mouth finds the sensitive spot behind my ear, licking and sucking the skin there until a shudder shimmers all the way to my toes. "You feel so fucking good, Billie," he whispers as he begins to move.

I let myself go, shutting my mind off, telling myself I can forget why I'm here for one night. I want this. I deserve this.

I do.

...

I wake up the next morning confused, unsure at first of where I am. But then it all comes rushing back to me in a flood of delicious memories and I fall back against the soft stack of pillows, closing my eyes with a smile.

Last night was…amazing. Magical. We talked long into the night, until we eventually fell asleep wrapped in each other's arms, but now he's nowhere to be found.

Sitting up, I push my hair out of my eyes and look around, spotting the white rose from dinner and a note from Connor resting on his empty pillow.

Meet me in the art room for breakfast. You've inspired me to paint again.

X—C

Giddy, I hurriedly get dressed and head for the art room. It feels like I'm walking on air the entire way. Are the birds chirping louder than usual? Is the rising sun brighter this morning? It certainly feels that way. My cheeks hurt, and I realize it's because I'm smiling so much. What's gotten into me?

Connor, the naughty voice whispers in my brain, making me giggle.

Luckily, it's early enough and hardly anyone is out yet. I can have a quick breakfast with Connor and then go back to my room to change into my uniform before classes start. I have plenty of time.

I glide into the art room, coming to a stop when I see Connor sitting at a small table in the middle of the room, his face as blank as the empty canvas nearby. On the table is Isla's yearbook and the dossier Peter and Whitney gave me.

My heart, my entire body, is in free fall. My brain scrambles to come up with an explanation, but I've got nothing. Absolutely nothing.

"What the hell is this, Billie?" Connor stands, waving at the yearbook and the dossier. "Who are you? Why are you at Wickham?"

"I never— I didn't want you to find out like this." Tears are already streaming down my face, dripping off my jaw, but I don't bother wiping them away. I'm devastated by the look on his face. He's angry, that much is obvious, but I can also see the hint of pain in his gaze. I betrayed him. Hurt him. After everything he said last night and what happened between us, this is how I repay him.

"Find out what, exactly? What are you, some sort of spy?"

I crack out a laugh, but there's nothing humorous about it. "I'm—I'm Isla's sister."

His incredulous expression says it all. "Bullshit."

"It's true. Our parents separated when we were young. I went to the States with our mom while Isla stayed here with our father. Peter Vale is my dad." I sniff, shaking my head once. "We're not close at all, and I hadn't heard from him in more than ten years before he called to tell me about Isla, but yeah. He's my dad."

Connor looks away from me, working his jaw. I can feel the anger radiating from him, and I want to throw myself at him. Fall to my knees and beg forgiveness.

But that would be a lost cause. I can tell from his body language that he's completely closed himself off from me. I've ruined everything.

"Peter Vale asked me to come to Wickham to try and figure out who hurt Isla and your sister," I admit, hating how my voice trembles. "We don't have much time left. Isla will be arrested by the end of tomorrow, but I know she didn't do it."

His gaze meets mine once more. "Who did, then?"

"I don't know!" I throw my hands into the air. "I'm still trying to figure it out."

Connor scoffs, shaking his head. "Good luck with that. If you don't know already, you're never going to be able to figure it out, Billie. If that's even your real name."

The tears come faster now, but I remain silent. There's no point in arguing. He's through with me.

"You need to leave." His tone is like ice, cold and unfeeling. "Leave this campus and go back home to the States with your sick mom. Is she even ill? Or was that another lie? It doesn't matter. You don't belong here. If you're not gone by the morning, I'm going to tell everyone who you really are and blow your supposed investigation wide open. I'm sure the police would love to know Peter planted someone with a fake identity on campus to, what? Impede their investigation? Sounds like a good reason to go to jail. And even if he's a shit dad, you can take it from me: watching your father get hauled away in handcuffs is the actual worst."

"What about watching your sister get charged with a crime she didn't commit? Do you think that comes close?"

He clenches his jaw and just looks at me, letting me hear my words play back in my head. I cringe, but there's no unsaying them. Connor will never watch his sister do anything ever again, good or bad. I can't believe I let something so insensitive slip out of my mouth.

He pushes past me and exits the classroom before I can say a word, the door slamming behind him like the final blow that sends me to my knees. I cry and cry with my hands covering my face. It's over.

Belinda Winters is no more.

CHAPTER NINETEEN

I arrive at the hospital in the early evening after ordering a car to London, adding the cost to the PETER PAYBACK note in my phone. Even if I failed in my mission here, I can't let myself go home poorer for it. It will be hard enough to put myself back together after I eventually shatter into a million pieces. Because that's how I feel—like there are fissures running through every part of me, and sooner or later, I'll fall apart in a catastrophic shower of glass.

I've been a mess all day. I can't eat. Can't stop crying. I even vomited at one point, overwhelmed by the swirl of emotions in my body. I'm a failure. A fraud. I'm trying to do good, and instead I hurt the people I care about most.

Like Isla.

Like Connor.

Leaving Wickham is the only way to salvage this whole horrible situation. Connor was right; if I stay and he exposes me, Peter could get in serious trouble. There may be no love lost between us, but that doesn't mean I want to see him put in jail or charged with a crime. Even if I think he deserves it a little bit, Whitney certainly doesn't.

Keeping my head down, I enter the hospital and head straight for the elevator, finding Isla's floor like a carrier pigeon flying to its coop. I wish I had a better message to bring her, but I'll have to tell her I failed. Still, I need to see her one last time before I leave. She has to know how badly I fucked everything up, if only so she'll understand how hard I've been trying to get it right. Not that she can hear me, but I need to get it out. Will purging my mistakes make me feel better? Probably not.

But I'm doing it anyway.

I find her room and slip inside before coming to a complete stop. Peter Vale is sitting at his younger daughter's bedside, watching her immobile body like the force of his concentration alone could wake her up at any moment. He glances in my direction and stands, his expression thunderous as he approaches.

"What are you doing here?" His harsh voice has me on the verge of tears, but I refuse to fall apart in front of this cruel man.

"I came to see her."

"Why? Have you discovered something? You should've called me. Our time is limited. Tomorrow is our last chance to file a formal injunction and stop the charges. How are you going to help us save Isla?" Peter is breathing hard, and there's a wild look in his eyes. Like he knows his entire world is going to come crumbling down around him if his daughter is arrested for killing her best friend.

"I don't know, okay?" I'm yelling, and I don't even care.

He's pushed me too far, though I was already on the brink of despair before I got here. "I don't know what to do anymore. All I've done is figure out who *didn't* do it. It wasn't Priya or Abigail or Julian or Connor. It definitely wasn't Sophia or any of the Harringtons."

Peter pounces on this information like a cat does a mouse. "You say it wasn't Julian, but what about Max? I haven't been able to stop thinking about what you told me."

I throw up my hands, moving past him toward the windows, trying to put a little distance between us. Peter's intensity is stifling, a fire taking up all the oxygen in the room. "He definitely hates you, but that doesn't explain how Emily ended up dead. Even if Mr. Ashworth wanted to get to you through Isla, I'd expect some sort of white-collar kidnapping scheme, or maybe he'd send Whitney some deepfakes of you with another woman. You know, to retaliate for your super funny joke at the last reunion," I explain with a roll of my eyes.

"The reunion." Peter scrubs a hand along his jaw, lost in thought. "Right."

He joins me at the window and stands there silently, staring out at the bleak cityscape like he can't bear to look at me. I study his profile, noting the way his once-sharp jaw is starting to soften around the edges. The version of Peter I'm most familiar with is the one in the picture of the four of us under the tree. All this time, I've been visualizing a ghost when I think of him. That man doesn't exist anymore. Hasn't for fifteen years. Now the man beside me is a different kind of specter. Haunted, rather than haunting.

"You didn't happen to hear anything else about the reunion, did you?" he finally asks.

"You spreading rumors about a man's loyal wife having an affair kind of stole the spotlight that night." My sarcasm is on full display, because I am so over this entire thing. The back-and-forth and the secrets and lies. It's exhausting.

Peter whirls to face me, clearly frustrated. "You think you're so clever, Belinda, but not everything is as simple as you make it out to be. Max Ashworth's histrionics served a higher purpose that night."

"So what, stroking your ego is a higher purpose now?" My voice drips with disgust. "Sometimes I wonder what Mom ever saw in you..."

Peter storms toward me, and I flinch, fear streaking through my blood. I'm afraid of this man, my father, for the first time in my life. I scramble to the other side of Isla's bed, using it as a shield. He stays on his side of the bed, but his expression is enraged. We glare at each other, and I refuse to be the one who looks away first. Until my phone buzzes with a text notification. The first one I've received all day. It's a message from Sophia.

Watson: *Statue is George Canterbury. Died in 2008. Mom wouldn't say more, just that Peter Vale led the fundraising for the memorial.*

George. The name tickles the inside of my brain, like a feather dragged against the soft skin of a palm. Then all at once, it's like someone flips that feather around and jabs me with the pointy end.

George and Daphne, 1994.

The photo in the library at the Pembrokes' house. Whitney's friend Daphne was a Canterbury before she was a Pembroke.

I glance up from my phone to find Peter staring lovingly at Isla, all the ire of a moment before replaced with worry and fear. "Does the name George Canterbury mean something to you?"

The effect is immediate. Peter drops his head, and his shoulders start to shake. Is he laughing at me and my incompetence?

But then he makes a weird noise in his throat before quietly saying, "George Canterbury. I should have known it would come back to him eventually. Why are you asking?" He presses his fingers to his forehead and starts rubbing at his temple, his sharp features in shadow.

"Isla was making notes in the back of her yearbook, about the llamas from 1998. Canterbury was one of the names on her list, and it took me until just now to figure out who he was." Sophia's timing couldn't have been more perfect. "The statue in the alumni garden, and…he knew Mom, right? There's a photo of your class, and his arm is around her shoulders."

Peter lets out a ragged sigh, his head still bent. When he finally looks up at me, I see he wasn't laughing at all. His eyes are red and filled with tears, and he looks at least twenty years older. It's not just the softened jaw. Now I see what I missed before: bruise-colored circles under his eyes, salt-and-pepper stubble on his hollow cheeks. "Maybe this is my punishment." He gestures toward Isla. "Maybe when you keep a secret for such a long time, the universe decides to keep one from you in return."

I'm confused. Is he all right? "What are you talking about? Should I get…a doctor or something?"

"No. A doctor won't fix this. Sit down."

I fall into a nearby chair, apprehension making me shiver. I scoot closer to the bed and take Isla's hand, imagining her giving mine a comforting squeeze. As if to say, *we're in this together no matter what.* But of course, Isla can't squeeze my hand. The machines that surround her bed continue to beep their steady, unchanging rhythms. I want to scream in frustration, but I restrain myself.

On the other side of the bed, Peter drags another chair close to Isla. He sits, resting his elbows on the edge of the bed and clasping his fingers together loosely. If I didn't know better, I'd say it looks like he's preparing to pray.

"George was in my class at Wickham—mine and your mother's. He was popular. An athlete, a scholar. Bit of a ladies' man, though he never dated anyone seriously. Your mother... She had the biggest crush on him. Got all moony-eyed and flustered whenever he was around. I used to tease her about it. But oh, I was jealous." Peter stares into the distance, shaking his head.

Peter, jealous? I can't imagine it.

"Some of us stayed in touch after graduation," Peter continues. "Me, Jonathan, and William; Samantha, of course, though she was at the University of the Arts London and I was at Oxford. George took to the wind a bit. I heard he took a gap year, deferred his university acceptance. I didn't give him much thought, if I'm being honest. But...your mother did."

My mind is racing. What is he trying to tell me, and what does it all mean? He's talking like this is a deathbed confession, and the morbidness of it makes me want to crawl out of my skin. Because Peter is still here, and Isla...Isla hasn't woken up yet. With every day that passes, the possibility that she never will looms larger and larger on the horizon.

"As it turns out, George and your mother reconnected about three months before the ten-year reunion for the Class of 1998. She was working at a gallery in London by then, and he just walked into her local one night. Pure coincidence. They had a pint together. After that, they went to dinner and, well. I've never asked for the details, as you might imagine. But things happened, as they do." Peter grimaces while I sit still in the chair, hanging on to his every word.

"It was wonderful seeing everyone at the reunion again. It was just like old times, all of us in the dorms. Of course, plenty of our classmates were married by then, starting families, thinking about the future. I myself had gone into the weekend hoping to reconnect with the woman I'd had a crush on since our school days. We'd been such good friends for so many years, and it seemed like we'd make a good team for whatever life had in store for us." He lifts his gaze to mine. "I'm referring to Samantha, of course. She was always the one for me, your mother."

I stare back at him, my mouth dry. My mind is awhirl with all the details he's confessing. I want to know more, but there's a small part of me that doesn't want to hear it. Like once I know everything, I'll be haunted, too. Like Peter. Like Mom.

"There was a dinner-dance the last night of the reunion weekend. And when I saw Samantha heading outside—for fresh air, I assumed, because it was hot as the devil's kitchen in that ballroom—I followed her. She took the path to the cliffs. It's a wonderful view, and I... Well, it seems so silly now. I thought it would make for a perfect backdrop to propose, you know? But when I got there, she wasn't alone. George was with her. We'd exchanged the usual niceties when we saw each other earlier that day. I met his fiancée, though for the life of me I've forgotten her name."

Alarm bells start to peal in my brain. They sound so real, I glance up at the machines hooked up to Isla to make sure my sister isn't completely crashing out.

But no, it's all just in my head. My heart is racing, too. I try to take a deep breath to calm down, but that doesn't help, either. It feels like something is coming for me—something big, with sharp teeth and sharper claws. I try to fight back the rising panic and terror by focusing on the scene out the window, but the quickly darkening sky offers no comfort.

Peter clears his throat. "At first I thought it was a coincidence—that they'd both had the same idea to visit the cliff and take in the view. I remember thinking it was strange that George's fiancée wasn't with him, but there was such a chill in the air, I decided she must have stayed inside. But then—oh, but then, your mother took his hands in hers. And the gesture was so *intimate*, Belinda. So tender. I had been waiting years for her to look at me the way she was looking at George."

The anguish in Peter's voice is obvious, and I feel terrible for him. I do. Seeing the two of them together must've been devastating.

"She pulled his hands to her stomach. And the smile on her face, it could have lit up the night sky, it was so bright. She was happy. Thrilled. George wasn't, though. He looked furious. Pulled his hands away like touching her was revolting. Even from where I stood by the tree, I could hear him clearly— that's how loud he yelled at her. *I'll pay for an abortion, but that's it. I'm engaged, Samantha. You can't think I'd blow up my whole life to what—raise a family with a starving artist no one's ever heard of? Absolutely not."*

Tears fill my eyes, and I wipe them away. How cruel George was, hurting Mom like that. I can't imagine.

"She was crying, and she tried to pull his hands back to her stomach again, maybe hoping if he could feel the baby move, he might...I don't know. Change his mind? But he didn't pull away. Instead, he grabbed her around the middle and forced her to the edge of the cliffs. I was moving toward them before I even knew what was happening. She was struggling, her feet scrambling on the dirt. She became a wild thing, but I suppose that's what happens to mothers when their babies are threatened. She stomped on his foot, and it must have hurt enough that he loosened his grip on her. She dropped to the ground where he wouldn't be able to push her. George wouldn't stop, though. He reached for her again, and she pushed his hands away from her, thrashing around, and then..."

Peter remains silent until I can't take it any longer. "And then?" I prompt.

"He went over." I gasp, but he continues, his voice dropping to a near-whisper. "Billie, he was there one second, and the next...gone. Samantha crawled to the edge. I'd never heard someone scream that way. Never heard a sound so pained and shattered come from another person. She was reaching forward, reaching like she could catch him, and I threw my body on top of hers to keep her from falling right over the edge herself."

Peter swallows so hard I can hear it, a *click* in his throat like a puzzle piece being snapped into place. He reaches for a plastic jug of water on the table beside Isla's bed and removes a plastic cup from an upside-down stack of them. His hands are shaking when he pours water for himself and takes a gulping drink before filling the glass again.

I watch him in total silence, too stunned to speak.

"She wanted to tell everyone what happened." He scoffs, shaking his head. "Always so honest, your mother. I convinced her she had a good reason to lie. The best reason, really." Peter watches me carefully. "You. What would happen to her baby if she went to prison? Even if we'd lied and told everyone George jumped over the edge himself, the story would never have held up to real inquiry. Neither of us was ready to lie like that. We knew we'd get caught.

"So instead, we went back to the party and I told everyone she'd said yes. That we were getting married. No one thought much of her tear-stained face or how stunned she seemed. They all thought she was happy. If only they knew."

Dizziness washes over me, like I'm the one standing at the edge of a cliff, looking down at a vast chasm below. I grip the arm of the chair like it can save me, like it can keep me sitting here instead of free-falling into the past.

George Canterbury.

Mom.

George's fiancée.

One night in London…

"Are you saying…George Canterbury is my father?" My voice is a choked whisper. The words hardly belong to me at all.

"I've always thought of him as more of a sperm donor, but yes. He was your biological father," Peter confirms.

The irony of his comment doesn't escape me. "Sperm donor" is exactly how I've thought of Peter over the years. A deadbeat dad who bowed out of all the hard work that comes with being a parent and left it—left *me*—to my mother.

But now our family's narrative has been flipped upside down. Peter just delivered the opposite of a villain monologue. It was actually a hero's monologue—the story of a love so strong, it inspired a man to cover up a crime. Because I can hear what Peter didn't say: Mom shoved George over the edge of that cliff. It might have been self-defense—scratch that. It was *definitely* self-defense. But she was responsible all the same. Peter married Mom knowing she was carrying another man's kid. He kept us both safe. But with that kind of devotion…

"Why did you leave us?" It doesn't make any sense. How could a man who loved a woman as much as Peter obviously loved Mom leave her six years after they got together?

"Have you ever loved someone who could never love you back?" Peter says. The lack of hesitation in his answer makes me realize this is a question he's asked himself many times before.

I think of Mom. Can a person sick with addiction love anyone at all? Because the most powerful force in Mom's life is alcohol. Did she start drinking because she was trying to forget something so horrific, only being totally numb makes it tolerable? I can't imagine dealing with the memories. They must still torment her to this day—to the point that she ignores all of her responsibilities, including me.

So yeah, I know exactly what it's like to love someone who can't love you back. Looks like Peter and I have more in common than I realized.

"I loved Samantha. Part of me always will. But I didn't realize that when I pulled her away from one cliff that night, I led her straight to another one. Her guilt over what happened was...immense. Terrifying in its hugeness. I could never compete with that, and I could never be enough. Not when the hole that night left inside her was so damn big." Everything about Peter is hollow right now. Like he scooped out his heart and misery and all of those past emotions and laid them bare, just for me.

But there's one thing I can't wrap my head around.

"How could you leave me alone with her? Why did you send us to America and keep Isla with you? I've essentially had to raise myself. I take care of everything. I take care of *her*. We needed you." *I needed you*, is what I want to say, but even in this moment, when so many hidden things are coming into the light, that feels too vulnerable. It feels like something that needs to stay in the dark. Because if I drag it out here, if I look at the shape and texture of it too closely, I'll see the words for what they really are: The devastation of a lonely little girl who's been missing her dad for the past eleven years.

But I guess the truth is, Peter's not my actual father. He never was.

Maybe I never should have been missing him at all.

"I wish I could change what happened, but I can't. And I'm sorry, Belinda. I didn't want you to go, but Samantha could no longer be here. She said it was too painful. The memories haunted her, and she even said that the cliffs...they were always calling her back. I worried she would go out there and... Well, I was worried we would never see her again. I tried to keep you with me and Isla, but she refused. She insisted on taking you from me and from your sister.

"I tried so hard to get her help. To convince her she should stay for the family, *our* family, but she wasn't interested in Isla. Or me. She only wanted you. The only tangible remnant of George." Peter leans back, thrusting both hands in his hair as he watches me. "Nothing was stronger than the guilt she felt over what happened. She saved you, but she lost a part of herself in that moment on the cliff. And you will never know how sorry I am. For all of it."

I am reeling. My entire life has been a lie. The man I believed was my father isn't. My real father is dead, thanks to my mother, though if she hadn't taken action, maybe neither of us would be here today. It makes me understand Mom's behavior throughout my life a little better, but I still have so many questions. They swirl and twist in my brain, questions about who George was, and why he'd sleep with Mom if he was engaged, and what she saw in someone who was so clearly awful. I want to know why she didn't fall in love with Peter at school, and what her generation called the friend zone, and what Mom felt in the moment Peter covered her body with his own, saving her and me from an almost inevitable demise.

But the biggest question of all, the one that pulses through my head like the beat of a powerful drum, is this: How does all of this connect to Emily's death and Isla being in a coma? Why was Isla tracing the Legacy List from 1998, and what could she have figured out for herself if Peter never told her about George?

I have vertigo again, though I'm still sitting in this chair, still holding Isla's hand. I rub my thumb over her palm and close my eyes, tracing the fine lines on her skin like they hold the answer to all my questions. *What did you know, Isla? What do you want me to see?*

My eyes slam open.

My heart pounds in my chest.

All the fine hairs on my arms stand straight up.

I lock eyes with Peter. His expression is racked with guilt and pain, and seeing him like this somehow confirms the idea that just shot through me like a bullet.

"Dad?" I hesitate after saying the word and swallow the sudden lump in my throat. "I might know what happened to Isla."

CHAPTER TWENTY

I wake up to a gentle hand shaking my shoulder, a woman's soft voice whispering my name. Not Belinda, either.

Billie.

I'm disoriented at first, my entire body aching as I slowly sit up. I fell asleep with my head resting on my crossed arms on the side of Isla's bed. Must've been exhausted to sleep like that for so long, but it also makes sense. The last few days have been an emotional roller coaster.

"Billie."

I glance up to find Whitney standing beside my chair, a small brown shopping bag in her hand. Diffused light from the windows on the far wall illuminates her silhouette, and my sleep-groggy brain supplies an observation my mouth isn't awake enough to keep to myself. "Tessa Thompson. You. Her," I babble, rubbing crud from my eyes. "You could be sisters."

"Aren't you sweet in the morning," Whitney says. "A little blind, maybe, but sweet. Good morning."

"Good morning," I return, though in an instant, I remember

there's not much good about today. It's Friday. My time is up, and I'm no closer to saving my sister from potentially being arrested.

Wait a second.

I *am* closer.

I need to get to Wickham. I need—

I start to rise out of the chair, but Whitney puts a firm hand on my shoulder, keeping me in place. "You need to eat something before you start your day. I brought coffee and an egg sandwich."

I sag into the chair with relief and accept the paper cup Whitney offers. I cradle the warmth as I take a tentative sip, heat from the liquid spreading through my hands and up my arms. "Thank you. It's perfect."

"Eat the sandwich," Whitney demands, though it's not a cruel command. "I'm sure you're starving. You never ate dinner last night."

I don't bother telling her I never ate anything at all yesterday. I was too upset, too nervous, too overwhelmed. I take the sandwich from her and unwrap it, the delicious scent of meat, egg, and cheese hitting my nostrils. My stomach growls, and I take a big bite. Then another.

The sandwich is gone in seconds. Usually I'd be embarrassed to wolf down food so fast, but I'm not this morning. The pleased expression on Whitney's face as she watches me eat makes me feel a certain way, and I realize it's the fact that she seems to get joy from taking care of me. I'm not familiar with that sort of thing, and it makes me sad.

But I have no time for sadness, I think as I wad up the sandwich wrapper. Whitney holds her hand out for it, and I give it to her, watching as she tosses the paper in the trash bin.

"That was delicious," I tell her. "Thank you again."

"Of course. I also brought you a change of clothes." She settles the shopping bag in my lap, and I peek inside. Yet another one of those soft cashmere sweaters—this one navy—and a pair of jeans, plus undies, socks, and shoes. Loafers. I would never wear any of this back home, but now it all feels… right. Not just for Belinda, either, but for me.

Billie.

I meet her gaze, wanting her to know my feelings are genuine. "You didn't have to do this for me."

"It's all right. I come every morning anyway, to see Isla. And, well…I wanted to talk to you. Peter told me the two of you worked through some things last night, and I'm so glad. When all of this is over—" She chokes on the last word and takes a second to compose herself, though her lips quiver. Like she's this close to completely breaking down, thinking about all the horrible ways this situation can end. "When all of this is over, I hope you'll consider joining us here. For the summer. And maybe even…beyond that. We would love to have you."

"But my mom—"

"Your mother will be welcome as well. There's a guest house on our property…Frankly, I think it's high time you're not the only one taking care of Samantha. I don't care if the past is painful for Peter or even for me. Her pain can't be allowed to destroy your present, or your future, Billie. Which reminds me, we must have a serious discussion about where you'd like to go to university." Whitney's smile is nervous, and she seems to brace herself for…what? My possible rejection?

"College?" I don't know why I feel the need to clarify.

Maybe because the opportunity has seemed so far outside my reality, she might have said *we must have a serious discussion about what color unicorn you want to ride in your magic princess parade.* Her words light the tiniest flicker of hope in my chest, but I don't let it grow into an all-out blaze. Disappointment is an ice bath on the coldest day of a brutal winter. No sense inviting it in. Better to keep my expectations low.

"Wherever you want. You can of course return to the States, but I have some wonderful contacts at—"

To hell with low expectations.

I leap out of the chair and wrap Whitney in a massive hug, probably squeezing her petite frame too hard, but I don't think she minds. She returns the embrace with a ferocity I don't expect, almost like she's holding both of us together when we're at risk of flying apart. We cling to each other, the steady beeps from the machines hooked up to Isla the only sounds beside the hiccupping gasps I try, and fail, to contain.

"Thank you. Just…thank you." I tighten my arms around Whitney's waist, and she lets me. Just stands there and takes it, as if she's enjoying this, and I firmly believe she does. She wants to help me. Wants to take care of me.

I love it. More than anything, I appreciate it. Whitney doesn't have to do this for me—didn't have to do any of the things she has for me since I arrived here—but she *wants* to. I'm not about to take that for granted, and I won't let my sister, either. When she wakes up, I'm never letting Isla complain about Whitney again.

As I pull away from Whitney, I catch myself. Not *when* Isla wakes up, but *if.* The reality is devastating, but I need to face it. I must resolve Isla's case and clear her name. It's why I came here, and yesterday's revelations have brought me closer than ever before to understanding the truth.

Even if the worst comes to pass—and I can't think about that, not right now—Whitney and Peter—*Dad*—deserve resolution. They deserve to know the truth. They've been great parents to Isla, and for that alone, I owe them.

"Your sister is a fierce hugger, too," Whitney says, halting the cascade of thoughts waterfalling through my mind.

"Yeah? I don't…I don't really remember that. Or much. We were in touch a lot until the past year, when I…I pulled away. Things were really hard at home and…" I trail off, too full of self-loathing to get the words out.

The touch of Whitney's soft palm on my arm is somehow full of understanding.

"She knew—knows—how much you love her. In fact, I don't think she'll be surprised at all to learn you dropped everything to come over here and help her. She'll think it's just the most natural thing in the world to find you here when she wakes up. I'm sure of it."

. . .

I use the shower in Isla's hospital room and get dressed, then climb into Peter's car, which he left behind for me. I tell Lurch we're headed back to Wickham. He keeps sending me curious looks in the rearview mirror, but he doesn't say anything.

Neither do I. I'm too nervous about returning to campus.

What if Connor holds true to his threat and exposes me to everyone? Would he really be cruel enough to do that? Not that the truth can hurt me personally, but it could definitely ruin my plans. Pressing just as heavy on my heart is guilt over the way my secrets hurt Connor. Our night together in the greenhouse glimmers in my memory like a mirage. I want so badly for it to be real, but it feels like that time belongs to someone else—someone who hadn't betrayed the boy she's falling for. I wonder if it feels unreal to Connor, too, when he looks back on our time together. We got so close, but all the time, I wasn't *me*. Not completely. That's got to hit Connor where it hurts the most, especially after so many of his friends refused to stand by him during all this stuff with his dad. Then I come along, somehow dodge his defenses, and proceed to completely abuse his trust.

Nice going, Billie.

I've lost Connor; I'm sure of it. But knowing it solidifies my already firm resolve into something so heavy, it could keep my feet grounded on the surface of the moon. If I figure out what happened to Isla and Emily, I'll at least be able to give Connor and his family some peace. It's the very least I can do after everything he's been through, everything I put him through.

A parting gift for the boy who deserved better than Belinda Winters.

Hell, he deserved better than Billie Vale, too.

Traffic is light in London thanks to the early hour, and when we arrive at Wickham, I know Connor will be in the dining hall. The moment we pull into the drive, I'm opening the car door and running across campus, ignoring the strange looks from the handful of students up and about at this hour. I'm too intent on finding Connor to worry about anyone else.

I enter the dining hall out of breath, frantically searching the room for his familiar, beloved face. I find him sitting alone at a table with his head bent over his phone and AirPods in his ears. I approach slowly, my stomach twisting into knots, protesting the breakfast sandwich I inhaled earlier. He doesn't notice me until I'm practically looming over him, and when he lifts his head, a grimace spreads over his face that leaves me a shaky, nerved-out mess.

"What are you doing here?" He plucks an AirPod from his ear, the weariness in his voice giving me the slightest bit of hope.

"I need to talk to you." Panic flashes through me when he stands. Is he already leaving? "Please, Connor. I need you to listen to what I have to say."

"I think we've talked enough." He starts to leave, and I chase after him as we exit the dining hall. I grab his hand the moment we're outside, and he lets me drag him around the other side of the brick building to a more private spot.

That he lets me take him there is another good sign, right? I've never been a superstitious person, but I guess it's true what they say—any port in a storm.

He lets go of my hand and turns to face me, his arms crossed in pure defensive mode. "You've got five minutes."

I take a deep breath and launch into the story of how I ended up at Wickham. His expression never shifts as I explain my background, my mom's dependency on alcohol, how resentful I became of Peter and Whitney and especially Isla. How I loved my sister in spite of it all, but I still couldn't deal.

Until Peter called me that one fateful day and said he needed me to help him figure out who tried to kill Isla.

"I did this for Isla, and for myself," I tell Connor, my voice cracking. "I didn't expect to fall for you when I came here. I had one mission, and you became an...unexpected and welcome surprise. I understand that you're angry with me, and you have every right to be. I want to give you time to decide whether or not you can forgive me. You deserve that—the chance to figure out if you can feel about me the same way I feel about you, knowing what you know now. But Isla is almost out of time, and I desperately need your help. If not for me, and if not for Isla...then for Emily. Because she deserves justice. They both do."

The entire time I'm speaking, his expression never changes. Not even a flicker of emotion in his eyes, nothing. His face is like a blank wall, his stance stiff. But now? In this moment, after I've told him why I came here and that he matters to me?

His eyes are a little softer, and he drops his arms to his sides. His jaw is still firm, his mouth still pressed in a hard line, but he doesn't look quite as angry as he did when he first saw me in the dining hall.

"I don't think I can help you," he starts, his voice hesitant. "I'm not equipped for this, and apparently, neither are you. This is bigger than us, Billie. Don't you see that? Doesn't Peter?"

I shake my head once, not about to give up now. "I left campus yesterday and headed straight to the hospital to see my sister one last time before I went back home."

His brows furrow. "You're going back to the States?"

His question lights me up inside. "You said I had to go

or— Never mind. That's not important right now. What's important is that Peter was there. We got into an argument. And then…he spilled his guts."

Connor leans against the building as I launch into a new story, giving him all the details from last night. Isla's list of the llamas from 1998 and all of the familiar names. Peter's story about the ten-year reunion and George Canterbury and how he's my biological father.

At that, Connor's eyes widen in what could be shock or alarm—hard to say which.

"You're a *Canterbury*?" he asks, and yeah, it's definitely shock. "That means Freddie is…"

"My cousin. I know."

"But I guess the question is, does *he* know? And if he does… If Isla told him…" Connor runs a hand through his hair, shaking his head a bit. Maybe trying to shake loose everything he thought he knew about his friend's family in order to make space for this new information. *Make space for me*, a hopeful part of my brain supplies. But I know better. I can't confuse Connor's interest in finding out what happened to Emily with forgiveness. Just because he seems to have found a temporary break in his hurt and anger doesn't mean he's ready to forget what I've done.

"I think Isla was trying to find a reason to bring me here," I tell him, sharing the revelation I came to last night after my talk with Peter. *Dad*. Trying to overwrite my feelings about Peter Vale is like trying to erase old computer code and input new commands on top of it. I've spent so long thinking about him one way. Realizing I was totally wrong…doesn't suck as much as I thought it would. I guess if you're going to be wrong about something, thinking your dad was an uncaring asshole for most of your life is a nice one to have been wrong about.

"She knew I was struggling. I feel like the worst sister in the world admitting this, but I'd been pulling away from her for the past year, and I wasn't exactly subtle about it. Things had gotten so difficult at home, and every path I tried to take led to a dead end. It crushes me that while I was trying to pull away from her, trying to insulate myself from seeing my sister's star rise, she was here, trying to raise me up alongside her. And it might have gotten her hurt. Emily, too, Connor. I don't totally understand how, exactly, but I'm so, *so* sorry she got caught up in this."

Shock ripples through me when Connor pulls me in for a hug, fierce and firm, like he can't help himself. I melt into him for a moment, savoring the feeling of his strong body so close to mine. He lets me go far too soon, and I immediately miss him. His warmth and strength and his delicious, soapy boy smell.

"It's not your fault, Billie. Lying from the second you arrived on campus? That's on you. But Emily's death? You don't carry the blame for that. I won't let you. Look what guilt did to your mum. And from what your dad told you, George's death wasn't her fault, either. For fuck's sake, he was threatening to *push her off a cliff.* From where I'm sitting, your mum, and you, and Isla, and even Emily are all victims of selfish men making selfish choices." His tone is bitter, the grimace on his face full of disgust, though none of it is directed at me.

I stare at him in silence, my heart turning over itself and my stomach fluttery in the best way. This boy doesn't blame me or Mom for what happened to his sister, though I'm more and more sure that our history—and the minefield of secrets it hides—is the reason Emily is dead. Instead, Connor's anger is aimed at the men who did this, and oh my gosh, I love that. Because his fury is warranted. Mom has been wronged for years, and so have I, through her. It's not fair.

But no one has ever said life is fair.

"We need answers, Connor. Figure out how the '98 llamas and George's death connect to what happened to our sisters."

"How?" Connor asks.

"We need to find Freddie."

CHAPTER TWENTY-ONE

Freddie has been a ghost on campus since his dad's arrest, but getting him to meet with us was easy. Connor sent him a text: *I know what you're going through, man. Let's talk about it.*

It worked. They agree to meet by the cliffside tree, which I suggested not for the drama but the potential stress Freddie might feel returning to the scene of the crime. But was there a crime at all? A seed of doubt took root in my gut when Dad told me what happened to George and Mom. None of that was premeditated, which definitely doesn't absolve George from being a murderous little shit, but it frames my mother's actions as self-defense. And a crime committed in the name of self-defense isn't a crime, is it? Though Julian was right and I've binged my fair share of *Law & Order* marathons, I don't have the faintest clue of the answer. Where's the spirit of Olivia Benson when you need her the most?

Connor and I trek out to the cliff in silence. We wait for Freddie under the tree, our thick coats doing little to protect us from the fierce wind whipping inland from the sea. It batters us even though we're sheltered beneath the branches, and I'm shivering. From the cold air, yes, but nerves, too. Gale-force anxiety matches the frantic weather.

My body knows a storm is coming.

The tree we stand beneath has been a steady presence in my life for as long as I can remember. A place of utter destruction not just once but twice. I'd love to banish this tree from my existence entirely, but unfortunately, that's not going to happen anytime soon.

"What if he doesn't show?" I check my phone for what feels like the hundredth time. Freddie is a solid ten minutes late.

"He'll show." The confidence in Connor's voice is reassuring, and he checks on me with a frown. "You're literally shaking."

"It's cold." I shrug. "And I'm nervous."

His face softens. "I've got you, Billie. You're not in this alone anymore, okay?"

His words offer some reassurance. I'm tempted to throw myself at him—for emotional support, sure, but also for basic shared body heat—when I spot a figure headed toward us. His steps are unsure and a little wobbly. When he draws closer, my nerves kick into overdrive.

It's Freddie.

He comes to a stop when he spots me, sneering before he pulls a flask from his inside coat pocket and uncaps it. He takes a long pull from the flask, which, if I'm not mistaken, is embossed with a family crest. I guess Pembroke pride persists even in the face of a criminal investigation. Freddie smacks his lips. It's still early in the day and he's already drinking? Great.

"What is *she* doing here?" He waves his flask in my direction.

Connor steps closer to me. "We're together now, Fred. When I told her we were meeting, she wanted to come."

"Of course she did." Freddie sways on his feet. He's more drunk than I realized at first—further gone than I've ever seen him, even at the party. His clothes are a mess under his coat, his white uniform shirt buttoned incorrectly, with big stains on the front. His eyes are bloodshot, and his words slur together when he speaks. "Thought you'd have run off by now."

Alarm bells start ringing in my head, reminding me of last night. The sound cuts through the wind screaming across the cliff edge. "Why would you think that?"

"Didn't someone go through your stuff? First day you were here, right. Terrible, having your privacy violated. Mother says those NCA fucks tore through Dad's office. Took the computers and statements and who-knows-what. Sucks that happened. Would be 'nuff of a reason for me to—what do you Americans say? Get out of Dodge?" He cackles like he just told the world's funniest joke.

But what he just said isn't funny. Connor sends me a curious look, and I nod once to confirm that yes, that's exactly what happened.

"Freddie, I never told anyone about that." I send him a pointed look, but he's unfazed.

He takes another sip from his flask, his lips wet from the liquor. "Right. Well. Priya… No, not Priya. *Me*. I should have taken the fucking thing and been done with it. But I figured they'd pull Isla's plug and you'd leave eventually, so what was the harm in letting you keep your sister's little book with all of her notes inside? Not like you could decipher that bunch of nonsense anyway."

Having confirmation that Freddie is the one who went through my stuff that first day feels good, like an open window in a drafty house has finally been closed, but it's also shocking. And scary. "You knew? All this time? Why didn't you say something?"

Freddie scoffs. "Please. What would that conversation have looked like, hmm? *Belinda, so good to meet you. We're cousins, actually. Ta!*" He chuckles, shaking his head. Seemingly lost in thought. "No, that would have been boring. Booooring. I left the book on your bed to see what you would do. Whether you'd run back to Daddy Vale or stick around. You chose to stay, which, I cannot lie, impressed me. Not sure why you didn't tell everyone you're Isla's sister from the start, though. You probably would've been more accepted, you know? Pitied at least."

Freddie keeps sipping from the flask. How much liquid can that thing even hold? He can barely stay upright, but somehow he keeps inching closer to us.

I don't like it. And from the way Connor steps forward like he's trying to protect me, I'm thinking he doesn't like it much, either.

"That's pretty messed up, Fred." Connor's voice has taken on a menacing depth. "Could make someone feel pretty unsafe, going through their stuff like that."

Feeling bold, I join in. "Yeah, *Fred*. Is making girls feel unsafe something you do a lot?"

Freddie's mean laugh sends a streak of fear down my

spine. "I'm not the one who went around threatening people, Belinda. No, that was your fucking *sister*."

I flinch at the fury in his tone.

"What are you talking about?" Connor sounds baffled.

"That little bitch showed me your picture." Freddie points at me. "She called you Billie, not Belinda. *Billie*. What a stupid name. I guess it runs in the family. Stupidity."

Now I'm as angry as Freddie seems. Maybe even more so. "You better watch what you say about—"

Freddie interrupts me. "Oh, save it, Billie. I'm just being… whatever I'm being."

"A drunk asshole?" Connor interjects.

"Yeah, yeah. That. But you know…I come by it honestly. My dad is…well." Freddie makes a tsking noise. "He's going to screw us all over in the end, isn't he?"

That much is obvious, considering he's been arrested. But I don't care about William Pembroke's crime at the moment. I need Freddie to focus.

"Why did Isla show you my picture?" My words are soft. My voice trembles. We're getting so close to the truth. I can feel it stalking through the scrubby grass around the tree, a snake slithering closer to its next meal.

"Because she had *eyes*, Belinda. She met Mother at one of our house parties last year and mentioned to me that she looked familiar, but I blew it off. Isla was a silly twit. But she was also too fucking smart for her own good."

I swallow hard. "What do you mean?"

"You know what I mean. She came to me and started pointing out…things. *Don't you see the resemblance?*" Freddie's voice pitches high, and I can only assume he's imitating Isla. "*Look at her!* She kept saying that. Over and over. *Look at her.*" He waves a hand at me. "Look at you. A Canterbury through and through."

I can't move. I'm too frozen with shock. He knows. But does he know *everything*? Last night, when I asked Dad if he'd ever told Isla the whole story of what happened the night of the reunion, he vehemently denied it. *I thought I'd be taking this secret to my grave* were his exact words.

Freddie staggers backward, glancing behind himself like he's looking for the something or someone who pulled him. But there's nothing there—just the wind and the cliff. He faces us once more. "She was a dog with a bone, my God. She kept trying to show me timelines and yearbook photos and Uncle George's obituary. And I kept telling her I'd never even met the man! He died before I was born. What do I know about any of this? It's not my problem. Wasn't my parents' problem, either."

That's where he's wrong. It's definitely his parents' problem, and ours, too. This revelation has the potential to change the course of all our lives.

Freddie keeps ranting. "Why should I care about my poor uncle George and this supposed illegitimate baby? As if he would've acknowledged it anyway. He was supposed to marry someone else. Mother married Father the year after she finished university, and she got pregnant soon after poor George's death. Legacy secured! All good." He lifts his flask like he's making a toast.

I remember what Dad said about how so many of their classmates were starting families around the time of the reunion. How it convinced Mom that George would be thrilled about her pregnancy. She was living in a land of delusion even then, considering George was engaged to another woman. I want to believe she didn't know—that she wouldn't have knowingly slept with someone else's fiancé. Not that the onus was on her to keep George's dick in his pants. That was his job.

"Did Isla tell you...that George was my biological father?"

Freddie's face scrunches into a disgusted grimace. "She did." He takes another swig from the flask. He has to tip it up nearly skyward to get at whatever's left. And while it's not great that he's finished the entire contents of that little silver flask, at least it's gone now. "I told her she was full of absolute shite. I mean, come on. I'm to believe Uncle George had the world at his fingertips but he decided to get in the mud with a fucking *nobody*? Because that's what your mum was. Is. Was. Is. Whatever."

He chuckles, and the sound makes me clutch my hands into fists. I want to smack him at the casually cruel way he's talking about my mother. I'm about to defend her, but Freddie keeps speaking.

"Nothing but a scholarship student. An *artist*, of all the fucking clichés in the world. Not a legacy, not even a politician's kid. Just a nobody. She was probably lying anyway, trying to get at that Canterbury money. Typical gold-digging bullshit."

My blood boils, my mind reeling. God, I can't stand listening to him anymore, but I have to. *We* have to, in order to find out the truth.

Connor finally speaks. "Hate to break it to you, Freddie, but Isla had the right of it all along."

"Bullshit." The word explodes from Freddie's lips along

with a healthy spray of spittle. So gross. "Say what you want, Belinda." He trips over his own feet, stumbling. "It doesn't matter anymore. Whatever Isla thought you supposedly deserved, well. It's gone now. Assets frozen. We'll probably lose at least two of the houses to cover it."

"What I...deserved? Freddie, what are you talking about?"

Freddie wags his finger at me, crooning, "Nuh-uh-uh." He shakes his head. "I don't *think so*, Belinda. Isla can't spread any more lies, and I'm not going to do it for her."

I take a step forward, but Connor rests his hand on my arm, stopping me from getting closer to Freddie. "Please, Freddie. I don't understand what you're talking about. Just—"

Connor interrupts me. "I do."

I glance over at him with a frown. Freddie scowls at him as well, but Connor is completely unaffected. His face is set in hard lines, his mouth firm.

"Isla figured out you were George's daughter, Billie. That means when he died, his trust should have gone to you. But it didn't. Right, Freddie? It went to Daphne. And Daphne—"

"Gave it to William to start Lumateg," I finish for him.

"Which means you're a very rich woman. Or...you should be, at least." Connor glances between me and Freddie. "Every Wickham family I've ever known invests with Lumateg. It's a huge fund. If money that was rightfully yours was used to seed it, I don't even know how to begin figuring out how much you're owed. But you can be sure it's an absolute fortune."

The vertigo that plagued me in Isla's hospital room comes back in full force. It doesn't help that the wind seems to push at me from every side, blowing me left then right, back then forward. Like it can't decide which way to send its power. I hold a hand out to steady myself, to try to quell the sensation that I could fall off my feet at any moment.

Then suddenly, an anchor.

Connor's warm hand wraps around mine, squeezing. The gentle, steady pressure feels like a clear dome dropped over this moment, shutting out the howling wind. We lock eyes, and he exaggerates his next inhale, letting me see the long rise and slow fall of his chest. I mimic him without hesitation once, then again. I let my awareness live in the space between his skin and mine. That's real. That's here.

That's safe.

I'm brought back to the moment when Freddie starts laughing, but I manage to maintain a sense of calm amid his rising hysteria. Irritation flits across Connor's face. We need to wrap up this conversation and somehow get Freddie back to Headmaster Harrington's office as soon as possible. Maybe he'll confess the rest there. Or maybe once he sobers up, the opportunity to learn all that Freddie knows will have passed.

I squeeze Connor's hand, and I hope he understands the message. *We have to stay.*

"Too late!" Freddie shrieks, making me wince. "We're all poor now, *cousin*. Not that anyone will believe you're George's child without proof. That's why Isla called me out here, you know. To have me spit in a tube for some kind of mail-in DNA test. She wanted to prove that you're a Canterbury and thought I'd go right along with it. As if I would."

Connor and I share a look. We're getting closer to the truth, and I don't want to stop the momentum.

"She went on and on about your pathetic life. Drunk mum—no surprise there. No college prospects. Working in a bar for minimum wage. I told her, *not my circus, babe.* Should have listened. Should have fucking listened! But instead she shoved that little tube right in my face! The audashitty." He slurs the word and shakes his head like he can dislodge his inebriation. "So I shoved her right back. She tripped over her own feet, and down she went!" At my look of horror, he barks out a laugh. "No, not *down* down. Just...she shtumbled onto her ass. It was quite funny."

He moves to drink from the flask again, remembers halfway through the gesture that it's empty, and tosses it to the ground carelessly. Like it's a plastic water bottle instead of an engraved piece of metal meant to last a lifetime. He ambles toward the cliff, and without exchanging so much as a glance, Connor and I follow him. We separate, fanning out on either side of Freddie, trying to put ourselves between him and the edge. But he keeps walking in circles, stumbling over his feet and completely unstable while mumbling incoherently to himself.

"I didn't even realize the little brat was here. Yours—" Freddie points at Connor. "Though I should've. Emily was always Isla's shadow, so I should have guessed she was lurking nearby, waiting to strike. The moment I pushed Isla, she came hurtling toward me. Emily. Screaming like a banshee. *Don't you put your hands on her!* So fucking dramatic. I stepped out of the way at the last second, but she couldn't stop herself in time and just..."

Freddie turns toward the cliff, gesturing at it like a conductor showing off the orchestra after a concert. Then he glances over his shoulder at us, a knowing smirk on his face.

Without warning, Connor leaps on Freddie from behind,

taking him down to the ground. He rolls Freddie onto his back and punches him square in the face once. Then again. Freddie doesn't even fight back. He just takes it, his eyes empty of emotion or reaction. I run toward them, tugging at Connor's shoulders until he finally gets off of him.

When I look at Connor's face, I see the anguish and the pain. He's crying, his heartbreak as obvious and acute as a broken bone. It breaks my heart. Tears spring to my own eyes, and I shake my head, desperate to hold them back. Both of us can't fall apart. Not now.

"Motherfucker killed my sister." Connor clasps the top of his head with both hands, turning his back on both of us like he can't take it anymore. Like a lie by omission, Freddie's crime is one of absence. He could have caught Emily as she ran, could have taken whatever blow she offered and stood in the way of her demise.

But instead, he stepped aside.

He made space for tragedy, when he could have stood in its way.

And somehow, inexplicably, he's managed to live with himself since then.

I think of all the times I've seen Freddie smile or laugh in the weeks I've been at Wickham. Jovial, at ease, puffed up with pride and his sense of self-worth. And all this time, he's known. He's carried the events of that day on this cliffside with him, and it hasn't slowed him down one bit.

I didn't know a monster could look like this, but maybe I should have.

"What happened next, Freddie?" I need to know.

Freddie rises to his feet, swaying a bit. His face is battered, thanks to Connor's fist. A bruise is already forming beneath his eye. "The screaming! My God, Belinda, the screaming was *immense*. Isla stood right at the edge, yelling for Emily, yelling for someone to help, yelling for me to call someone. She wouldn't shut the fuck up! My head was throbbing from it all." He touches the side of his face. "Quite like now, actually."

He's so casual about it all. He disgusts me. To my right, I can literally feel the frustration coming from Connor in thick, hot waves.

"And then?" I prompt, Connor turning to face us both once again.

Freddie frowns. "And then…what?"

I keep my voice steady. "How did Isla end up sprawled on a ledge thirty feet down? How did my sister end up in a coma?"

Awareness lights up his face, and he rears his head back. "Oh, that's simple." He pauses, that tiny smile reappearing on his smug face. "I pushed her."

CHAPTER TWENTY-TWO

I'm blind with white-hot rage at Freddie's nonchalant confession and his smug, shitty tone.

I pushed her.

With the words echoing in my head on repeat, I lunge toward him, a snarl ripping from my throat. Grasping hold of Freddie's coat's lapels, I snarl as I lift my knee, nailing him square in the crotch. Freddie doubles over with a howl, clutching himself, and I'm about to knee him in the nose when Connor tugs me back at the last second. He wraps his arm around my middle while I kick and scratch at Freddie, screaming at him.

"Fucking bitch! Get your whore under control, Wells!" Freddie staggers to the side and bends over. He rests his hands on his knees and begins to retch with a groan. He heaves and curses, and all I want to do is hurt him again.

Hurt him the way he hurt Isla. The way he hurt Emily.

Fuck it—those hurts are too good for him.

"Why?!" I yell, my voice animalistic, unrecognizable to

my own ears.

In contrast, Freddie's voice is smooth as silk. "She was screaming, as you may recall," he says. "Kneeling on the edge, yelling to Emily. *Emily! Talk to me, Emily! Are you okay?* Like I said—stupidity really seems to be a genetic inheritance in your family. Anyway, she was there. She was wailing. She was...trying to prove you're a Canterbury. So I helped her reach Emily. Or I tried, anyway. Didn't take the way I hoped it would."

"You're a fucking monster!" I scream, swiping at the air with all the power I can muster. I dig my feet into the dirt and try to break Connor's hold. If I can get to Freddie, I can rake my nails down his face and pull his hair and make him *hurt*, make him feel some kind of pain, make him show me he can feel anything at all.

"Billie. Baby. Calm down." Connor's even voice is soothing, and I focus on the sound. Taking a deep breath, I relax in his hold, but he doesn't let me go. Which is smart because I would've launched into a new beat-down on Freddie if given the chance.

"He's not worth you possibly hurting yourself," Connor reminds me, and I nod, though I can't speak. I'm breathing heavily, anger coursing through my blood and making it run hot. He killed Emily. He almost killed Isla. And he doesn't give a shit.

I hate him.

Worse? I'm related to him. He's my cousin. If they're all as bad as Freddie, I don't want to claim his family as any part of mine.

Freddie is still hunched over and clutching his stomach

while he wheezes like he can't catch his breath. *Good.* "Miserable whore." He glares at me. "How dare you?"

I start laughing, and it sounds hysterical. I *feel* hysterical. Out of my mind and body. Like none of this is real. "Getting uppity on me now, Fred? Give me a break."

My taunting tone has him lurching toward me, and he trips over a rock. He stumbles backward, his eyes going wide as he throws his arms out. He's precariously close to the edge, and as if on instinct, I tear out of Connor's grip. Running toward Freddie, I grab hold of one of his flailing hands and keep him from tumbling over the cliff's edge.

Adrenaline gives me the strength to pull Freddie forward, but at the last minute, Connor forces me to let go. He grabs hold of my shoulder and whips me around to face him while Freddie writhes on the ground.

"We can't let him fall—" I start, and Connor shakes his head once, his expression grim.

"He's drunk." Connor's eyes are wild, his breathing heavy while his whole body vibrates. "We saw it happen, Billie. He stumbled too close to the edge and...fell. We couldn't save him in time."

My eyes go wide. "No. Connor, we can't."

Connor's face crumples, and I see the misery in his turbulent gaze. "He let my sister die. Just stood by while she went over the side and did nothing to help her. He could've said something. He could have brought my family some peace. Even if he made up a story about how it all unfolded, that's the least he could've done. But he didn't. Instead, he let my sister die, and he's letting your sister take the blame so he can get away with it. That has to make you angry, Billie. Right? You *hate* him. I hate him, too. He doesn't deserve to live after what he's done to our families. Don't you want to make him pay as much as I do?"

"Of course I do! But my entire life has been shaped by what happened when some callous asshole went over the edge of this exact cliff and the two people who knew the truth never said anything. Do you really think we can lie about this for the rest of our lives?" I stare at Connor, trying to implore him with my own earnest gaze, but there's nothing but firm resolution on his face.

"Absolutely." A muscle in his jaw jumps. "I can keep a secret."

I slowly shake my head. "You think that now, but I've seen the way guilt can eat someone alive. How it leaves them a shell of who they used to be. Guilt like that can end a marriage. Destroy a family. A secret this big can make someone turn to alcohol or substances to numb them so they can't remember what happened. Or how they're responsible. Do you really want to do that to yourself? To me?"

Connor closes his eyes for a brief second and presses his forehead against mine. When he opens his eyes, tears streak down his face. I feel them drop onto my own cheeks. Whatever ends up happening, we're bonded forever by the tragedy that unfolded on this cliff, both in the past and the present. No one else will understand what happened or what we've been through. How it feels to stand on this cliffside with the wind at our backs while we decide whether or not Freddie Pembroke should die.

I felt a connection to Connor from the moment we first met, but this, right now, is on a whole other level.

I press my palms against Connor's chest and detect the frantic beating of his heart. I couldn't live with the guilt. I've witnessed it firsthand, just like I told Connor. It's a terrible thing, watching someone you love destroy themselves bit by bit, day by day. All because there was something weighing heavily on them. Secrets are a terrible burden I wouldn't wish on anyone, and I've already carried more than my fair share these past two weeks. I wouldn't wish the burden of a secret like this on my worst enemy.

Which is to say, I wouldn't wish it on Freddie Pembroke.

"Billie." Connor's voice is a rasp, and I lift my gaze to his. The sincerity that blazes in his eyes makes my heart jump. "I love you, Billie. You have to know—"

Out of nowhere, Freddie appears, looming behind Connor with a giant tree branch in his hands. He swings it with a grunt, straight into Connor's knee, sending him to the ground.

"Fuck!" Connor roars, clutching his knee.

I kneel down to help him just as Freddie swings again, the branch making contact with Connor's head. He slumps forward, his body limp, and I'm screaming.

"No! *No!*" Over and over again.

"Shut the fuck up!" Freddie yells, and I jerk my gaze to his. He clears his throat, his expression evening out. "You know what happens to girls who start screaming on this cliff."

I jump to my feet, never taking my eyes off Freddie. Hatred curdles my stomach, and as if he can sense it, he smiles. His pupils are dilated, his breaths quick and shallow. It's obvious he's not in his right mind. How am I going to rescue Connor now that he's down? How am I going to rescue myself?

Without a word, Freddie takes a menacing step toward

me, and I shuffle back toward the tree. I reach inside my coat pocket, searching for my phone, but I can't find it.

"Wrong way," Freddie snaps.

"Excuse me?" I pause.

"You're walking in the wrong direction." He gestures toward the ledge with the branch.

I'm incredulous. "What makes you think I would step anywhere near the edge of a cliff with you nearby? You just told me you pushed Isla from that same exact spot."

"You're going to walk over there and jump." Freddie's voice is eerily calm, despite the snarl on his face and the giant branch he's wielding. "Or I'm going to crack open Connor's head like a fucking melon."

The image his words conjure up fills me with despair. I fight to remain calm, forcing my lungs to accept a deep but ragged breath. "You actually believe I would trade my life for his?"

Freddie hoists the branch over his head and slams it down on Connor's arm. The chilling sound of bone snapping rings in the air as Connor gasps awake before he starts screaming with pain. But it only lasts for a second before he goes quiet, though I can tell from the rise and fall of his chest that he's still breathing. I'm filled with a sick sort of relief that at least he's not lying there awake and suffering. And at least he's alive.

"So fucking predictable." Freddie stalks toward me, dragging that branch along with him, and I keep moving, shocked to find I've already closed half the distance between myself and the ledge. "Someone like you is never going to be more than a pawn in the games of better men, Belinda. Of course you'll trade yourself for Connor. Who even are you?

No one. Just like your mother, a nobody from nowhere. But Connor? Ho, ho, *the* Connor Wells! The golden boy! The Wells family just got their lives back—minus Emily, but hey, at least Dad isn't in prison anymore. It'd be a damn shame if Jonathan just went through all the trouble of fucking over my dad, only to lose his son the very next week. Now *move*."

I take another step back, getting closer to that edge, Freddie keeping pace with me. My entire body trembles, and I swallow down the fear that's gathered like a lump in my throat. "What's the point of making this easy for you? And why do you think I'd believe for even one second that you'll let Connor live if I jump? You'll just keep beating him, or you'll push him over the side, too."

The thought of Connor dying has tears streaking down my face. I can't imagine him gone. I can't imagine me gone, either, but here I am. On the edge of a cliff with a killer. Everyone knows that history repeats itself, but somehow I never saw this coming. In this story, the end result is always the same, no matter how much time passes.

Someone dies.

Freddie makes a tsking noise, as if he's disappointed in me. "Come on now, Billie. That would be a bit too suspicious, don't you think? The heroic whistleblower's son dies with the traitor's son nearby? I may have lost almost everything, but that still leaves something for me to build from. And I wouldn't thrive in prison."

"If you leave him alone, Connor will eventually wake up and tell the police everything," I remind him, my brain scrambling. Reasoning with a boy who's completely out of his mind isn't easy.

"Oh, don't worry. I won't *kill* him, but I suspect he'll suffer the kind of head injury that leaves his testimony extremely unreliable. After all, when I first ran out here, I saw the two of you arguing. Lovers' quarrel, you know? It went from sweetly romantic to *very dramatic* in a matter of minutes. You attacked him, and I did everything I could to intervene, but my goodness, you're a violent little thing. Typical American. Anyway, we all three tussled, you smashed the side of Connor's head with your big stick, then when you realized what you'd done, you threw yourself over the side. It was very tragic. I'll probably need therapy."

His laughter fills me with anger. "That's completely ridiculous. You can't guarantee Connor won't remember—"

The laughter stops. "You're right. Guess I'll beat him until he's in a coma, too. Like Isla. A perfectly matched set—maybe they could share a hospital room. I'll definitely leave him alive, Belinda. It's the only guarantee I'm willing to make." He lifts the branch over his shoulder with a wince. "But I'm done talking now. You have five seconds to fulfill your life's highest purpose by shutting up and jumping already. Five…"

I take another step closer to the edge and glance over my shoulder, shuddering. The wind is stronger here, whipping my hair across my face and making it difficult to see. The angry roar of the sea below reminds me of a wild creature with its mouth gaping open, eager to swallow me whole.

Am I really going to die like this?

"Four," Freddie calls, the glee in his voice obvious. He's enjoying every minute of this, and I hate him for it. I hate him for everything he's done.

I think of sweet Isla. How she was only trying to help

me. Look where it got her. I'd give anything to see her wake up again. My poor, guilt-ridden mother, who can barely live with the weight of what she knows all these years later. I hope she gets the help she deserves. And then there's my dad and Whitney. Will they be okay if I die? No. They won't. Just when we were getting closer, any chance at being a real family will be gone. Banished for good.

Connor's face flashes in my mind, and I'm sobbing. He could have had such a beautiful life, and maybe he would have, if I hadn't walked into it. But now he's like me, at the mercy of a drunken madman. Because I'm sure there is nothing about Freddie that's grounded in reality anymore.

That might be why he never thought to look behind him, toward the road that leads to the Harrington estate.

"Three…" Now Freddie sounds annoyed. "You're taking too fucking long, Belinda."

I take another step.

If he had looked behind him, maybe he would've seen the faint blue-and-red sheen of police lights coming closer. Heard the wail of their sirens just above the roar of the wind. They're not going to get here in time to save me, but chances are good they'll arrive before Freddie can do any more damage to Connor.

"Two, one, *go*!" Freddie's eyes are wide, and he raises the branch in front of him. I take a step back, the ground soft and crumbling beneath my feet. My hair flies across my mouth with the wind. Our gazes lock.

"Freddie?" My voice is soft. Calm. I brush my hair away with a trembling hand.

"What?!" he snaps.

"When Connor wakes up, will you tell him I love him? Please. Could you at least do that for me?"

Freddie smirks and shakes his head. "You mean, will I rub salt in the wound? With absolute pleasure, Belinda. Now you've delayed this as long as you could. Your time is up."

He runs toward me, holding the branch straight out, poised to push me right off the edge. When he's close enough that I can feel his movements disrupt the air around me…

I jump.

CHAPTER TWENTY-THREE

Freddie believes I'm weak. That I'll listen to his maniacal nonsense and jump to my death merely because he says I should.

I don't think so, Fred.

What I've learned so far in my life—and especially the last two weeks here at Wickham—is that more often than not, you have to stare down what's coming for you and get right in its face. If my mom and dad had confronted the truth instead of running from it that fateful night at their ten-year reunion, my life—and Isla's—would be so much different.

Connor's father stared corruption dead in the eye and made the difficult choice to take action, even at the expense of his family's well-being.

It feels like a lifetime ago, but just this morning, Whitney said she's done ignoring Mom's disease and the way it's robbing me of my own life.

Sophia confronted me unflinchingly after overhearing my phone conversation with Peter. It goes to show that pretending problems don't exist doesn't make them go away.

No. Ignoring them only makes your problems worse.

For the past few minutes, all of these thoughts rocketed through my mind, bolstering me with strength as I stepped closer to the cliff's edge. I knew I needed to remain calm and wait for my opportunity.

Wait for Freddie to underestimate me. Or, more accurately, overestimate himself.

He doesn't see me coming, doesn't expect me to spring toward him at the last second. I leap onto him like a tiger taking down my prey. Once I get inside the reach of that branch, I bend down low, then explode upward, ramming my shoulder into Freddie's chest and knocking him to the ground.

I go with him, using my momentum to roll both of us away from the edge. Freddie is yelling, but I remain quiet, containing my strength as I wrap myself around him like a feral koala. There's no way I'm about to let him go. That cliff has taken enough from me, and I'm not about to let it take away Emily's and Isla's justice. I'm not going to let it take another life, either—even if that life belongs to a piece of shit like Freddie Pembroke.

Freddie is howling his displeasure as he struggles to get away from me. He manages to roll us again, so the bulk of his weight presses me down into the scrubby grass and makes it hard to breathe, but I tighten my grip. I'm hanging on for dear life—mine and Isla's. I can't let go, can't let him get away. I have his arms pinned tight to his sides, my legs wrapped around his hips, my ankles locked together behind his thighs. I've learned a thing or two about facing problems head-on, but I've always known how to ride out a storm. That's all I have to do now: *hold on.*

Red and blue lights streak across the landscape, and I hear footsteps pounding toward us. I glance over to see the police car parked only feet away from us, along with an ambulance. I nearly sag with relief, though I still don't let go of Freddie.

We're going to be saved.

"Billie!" I hear Sophia's cry, filled with worry and devastation. She's running toward us with her parents right behind her, but one of the police officers halts their progress as the other one jogs toward us.

Without hesitation, the officer grabs the back of Freddie's coat and pulls him off me. The man has his handcuffs out already, and he yanks Freddie's wrists together to pull them behind his back. I collapse into the grass, my limbs heavy as lead and my breath coming in great, heaving gasps. I never take my eyes off of Freddie, who curses and thrashes but is no match for the officers—there are two of them now. I collect myself enough to stagger to my feet, silently watching as the officers drag Freddie to the police car.

Sophia pushes past the other officer and comes to me, wrapping me in a quick, full-bodied hug before she pulls away. She keeps her hands on my shoulders as she scans me from head to toe. "Are you all right? Well, obviously you're not *all right* all right, but are you injured?"

She pulls me back into a hug before I can answer, her embrace gentle but all-encompassing. I close my eyes as I slip my arms around her. We cling to each other for a long, quiet moment as chaos erupts all around us. I open my eyes in time to see two paramedics run to where Connor is lying on the ground. They kneel on either side of him, speaking in low tones as they begin to check his vital signs.

I disentangle myself from Sophia's hug. "I want to go to him."

She keeps her arm around my shoulders and steers us toward where Connor is laid out. He's not even sitting up, his long body sprawled across the ground, and my heart cracks wide open in my chest.

"He was hit in the arm with a heavy branch," I tell a female paramedic as we draw closer. My voice shakes, and I'm scared. I witnessed what Freddie did to him, and the damage could be severe. "I think I heard a bone break? And...he was hit in the side of the knee, too. He fell when it happened. I—" My words are cut short by a dry heave that doubles me over. Remembering the sounds of impact—branch to knee, branch to arm—turns my stomach something fierce.

The EMT checks in with her partner before rising and coming to me. "We just gave your friend something for his pain. Once we finish splinting his arm, we'll head straight for the hospital. Can you tell me what happened to you?"

She looks in my eyes with a flashlight while I start reciting, in fits and starts, what happened. She continues to check me over, looking in my ears and nose, palpating my head for bumps, putting gentle pressure down the lengths of my arms.

"Did you hit your head? Lose consciousness?"

"No, nothing like that. But can I— Can we go with him? With Connor. His name is Connor—"

My father materializes out of nowhere, heading straight for us. His face is etched with worry, and I swear he has new wrinkles. And am I losing my mind or is he also grayer at his temples? This poor man. The entire ordeal has probably aged him considerably in a short amount of time.

"We'll follow you to the hospital," he tells the paramedics, his voice gruff. "I've already called our family doctor. He'll be waiting for us—waiting for *my daughter*—when we arrive."

My knees buckle at hearing my dad claim me as his daughter in front of everyone. I'm grateful Sophia's got a hold of me or else I'd probably collapse. He's never done that before. When our gazes meet, I see all the concern in his eyes. I want to go to him and give him a hug, but Headmaster Harrington approaches at that exact moment, so I remain by Sophia's side. The two men shake hands before speaking to each other in hushed tones. I turn away to check on Connor, only to see he's awake.

I break away from Sophia's hold and run—okay, half stumble—to his side. Falling onto my knees, I carefully brush a few stray dark-brown strands of hair away from his forehead. He cracks his beautiful gray eyes open wider, though his lips remain pressed in a pained grimace.

Relief shoots through me at seeing him awake.

"You're a difficult girl to impress," he murmurs.

I frown. "What do you mean?"

"I get taken out by a drunken Freddie wielding a *branch* of all fucking things, and then you charge at him like a linebacker." He tries to shake his head but winces as if the movement hurts. "Unbelievable."

"Try not to move too much." I drift my fingers across his cheek, savoring how warm his skin is despite the chilly wind whipping around us still. "And what do you know about linebackers? Does the King let you watch football?"

"Ha. Ha," he deadpans, and the relief I feel knowing he

can still laugh in such a chaotic, dark moment is a balm to my aching soul.

He closes his eyes briefly. "I saw everything. You were magnificent, Billie. So brave."

I press my fingers to his lips, feeling like I'm this close to bursting into tears. "You were brave, too."

"Miss, please back up. We need to get him into the ambulance," the male EMT says.

Rising to my feet, I take a few steps back to give the paramedics the room they need. Sophia and I watch as they roll Connor onto his right side, wary of the sling on his left, and slip a board beneath his body. Another paramedic appears with a gurney. The woman counts to three, and they lift Connor up and onto it. His eyes are squeezed shut, and I hope against hope that the pain meds are starting to work.

He opens his eyes and reaches toward me with his good arm. "Don't leave me, Billie. I need you."

Tears rain down my face. "We're right behind you. I promise."

"I've called your parents, Mr. Wells," Headmaster Harrington says. "They're already en route to the hospital." He nods to the paramedics, turns on his heel, and heads straight back to the police.

The paramedics wheel Connor to the ambulance, and my father approaches Sophia and me, his expression grim. "Come on, girls. I'll drive you both to the hospital. Sophia, your father has to stay here and deal with...all of this."

The three of us turn our heads toward the police vehicle where Freddie is sitting in the back seat. Headmaster Harrington is talking to one of the officers, and they wear matching serious expressions.

Dread coats my insides. I'm going to have to talk to the police and tell them everything. But that's a good thing. Being a live witness means I can give them every little detail. What Freddie said and did—and he said and did *a lot*. So much destruction, and an unnecessary death. I can never forgive him for what he did to any of us. But he won't get away with his crimes. Hopefully, he'll be locked up for a long time.

Looks like the Pembroke men have a lot to answer for.

We follow my dad to his car, and I pause beside the passenger door. My entire body begins to shake so hard that I can't even reach for the handle. Sophia takes charge and encourages me into the back seat before sliding in beside me and shutting the door. She buckles my seatbelt for me like I'm a little kid, and from out of nowhere she has a thick blue blanket in her hands, which she tucks all around me. I'm immobile, overwhelmed with emotions, yet also grateful she's taking care of me.

My body slowly relaxes against the soft leather seat, and I close my eyes when the car starts moving. My mind offers up a memory of winding roads and hairpin turns on the route from Wickham to the hospital, and some self-protective instinct tries to pull me into sleep so I can avoid experiencing it. Shivers of adrenaline periodically race through my fingers, making them twitch. My father and Sophia begin to speak.

"God, that was too close." Dad's voice is ragged.

"My father said the same thing," Sophia murmurs.

"You've been a good friend to Billie, Sophia. Thank you for that, and thank you for telling Percy in time for him to call me. I'm glad she brought you into her confidence. She's had to keep too many secrets during her time here."

"I'm glad, too. When she told me what she and Connor were planning, I took it straight to my parents." Sophia pauses. "I hate to think what would have happened if we hadn't gotten there in time."

I'm half asleep thanks to the gentle rocking of the car and the warmth filling the interior, but Sophia's words perk me up. "You finally decided to be the snitch those assholes think you are, huh?"

Sophia actually laughs, and I savor the joyful sound. "Hell yeah, I did. And I'd do it again in a heartbeat. I can't believe you and Connor thought confronting a potential killer at the scene of his crime was a good idea."

"Um, not potential," I whisper.

The car goes eerily quiet as they absorb what I said. What it means.

"Are you saying Freddie…confessed?" Dad asks.

I'm drifting. It's all been too much, and I can barely think, let alone talk. "Mm-hmm."

My father asks another question, but I can't make out what he's saying. The darkness is too strong, and I finally let it pull me under.

...

Once we arrive at the hospital, we're met by Whitney, who was visiting with Isla when Dad called her to explain the situation. A nurse's assistant escorts me to a private room, where Whitney insists on staying with me while I get checked out. My father goes upstairs to look in on Isla, and Sophia goes with him, telling me she wants to check on her Little.

Whitney fusses over me while we wait for Dad's doctor to appear. She gives me water and requests pain medication when another nurse comes in to check on us. I sit on the edge of the examination table in a haze, slumped over in exhaustion. I just want to lie down. Rest. My head hurts, my entire body aches, and while I don't see many physical injuries on me, I feel beat up inside.

Thank God the worst is over, though there's still more to come. I have to talk to the police as soon as possible—tell them what Freddie confessed, so they don't file formal charges against Isla. As long as I have my family and Sophia and Connor standing by my side, I'll be okay. It feels so good, that realization. I've been on my own for so long that bearing the weight of the world on my shoulders has practically become second nature. But now I feel like I can share the load. I can let myself get taken care of, instead of doing all the caretaking. I don't love how this all came to pass, but that, at least, is a positive outcome.

"I'm so glad you're okay." Whitney cups my face with delicate hands, her tawny brown eyes brimming with tears. "I was so worried about you. I told Peter countless times maybe it wasn't a good idea, having you out there, but look at you. You did it. You figured out everything."

I lean into her palm and close my eyes so I don't cry with her. "I had help. Isla left plenty of clues."

"Take the credit where it's due, Billie." She leans in and presses a soft kiss to my cheek just as the door opens and the doctor strides in.

He looks me over with the usual poking and prodding. He worries at first that I might have a cracked rib but, after a few extra pokes, tells me he suspects it's just "a god-awful bruise."

"You're going to be sore, young lady," he warns me. "But you'll be all right. Acetaminophen, ice on the worst of the bruises, twenty minutes on and twenty minutes off for the first twenty-four hours."

The doctor is just about finished with my exam when the door swings open again, Sophia barreling inside and skidding to a stop.

"Young lady, you can't just run into an examination room without knocking," the doctor chastises, but Sophia completely ignores him.

"She's awake! Isla's awake!" Sophia practically screams.

With zero hesitation, I'm hopping off the table and running out of the room with Sophia, Whitney just behind us. We enter the elevator and ride up to Isla's floor. Whitney is clutching her hands in front of her, dead silent. I'm too stunned to speak. But Sophia chatters on, practically vibrating with excitement.

"We were sitting on either side of Isla's bed, and Peter was talking to her, telling her how much he misses her, when we heard a soft groan. He went silent and looked at me. 'Did you hear that?' and I said yeah, I definitely did! Then Isla said, 'Mum?' so I ran downstairs to get you while Peter stayed in Isla's room. He pressed the call button for the nurse," Sophia explains, bouncing on her feet. "I can't believe it!"

I can't, either. This is the moment we've all been waiting for. The timing is impeccable.

The elevator doors slide open, and Sophia darts out while

Whitney hesitates. I check her face and find she's struggling to keep it together. When she holds out her hand toward me, I take it. We keep our hands linked, staying together as we head for Isla's room. The corridor feels as long as a football field, like the distance is growing with every step we take. Exhaustion is settling into my bones, but my heart is racing at the prospect of seeing Isla awake.

Inside Isla's room, it's pure, controlled chaos. Two nurses are there, checking Isla's vitals and adjusting her IV bags. My father's face is a study in joy. He's lit up from the inside, his smile wide and full of utter relief. Whitney lets go of my hand to rush toward him, and he holds out his arms, though he only wraps one around his wife. The other he opens toward me, encouraging me forward, and I go to him. He hugs us both, murmuring. "Our family is together at last."

"We'll let you stay," one of the nurses tells us. "The neurologist should be here at any moment. He'll want to check on Isla here. Run some tests. But so far, she looks great." She aims a warm smile at our little tableau, then follows the other nurse out of the room.

"I'm going to grab a coffee," Sophia announces as she starts to exit the room. "Let me know if you need anything."

"Thank you, Sophia." I smile at her, and she offers one last wave before she walks out, closing the door behind her.

I sag against my father's chest, and Whitney does the same. I've never felt such relief and happiness before in my life. Isla is finally awake, and hopefully she's going to be okay.

I watch my sister, my eyes greedy for the sight of her. I step closer to her bed while Whitney and Dad stand by her on the other side. Even though her eyes are closed again, there's color in her cheeks and she definitely looks more vibrant than the last time I saw her. She opens her eyes slowly, like there are bricks weighing down her eyelids, and she turns her head toward Dad and Whitney.

Her eyes are full of tears when she asks, "Emily? Please tell me…"

We all share a look, but it's Dad who lets Isla know Emily isn't with us anymore. He doesn't go into too much detail because one of the nurses warned she'd be in a fragile state at first, but Isla falls apart anyway.

Once she composes herself, she murmurs, "There's so much I need to share with you. I—"

"We know, Isla," I say, interrupting her. "I followed your clues. We figured everything out. About George. About Mom. About…me."

Isla's eyes are closed again, though tears still slide down her cheeks. She parts her lips and whispers, "Good." But then she seems to doze off.

"Get some rest." I take Isla's hand and press a kiss to the back of it. "I'll be here when you wake up again." Then, with a glance up at Whitney and Dad, I say, "I'll be here from now on."

...

My dad told me Connor's room number, and I find it easily, since it's on the same floor as Isla's. I slip inside, grateful to find it's empty save for Connor, lying in the hospital bed with his eyes closed and his arm in a sling. Whitney told me he had surgery on his arm, and his parents were by his side until just a few minutes ago, when they left briefly to grab some dinner. I stand in the doorway for a moment and just take him in, trying to contain the emotions that want to sweep over me and drag me under. He's going to be okay.

We all are.

"Have you turned into a stalker?"

I blink myself back into focus at the sound of Connor's amused voice. "Excuse me?"

"You're being such a weirdo, just staring at me over there." He lifts his good arm and gestures at the space between us. "Or did they declare I have a contagious disease and you can't come near me?"

Rolling my eyes, I hurry to his bed and lean over, pressing a quick kiss to his cheek. "So bossy all the time."

"I use humor to mask my real feelings," he admits, his lips curving upward.

"You do not. When I first met you, you were incredibly standoffish."

"It's because I thought you were hot." His smile grows, and mine does, too.

I don't bother mentioning that I know what it's like to close yourself off to protect your soft, vulnerable heart. That I'd recognized another wounded animal limping through the world all by itself. Knowing what happened to Emily won't bring her back, won't heal the pain, but it might ease the hurt.

Freddie will pay for what he did, to Isla and to Emily. I'll make sure of it.

Pulling up a chair, I sit as close to Connor as I can get

and study his beloved face. He's a little beat up, with all sorts of scratches and bruises forming across his face and arms. "How's the arm?"

"Broken in two places. And I have a concussion. I'm a right mess." Connor chuckles until he winces. "I can't laugh, either. Hurts too much."

"The doctor thought I had a broken rib," I admit.

He swivels his head in my direction, wincing at the quick movement. "Do you?"

He sounds like he can't bear the thought of me being injured, and I want to swoon. "No. Just badly bruised."

Connor exhales slowly. "Good."

"Were you worried?"

"I always worry about you, Billie. You have this way of getting yourself into...dangerous predicaments."

"Not anymore." I take his hand and lace our fingers together. "Freddie is going to jail. My girl-sleuth days are behind me."

"Think he'll share a cell with his dear ol' dad?"

I shake my head. "Doubtful. But they're both behind bars where they belong."

"Thank God," Connor breathes, closing his eyes. He seems drowsy.

"Are you in pain?"

"Not too bad. A little bit," he admits, his eyes still closed.

"Want me to sing something to make you feel better?" I want to laugh, but I try to control myself.

He cracks one eye open and scowls. "Someone already tried to murder me today, but thanks."

I get a case of the giggles, and he tugs on my hand, forcing me to stand. I lean over him, our faces close as I stare into his eyes. The moment goes from light to somber in an instant. "I know we…said things. On the cliff. You were practically delirious with pain and we had both just experienced something so…terrifying. So, so scary. But I almost lost you up there, Connor. So I know I really mean it when I say I love you. I just wanted you to know it's still real for me. Even after everything."

"I almost lost *you*—and I love you, too, Billie." His expression is grave. "Fucking Freddie."

"Fucking Freddie," I whisper, leaning in to deliver the softest kiss to Connor's lips. "My sister is awake."

"What?" He's so loud I need to lean back as if he's a one-man bomb blast. "You waited this long to tell me?"

"I wanted to check on you first and make sure you're in one piece." I shrug one shoulder. "The doctors think Isla's going to be okay."

"This is wonderful news." He shifts and lifts his arm, settling his hand on my cheek. "The best news ever. What a day."

I rest my hand over his and nod. "What a day is right."

"Plus, with the discovery of your birth father…" Connor's voice drifts, and we stare at each other for a long moment. "You're a Canterbury now."

A sigh leaves me, and we drop our hands. "Yeah, about that."

Connor frowns. "What about it?"

"I know out on the cliffs I told you that secrets ruin lives. But this is one I think I'd like us to keep," I explain. His frown deepens, and I continue. "Those of us who know, know. But

I'm in no hurry to stake a claim to the Canterbury fortune, Connor. I'm a Vale. It's who I've always been. It's who I want to be."

His frown disappears, replaced by the sweetest smile I've ever seen. "Billie Vale, then."

"Yeah." My nod is firm, the smile stretching my mouth so wide it almost hurts. "Billie Vale."

EPILOGUE

I'm a bundle of nervous anticipation as I stand in front of the window and stare outside, eager to see my father's car pull into the drive. He's bringing Isla home from the hospital today. She might've woken up from her coma a few weeks ago, but she had to stay in the rehabilitation wing before they'd allow her to come home.

It was scary at first—how her injury seemed to have erased so much of her brain. She struggled to find the words she was looking for and kept jumbling the timeline of events leading up to the night on the cliff. But the doctors assured us she'd be okay, and…they were right.

Isla was a quick study. She relearned how to walk and talk and feed herself by going to hours of physical therapy, and she never gave up. She also worked on improving her memory with a variety of guessing games and looking at lots of photos of familiar faces. Like her family. Her friends. Students at school, as well as teachers. She got the hang of it at a rapid-fire pace, able to identify people, places, and things within seconds. Her determination won over everything else—she wanted to go home. She wanted to feel like herself again.

She also started seeing a therapist. I have, too. All of us Vales have, actually. Going through something so traumatic weighed heavily on all of us, and we desperately needed someone objective to unload our pain and feelings on. Someone to help us process everything that happened and come to terms with who we are on the other side of our experience. It's helped me a lot.

"He should be here soon." I whirl around at the sound of Connor's voice. He stands in the open doorway with his shoulder propped against the doorframe. "I just spoke with Whitney. Your father called and said they're five minutes away, if that."

I don't move from my spot at the window. "I want to see his car the minute it gets here so I can go out and greet them."

Connor approaches, settling one hand on my shoulder as he stands behind me. "You're a good sister."

I lean into him, savoring his strength. "I'm nervous."

"Why?"

I turn to face him and rest my hands on his chest. He looks good. You'd never know he got the crap beaten out of him only a few weeks ago. The bruises and scratches are gone, though his healing arm is still in a cast, which he hates and can't wait to get rid of. He says it itches terribly, and more than once I've had to scold him for trying to shove all manner of pseudo-sharp objects under the cast to scratch with. Whitney explained that most men—not all, but definitely my dad—are huge babies about injuries, illness, and physical discomfort in general. She might be on to something.

"I've never lived with them—all of them—before. The last time Isla and I lived under the same roof, I was six years old and she still wore pull-up diapers at night. What if we don't get along? What if she resents me being here?"

"She won't." He tucks a strand of hair behind my ear. "I'm pretty certain she's excited to get to know you better."

I frown. "Who told you that?"

"Isla." He shrugs. "What can I say? We text each other a lot."

Right. Once Isla's neurologist cleared her to look at screens, she started texting Julian and Connor. The first because she was ready for him to get his head out of his ass and go public with their relationship, and the second because she needed to bond with someone over her grief about Emily. I wish I'd known her. From the stories I've heard, she was an amazing human—funny and bright, with an unrivaled passion for baby animals and *Love Island*. Regardless of the details, she was someone loved by two people I love. That's all I need to know to understand the world lost someone precious when she died.

"Don't be nervous," Connor reassures me when I still haven't said anything. "They're all glad you're here. Even your mom."

"You're right," I say with a sigh. I'm staying in England for the time being. Mom has moved to an outpatient rehab program, and her new roommate—surprise, it's Doug—is helping her navigate her new sobriety. Doug offered to let me stay with them, but everyone, including me, thought it would be better if I stayed on this side of the Atlantic for now. Besides, if I'm being honest, I'd much rather be here. Mainly because of Isla and Connor. Well, and my dad and Whitney, too. And Sophia.

It turns out there are a lot of reasons for me to live here. It feels so good, realizing I'm starting to put down roots.

"It's going to be great." Connor dips his head and settles his mouth on mine for a too-brief kiss. "This is the perfect chance for you and Isla to spend time together. You should cherish that. I wish I had more time with my sister."

I immediately feel terrible. "You must think I'm selfish."

"No. Never." He shakes his head. "It's normal for you to feel apprehensive, but I think everything is going to work out just fine."

He kisses me again. And again, until we get a little too caught up in each other. We only break apart when Whitney clears her throat extra loud.

"They're here," she announces as she walks toward the front door.

Not even the delicious, familiar heat of Connor's mouth is enough to keep me from running to the door. Whitney opens it, and I scoot out before her, racing down the steps and making my way to the passenger side of Dad's car. I open the door for Isla and make a sweeping gesture.

"Welcome home!" I practically shout.

Isla climbs out of the car with a dazzling smile on her face, and before she can say a word, I pull her in for a hug. We hold on to each other for a long time, saying nothing, though it feels as if we're communicating with each other anyway. The relief that I feel at having her here, out of the hospital, is immense to the point of overwhelming. I can barely speak because I'm so overcome with emotion. I'm grateful that she's finally home and that we're all together.

So grateful.

We finally break apart, tears shining in our eyes as Whitney makes her approach, pulling Isla into her embrace.

"Oh, sweet girl. We're so glad you're home," she murmurs into Isla's hair.

It's almost the same exact thing Whitney said to me when I came back to their house for the first time. I heard the sincerity ring in her voice when she said it to me, and I can hear it again, now. In this moment.

We enter the house together, Connor waiting for us in the foyer. When Isla spots him, she gives him a big hug. After she pulls away, they share a sad smile, and Isla wipes the tears from her cheeks before she turns to face us.

"The Harringtons will be here soon," Whitney announces. "We wanted to make sure it was just family greeting you home first. Didn't want you too overwhelmed."

"Thank you." Isla's voice is soft, and she tilts her head back, taking everything—including us—in. "It feels good to be home."

...

Whitney had the luncheon for Isla's return catered so she didn't have to do anything in the kitchen beyond make Isla her favorite chocolate cake for dessert, which she did earlier this morning. The Harringtons are sitting at the table with us, and they brought Julian along with them. Our father has come to terms with the fact that Julian and Isla are in love, despite the veritable blood feud between him and Max Ashworth. But Dad can't deny that since the day she woke up, Julian has been at the hospital by Isla's bedside whenever he didn't have school. He's been helping her walk the corridors and playing memory games with her. Bringing her stuffed animals and flowers, or her favorite sweet treats. The way he looks at her and how he takes care of her...none of us can deny it.

Julian cares about Isla deeply, and she feels the same way about him.

We're making idle conversation after we finish eating, when Headmaster Harrington sends Connor and me a pointed look from across the table.

"I hear you two are going on a few university tours soon."

Connor and I share a look before I answer for both of us. "We are, and I can't wait. We've come up with a fairly extensive list, scheduled private tours at most of them...we even have a list of historical sites to visit en route. No hasty decisions from us, I can promise you that."

"I think that's a wonderful idea." Mrs. Harrington smiles at me.

"I'm just glad you're staying here," Sophia says from where she's sitting by my side.

Reaching out, I rest my hand over hers. "Me too."

"I'm also taking her around London to show her the sights," Connor adds. "Claims she wants to get to know the city better."

"Oh yes. I'm going to make him take me to every tourist landmark there is." Connor groans, making me laugh. "He'll have to ride the hop-on, hop-off bus while doing it, too."

"Sounds like a nightmare," Connor mutters, shaking his head.

"As long as I don't sing, you'll be fine." I elbow him in the ribs, making him chuckle.

"We should all go together," Isla suggests, sending a look to Julian, who nods his encouragement. "That could be fun."

"You should come with us, too," I tell Sophia.

"I would love that." Sophia beams.

Whitney excuses herself to the kitchen to prepare the chocolate cake, and Mrs. Harrington goes with her. My phone rings in my pocket, and I pull it out to see MOM flashing across the screen with a FaceTime call. I answer it immediately.

"Billie! You look so pretty," Mom greets me.

I feel my cheeks heat at her compliment. "Hey, Mom. So do you."

But "so pretty" doesn't even begin to cover it. Mom looks amazing. Her eyes are bright, and her skin isn't as sallow as it was before she went to rehab. Her cheeks are full, too, like she's been eating regularly again. I've never seen her look better.

"Thank you. We just wanted to check in." She waves a hand to someone off-screen, and Doug appears, a smile on his face as he raises his hand to me in greeting. "Doug reminded me Isla is supposed to come home today."

"She's here already. We were just having lunch." I flip my phone's camera and aim it at Isla, who waves.

"Hi," Isla tells her with a smile.

Their relationship is tentative at best, but I believe it'll grow stronger with time. Isla wants to get to know Mom better at her own pace, but she told me it makes her nervous, letting our mother back into her life. I don't blame her, and neither does Mom, so they're going to take it one day at a time. It's all they can do.

"Got my chip today." Mom holds up the Alcoholics Anonymous milestone chip in her hand. "Thirty days sober."

"Congratulations." I smile at her.

"Whitney texted me last night. She mentioned she has some friends who own art galleries here in the city. Once I finish a few paintings, she's going to talk to them, see if she can get my work in a gallery for a showing," Mom explains.

"That's so exciting." I laugh, my joy for Mom's improved health—her improved *life*—bubbling through me. "Better get to work!"

"I'll keep on her," Doug says, beaming at Mom.

Doug didn't waste any time once I left for England. I didn't think anything of it when he asked where Mom was—in fact, I was happy to have someone stateside who might pop in to visit every now and then. But Doug understood the assignment a little differently. He visited Mom every day, supported her in her recovery, and moved her into his apartment once she was ready for an outpatient program. Most impressive of all? He finally sold that shitty bar. He told me a man who loves a woman who struggles with alcoholism doesn't come home from work smelling like beer. It was that simple for him.

I'm so, so happy for them both. It's reassuring, knowing Mom has Doug to take care of her. And in her own way, Mom will take care of Doug, too.

Doug is a good man. My mom is lucky. So am I.

We say goodbye and hang up the call when Whitney enters the dining room carrying the cake, which is covered with lit candles. When Isla spots them, she begins to laugh.

"It's not even my birthday," she teases when Whitney sets the cake in front of her.

"We're celebrating your return home." Whitney's voice is hushed, and her eyes are glassy. "Candles felt…appropriate."

"I encouraged her to do it," Mrs. Harrington adds with a laugh as she settles back into her chair.

I glance around the table, my gaze lingering on each familiar face. I care about all of the people sitting at this table. They've all become a part of my family, even Julian. I can't imagine my life without any of them, especially Isla and Connor. That I came so close to losing both of them has brought crystal clarity to my life. I'm learning how not to be alone anymore—how to let myself love and be loved. I'm coming to terms with the fact that pushing people away doesn't prevent them from hurting you—it just makes you miserable all the time. And in what might be the greatest irony of all, being Belinda Winters taught me what it really means to be Billie Vale.

Sister.

Daughter.

Friend.

Girlfriend.

And soon, college student. I'm really excited to add that identity to the list.

I'm surrounded by family. People I adore and love. I scan the table, letting my gaze linger awhile on each person. When I finally get to Connor, I discover he's already looking at me. Waiting for me to see the love shining in his eyes.

I lean my shoulder into his and whisper, "I love you."

He drops a kiss on top of my head. "Love you, too, Billie."

"Even when I sing?" I bat my eyelashes at him.

He laughs, leaning in so his mouth hovers above mine. "Yes, even then."

ACKNOWLEDGMENTS

This book. This project! I can't lie, it was a struggle and a battle and it wrecked me in a variety of ways. But finally, *finally* we've got it right. I hope you enjoyed Billie's story. She's such an independent little badass and I love how we made sure she got everything she deserved. A family. A best friend. And the hottest boyfriend on campus.

I want to thank everyone at Entangled Publishing for putting in the hard work to get this book published. There is one person I want to mention in particular: Rebecca Heyman, you helped me so much with this story and it wouldn't exist without you, so thank you for guiding me through it all.

Always have to thank my agent, Georgana Grinstead, for keeping me sane when I was losing it (which was often). And to my family for also putting up with me and this project over the years (I'm not kidding). It's finally done! I want cake. My friend Marni Mann suggested I deserve a party and she's right.

Finally, to the readers: I hope you enjoy Billie's story. It's a bit of a diversion from my usual books, but there's plenty of romance, I promise! I can't do this writing thing without you so thank you for reading this book. I appreciate you more than you'll ever know.

THE WALL WAS BUILT TO KEEP THEM SAFE. OR SO THEY THOUGHT.

For as long as seventeen-year-old Apothecary Rose Allgood can remember, the towering stone Wall surrounding Noah's Valley has protected her people. No one leaves. No one fights. And no one questions why.

But their paradise has been hiding its thorns. When Rose's mother becomes the Valley's first murder victim and her twin brother is swiftly condemned, she alone is searching for the killer. Determined to find the truth and forced to ally with the son of her nemesis to solve the crime, Rose follows a trail of hidden messages, forbidden knowledge, and whispers of a past no one dares remember.

The deeper she digs, the more certain Rose becomes that her mother's death was no accident. That the Wall isn't just keeping something out.

It's keeping something in.

Fans of *The Hunger Games*, *The Grace Year*, and *The Maze Runner* will devour *The Verdant Cage*—a chilling dystopian thriller about what it takes to rebel when you discover your entire world is a lie.

NYT bestselling author Monica Murphy returns with a deeply romantic story about the most popular girl at school—and the boy who becomes completely obsessed with her.

Wren Beaumont is a model student. Kind, clever and beautiful, she is loved by everyone at Lancaster Prep.

Everyone but brooding campus bad boy Crew Lancaster.

Son of the family who own the school, Crew's life seems easy—but with an overbearing father and high expectations, it's anything but.

Which is why he has no time for people like Wren.

But when their lives unexpectedly collide, Wren discovers there's more to life than good grades - and Crew finally understands what it's like to care about someone other than himself...

Could they—should they—become the school's most unlikely couple?